DEDICATION

To my parents, who always believed in my book, even when I had lost all faith in it.

ACKNOWLEDGEMENTS

Since I am not Richard Castle and do not get a chance to work with a New York City police detective on a regular basis, I had no idea how to set up many of the scenes in this book.

So thank you to Donnie Conley, police chief of Dayton police department. I'm so thankful I was able to ask you anything about the police profession and you came up with the answers for me, no matter how odd the situation.

Thank you to all my reviewers, including members from the Christian Writer's Guild, Brenda Risner, Kay Walsh, Kristen Huffman (for whom I named K&T Diner), Ruthie Voth, Laura Wyant, Jeremy Keegan, Jennifer Twitty, and several others. You all gave me honest feedback, sometimes brutally honest. But it helped the end product.

Thanks to the best editor ever, Toni Ressaire. You painted my fading dreams in the brightest colored reality. I'm so thankful for you.

Thanks to my dear husband, because you didn't give up even when I had.

And most of all, thanks to God, who took this broken vessel, dusted it off, fixed the leaks and put it to use. Help me to always use my writing for Your glory.

CHAPTER 1

Jack and Jill went up a hill
To fetch a pail of water.
Jack fell down and broke his crown,
And Jill came tumbling after.

Jill sighed as she replaced the receiver. Hectic days comprised the majority of her weeks at Bradley, Bradley & Dunn, PLC and today was no exception. The phone had rung non-stop for the last two hours and the stack of papers in her inbox looked taller than when she had arrived that morning.

"Jill!" William Bradley's voice boomed through the adjoining door of her office.

She jumped. "Yes?"

"Have you finished typing those notes yet on the Hargrave case? I'm due for that hearing at... uh..." Jill heard him fumble through some papers on his desk.

"Two-thirty," Jill finished for him. "Yes, Bill, I'll have that on your desk in 15 minutes." She turned to the computer and started typing.

Fifteen minutes later, her back ached and her fingers tingled, but she had completed the dictation. She packaged it, placed a binder clip along its top edge and carried it in to Mr. Bradley's office. He was sliding his arms into his suit coat. Jill laid the packet of papers on his desk and waited for his approval. His eyebrows lowered as he frowned at her work. "Thanks, Jill."

"No problem." She pivoted on her heel to return to her office.

"Jill?"

She turned. "Yes?"

He smiled as his brows slid back up on his forehead. "My sister wants to know if you're coming out to the lake this weekend for the usual grilled steaks."

"Yes, sir, I'm planning on it. You can tell Doris I'll bring a salad this time."

"I will. Maybe you can bring that young man from church that follows you everywhere."

Jill laughed. "Bill, you know I'm not interested."

"Well, it was worth a try anyway." He finished shrugging on his jacket. He lifted the notes again and glanced once more through the pages. He looked up. "See you after the hearing." Jill recognized her dismissal. She opened his office door and walked down the hallway to the restroom.

In the restroom, she rifled her hair with her fingers and blew her bangs out of her face. She stared at her reflection and pulled up the spigot to get cold tap water. She cupped her hands, allowing the water to run between her fingers for a few seconds. She rubbed her hands together, a thoughtful exercise that she repeated again and again. She leaned her hands on the edge of the sink basin and gazed into her own earnest blue eyes. Mirrored in them, she saw regret, fear, self-hatred. She sighed, turned off the water and grabbed a paper towel to dry her hands and adjusted her blue knit top before opening the bathroom door.

Jill took a step around the corner and stopped short. She caught her breath and backed up swiftly against the bathroom door. Gathering courage, she edged forward and peeked around the corner. At the end of the hallway, a burly man gripped the collar of a man much smaller than he was. The small man's face turned purple as he gasped for air. Neither man had seen her, and Jill didn't recognize either of them.

What are they doing in the back hallways of the firm?

She could hear their urgent whispers. The small man's voice was barely audible as he fought for breath. "…not able to do it, Elliot… too complicated…I *know* the plan was murder. I blew my chance." His plea was unmistakable.

Jill drew a sharp breath and willed herself to be still. *Murder? What are they talking about?* A strange accent cloaked the man's words. *British?* Her brow furrowed. *And why are they talking about murder in such a public area? Well, I guess it's not that public.* The hallway was at the very back of the firm. Mr. Bradley's office suite was closest to the rear of the building and the rest of the offices had convenient access to the front bathrooms. As a result, this hallway didn't get a lot of traffic. The firm had authorized an extra room to be built at the end of the hallway for storage, but the lawyers had yet to fill it. Jill suddenly realized that she was very much alone and her only way out was past the two men.

Elliot thumped the small man's head against the wall. Twice. Jill cringed. "Don't you tell me that," Elliot whispered. "The plan will work. But now someone else has to do it since you were clumsy enough to mess up a well-laid situation. You're worthless to her cause. She's going to be unhappy, Topper." Another thud followed. "We've got to get out now." Urgency laced Elliot's words.

Jill held her breath as she listened to the men's footsteps fading down the hallway. She swallowed and waited until she was sure they were gone. Dead silence reigned in the hall. Jill took a deep breath and squared her shoulders. Her hands trembled and she interlocked her fingers to keep them from trembling. She peered once more around the corner. The hallway was empty. She breathed a sigh of relief and hurried back to her office. Her head spun.

"Bill?" Hearing no answer from his office, she realized he had probably already left for his hearing. She sank weakly into her office chair and wrapped her shaking fingers around the leather armrests.

Who are they going to murder? Why? Her head felt light and her ears pounded. *I need to talk to someone.*

She didn't feel comfortable using the company phone to call the police, so she rummaged in her purse for her cell phone. After a moment, she realized she had left it in Mr. Bradley's office that morning. She pushed herself out of her chair and walked to his office door. She stopped short in the doorway.

William Bradley lay slumped over his desk, his head resting on his arm. "Bill!" Jill touched his hand. He didn't respond. "Bill!" A pool of dark liquid soaked his desk calendar. Her voice rose to a shriek. "Bill!" Jill grasped his head between two shaking hands and turned it to one side. His glassy eyes were wide and staring. A bullet hole through his forehead still leaked blood and matter. The pool even now seeped over the edge of his desk, gathering and dripping onto the plush carpet below.

Jill screamed. "Help! Someone help!" *He's not dead. He can't be dead. Bill, you're not dead.* Feet pounded in the hallway. Her stomach wrenched and she tasted bile rising in her throat. She backed away, shaking her head, and squeezed her eyes shut.

Mr. Bradley's office door burst open. "What the... Jill? What's going on here?" Mr. Dunn's voice thundered in her ears. She turned her back on him and stumbled toward her office.

The afternoon sunlight filtered through the dusty blinds of Jill's office. She ignored the sounds of officers in the hallway. Discussing things. Eternal discussions. She slid her eyes shut, knowing the interrogation would come soon. She wanted to hide. She wanted her mother. Her thoughts drifted.

"How do I look, Mom?" Jill twirled in the doorway to her mother's bedroom. She went to stand in front of her mother's mirror. The evening gown she wore shimmered a midnight blue. It collected glints of light from her mother's lamp and reflected in her eyes. Her blond hair met her waist, each strand shining with a light of its own.

"Gorgeous, as you well know." Irene smiled. "I like the way you left your hair."

Jill pulled the heavy curls over one shoulder. "Well, I don't like it much when it's up. It's too heavy. Do you know how long it took me to get this much curl in my hair? And how many bottles of hairspray I used?"

"I have a pretty good idea. You've been in that bathroom all afternoon. I just hope David appreciates the effort."

Jill smiled and sighed as she sank onto the bed beside Irene. "I'm in love, Mom. I'm going to marry him." She turned to face her mother.

Irene stroked Jill's arm, her eyes gentle. "I'm glad he makes you happy, Jill, but you've only known him three months. Just be careful."

Frustration laced Jill's voice. "Yes, Mom. But you've told me you liked him the times I've brought him home."

"You're right. I have. So maybe it'll turn out okay." Irene drew a deep breath and exhaled. "I pray he makes you happy." She fingered Jill's necklace, a blue sapphire set in a heavy ring that she had always said brought out the blue in Jill's eyes. "If

David truly is everything you've told me, I'm happy to gain him as a son. Just give it some time." She paused. "I'm sure your father would have liked him, too." Her voice shook.

Jill's eyes blurred. She snatched a tissue from the nightstand and dabbed at the wet corners. "Well, Mama dearest, I believe David is all that I've told you, and if he proposes tonight, well, I love him." She shrugged. "You know I'll accept."

Irene smiled, but Jill could see doubt clouding her mother's eyes.

"And I'll pray for wisdom for you—to choose well and to love strong if that's God's will."

"I love you, Mom." Jill hugged her mother. The doorbell rang downstairs and she pushed herself off the bed.

"Get going." Irene swatted her on the rear. "And wake me up when you get back. I want to hear all the juicy details."

Jill resolutely ignored the undertone of warning in her mother's voice. She was determined to enjoy her evening with the man she'd convinced herself that she loved.

"Excuse me, ma'am."

Jill jerked, returning from the past, and faced the officer in the doorway.

"We're ready to ask you some questions now, if you don't mind."

Jill nodded and took a deep breath to calm herself.

The afternoon crept by. Jill answered countless questions in her office, but her mind was sluggish. "You're sure he was positioned like that when you found him?" "Tell me again what the two men in the hallway said." "Are you sure you had never seen those men before?" At one point, the police left her alone for a few minutes and Jill rubbed her temples. A headache throbbed and wouldn't go away. She closed her eyes, desperate to sleep, but the noises and distractions kept her awake.

Ever since Jill's childhood, she had used sleep as a defense mechanism. After her father overturned the big rig, she had slept for weeks. And now Bill was dead. He and his sister, Doris, were second parents to her in the last two years that she had worked for the firm. She'd spent hours at their homes and both had given her keys to their properties. Now hopelessness settled in. Bill's glazed eyes and bleeding forehead were all she could see. She snapped her eyes open.

A small slip of turquoise paper grabbed her attention. The paper was from a sticky pad, folded over and stuck to the base of her office chair above the wheel bearings. She leaned over to pick it up. Unfolding it, she saw her name and a carefully printed message. Her brow knit. The note read:

> *Jill,*
> *Both kings and commoners all alike*
> *Use this device much as a tool,*
> *The commoners to send a note to post,*
> *The kings to make a rule.*
> *(859) 185-1919*
> *218-9147*
> *(251) 521-1819 5111*
> *Don't let what happened to Wolsey happen to you.*

What did it mean? The note made no sense. Who was Wolsey? And what did he have to do with her? Jill bit her lip.

The connecting door to Mr. Bradley's office swung open and Jill hastily stuffed the note in her pocket. An officer entered the room and sat down to face her. "Just a few more questions and then you can go home." His voice was kind. She nodded. A twinge of guilt nipped at her mind. She really should give the man the note. For no reason she could explain, she ignored the thought.

Jill opened a can of ravioli that night for supper. She stared at it steaming on her plate. Her stomach rolled. She grabbed her spatula from the drawer and scraped the food into the trashcan. The picture of a dead man burned itself into her brain. In desperation, she flipped through the TV channels for escape, but Mr. Bradley's glassy, dead eyes still stared at nothing. She hit the power button on the remote and dragged herself to bed.

Somewhere in the darkness a child screamed. The jarring sound bit into Jill's consciousness and she clutched her stomach. The pain was intense. Was there no relief? Where was the baby? She struggled to see through the darkness. Confusion filled her.

She couldn't remember where she stood.

The next moment, she sat in the doctor's office. A white-clad nurse leaned over her, patting her hand. "It was just a fetus. You did the right thing." The words echoed in Jill's head. "The right thing… right thing… right thing." Tears seeped from under eyelids that were sealed shut. The doctor's telephone rang and her nerves shattered. The nurse ignored it and continued to pat Jill's hand.

Jill's sobs grew stronger. "I'm sorry! I'm so sorry. God, please, let me take it back." Why wasn't the nurse answering the phone? Get the phone, she tried to tell the nurse, but her mouth muscles wouldn't work. She felt the firm pillow behind her head. What?

The phone kept ringing. Jill fumbled for the receiver as she wiped sleep from her eyes.

"Hello?"

"Jill?" An unfamiliar voice.

"Who is this?"

"Why don't you check out your front porch?" There was that accent again.

Jill sat bolt upright as the line went dead. Her pulse pounded in her ears. She slipped out of bed and felt her way to her bedroom window. She cracked open the blinds and peered into the mist. Nothing. The woods around her house remained gloomy and still. She released the blinds and tiptoed down the hallway into her living room. She stared at the front door. The deadbolt was still in place.

Jill, this is a dream. You're dreaming. Go back to bed. Ignoring her own advice, she slipped over to the living room window.

Cracking the blinds, she scanned the woods again. Still nothing. She glanced at her porch. In the darkness she could see the outline of a large basket with a lid. It reminded her of the clothes hamper in her bedroom.

Her breath came in swift, short spurts and her heart thudded in the silence. *God, what should I do?*

Dread filled her. An umbrella leaned against the wall next to the door. Jill gripped it with one hand, raising it above her head. With her other hand, she slid the deadbolt back and turned the doorknob. The door opened. No movement from the tree line. Jill paused as adrenaline pumped in her veins. Suddenly, she grabbed the basket and dragged it backward into her living room. It weighed a lot. Jill let go and slammed the door shut, sliding the deadbolt home and snapping the chain in place, too, just in case.

Her legs felt like jelly. She sank onto the floor and gasped for air.

After a moment, she crawled back to the living room window. Peering out, she scanned the tree line again. Nothing. She let the blinds fall back in place and crawled over to her TV cabinet. She pulled a flashlight from the lower cabinet. Flipping it on, she pinpointed the basket with the weak light. A typical wicker basket; a latch attached the lid to the base.

She glanced behind her, shivers racing up her spine. Her fingers trembled. Despite her better judgment, she reached for the latch.

The latch lifted easily. Jill eased the top up and leaned closer. Her eyes narrowed in confusion and she lifted her flashlight higher. Jill stared with horrified fascination. Her light played off of two coppery eyes. A long, serpentine body wrapped in large coils filled the basket.

CHAPTER 2

Jeff Siegle squinted his eyes against the glowing evening sun as he watched the boys. They sprinted up and down the soccer field, their legs a blur of motion.

"That's it, Brian! Good pass! Way to look for your teammates!" He grinned as his oldest son looked at the sidelines and waved. "Now, Brandon, it's your turn. Let's see what you can do!" His second son played forward left, though in the "Mini-Soccer" community league, it was hard to tell who played what position. Boys and girls under ten years old from the community made up the team and most of the children just chased the ball. Jeff did think that both of his boys showed extra talent in sports, especially soccer. Of course he was prejudiced, but Brian could already out-dribble Jeff, and Jeff had started for his soccer team in high school. *Or maybe I'm getting old.* He smiled wryly. *Thirty-two isn't a babe in arms anymore.*

Brandon lowered his sandy blond head and raced toward the ball. He reached it first before anyone else and kicked it to a teammate. His body tumbled head over heels on the turf. Jeff hooted. "Nice play, son!" Brandon grinned. He pushed himself up and wiped some blood from his knee before charging after the ball again.

"Jeff, keep it down over there. People might think you're proud of your boys."

Jeff grinned at Bob Saint, a friend whose son also played on the soccer team. "Yeah, that would be the end of the world, wouldn't it?" He laughed. "I told the boys I'd treat them to ice cream after the game if they played their hardest. Looks like they took me seriously." He squinted back out at the field where the team sweated in the warm July evening.

"Ice cream's a good incentive. Sandy said she'd make homemade ice cream for Evan when we get back to the house. You all want to drop in?"

"Thanks, Bob, but the boys have had a lot going on lately and I need to get them to bed early." He felt his smile weaken.

"Well, the invitation's open if you change your mind." Bob clapped his hands as one of the boys kicked the ball at the goal. "Stay in there, Evan!"

Jeff clapped too, but his mind wandered. *It's only been a year since Cindy died. You're allowed to give yourself some time, Jeff. You'll get through this.* He sighed. The pain wasn't as intense anymore and he could sleep through the nights now. He missed her, but life had moved on.

He rested on his hips. *It's not really me that I'm worried about anyway. Brian and Brandon need a mom, and I'm not cut out for the job.*

Brian ran by backward, trying to get open for a pass. Jeff clapped and gave him a thumbs up. His thoughts returned to his problems. Brandon had asked him last night if his mommy was ever coming back.

Jeff had squatted before his young son. *"She's in heaven, bud."*

Brandon had nodded. "But can we get another one that lives down here on earth?"

Jeff kicked a tuft of grass. *What kind of position does that put me in? Should I consider remarrying, even if I can't love again?*

Jeff's heart ached as he thought about the lonely house he and the boys would return to that evening. He chewed on his lower lip. *My kids need a mom. But if I'm not ready for love, how is that fair to the woman?* The conversation with Jeff's pastor from the previous weekend drifted through his head.

"Don't forget, Jeff, love is a choice. If you do choose a woman to be a mother for your kids, love could easily follow if you allow it."

Jeff had responded with frustration. "But what do I know about finding a mother for my kids? So many things could go terribly wrong."

Pastor Wyman had smiled. "You found Cindy the first time, didn't you?"

"Cindy was special. The woman had the gift of grace—didn't care about my past and all my mistakes. She just loved me for who I was."

"I don't think you're being fair to a lot of Christian women out there, Jeff. Many

Godly ladies have their hearts in the right place and would welcome a chance to raise two adorable boys. Give God the benefit of the doubt. He'll show you the right one in the right time."

Jeff had thanked the pastor and left, but the words had stayed with him all week.

"Game's over." Bob clapped heartily as the shrill whistle blasted three times.

"See ya, Bob." Jeff jogged onto the field to congratulate his two young sons.

Jeff gripped the wheel of the truck, his mouth fixed into a smile as his sons discussed the game.

Brian caught his attention with a comment. "Mom would have been proud of us, wouldn't she, Dad?"

Jeff reached over and ruffled his son's hair. "Yep. She always thought you guys played really well."

The boys continued to chatter, but Jeff allowed his mind to drift again. *God forgave me for my past and Cindy did too, but could someone else once they knew?* He allowed his thoughts to wander over previous years.

Richard blinked in disbelief. "Your parents don't know you're spending the night with me?"

"No." Jeff frowned at him. "And don't look at me like that. I know you sneak out all the time, too."

"Yeah, but I'm usually in my bed the next morning, so they don't think I left."

"My parents can't stop me. They've given up trying."

"Whatever happened to the goody-goody Jeff from middle-school? Mr. You-Can't-Get-To-Heaven-Without-Jesus?"

Jeff gritted his teeth. "How about shutting up for awhile?"

Richard waved aside the comment. "Up for a game?" He dropped to his knees and dug under his bed.

Jeff grinned as his friend tugged a box into the light. "What is it?"

"Ouija Board." Richard lifted the lid. He pulled out the smooth play board and carefully laid the pointer on top.

"You want to play dumb stuff like that?"

"It's not dumb!" Richard's face flushed. "Besides, Gloria and Shawna are sneaking over and they wanted to play. It's the whole reason they're coming."

Jeff swallowed. "Shawna's coming?"

Richard cackled. "I knew you liked her. Why didn't you say so?"

"I'm not saying anything." Jeff heard the snap in his words. "When are they coming?"

A tap sounded on the window and Richard jumped. "Looks like right now." He hurried to open the window for the girls. "Evening, ladies."

Shawna accepted Richard's help to crawl in the window. She crossed the room and knelt beside Jeff. "Look, Gloria." She glanced up. "I've never seen one this fancy." She felt the edge of the board and picked up the pointer.

Gloria knelt beside Shawna, leaving Richard standing beside the window. He shut it with a snap.

"H-how do you play?" Jeff's eyes traveled over Shawna's long, thick hair.

Gloria stifled a giggle as Shawna stared at him. "You mean you've never played?" Jeff felt his face flush. He stared at the game board.

"Well, silly, let me show you." She took his hand and placed it on the pointer. Jeff felt the softness of her hand and forgot everything else.

"Dad, did you see when that one guy tugged my shirt? That's not allowed, is it Dad? But I kept on going and I got the ball. Did you see, Dad?" Brandon's high voice interrupted Jeff's thoughts. His sons' excitement was contagious.

"I sure did, Bran, and I was proud of you. You too, Brian." He winked at them as he turned into McDonald's parking lot and stopped the truck. "Milkshakes only. No cones." His boys could be sloppy with uncovered ice cream.

"Yippee!" Brian was the first one to tumble out and Brandon followed after. Jeff climbed out and slammed the door twice to get it to shut. *I need a new truck.* He scratched a rust spot on his '88 Ford. His cell phone vibrated in his pocket and he flipped it open.

"Hey, Bonnie, what's up?"

His sister-in-law cried softly. Her words slurred together.

"Wait, Bonnie, start again. I can't understand you." He kept his voice calm, but his heart beat quickly. *What in the world is wrong?*

Bonnie tried again, her voice choking on her tears. "John's been shot. He's in the hospital." Her voice shuddered. "I still don't know how bad it is. The doctor's in surgery with him right now."

Jeff was speechless. His brother had worked on the police force for several years and the family had dealt with a few scares before, but never anything like this. Jeff found his tongue after a long minute. "Do they know who did it and why?"

"No." Bonnie took a deep shuddering breath. "It wasn't even in the course of duty. Jeff, it had to have been intentional."

Jeff felt as though a boulder rested in the pit of his stomach. He rubbed his hand over it.

Bonnie's voice quavered. "He'd left the station for the day. He was only on duty till six today. The hospital called about an hour ago and told me." She paused. "Jeff, who would want to kill my husband? And why?" She began to cry again.

Jeff checked his watch. It was ten till eight, so his brother had been shot in the last two hours. *She should have called me right away.* He watched his excited little boys waiting inside the restaurant, grinning at him through the glass doors. Innocent, like his brother. *Who would have done this?*

"Bonnie, did John have any enemies? Did he mention anything about a hard case that he was trying to crack?"

"No." Bonnie sniffed. Jeff heard her blow her nose. "You know that confidentiality is a big deal with the force. But I'm sure he's made some enemies. I just don't know who."

Jeff ran his hand through his hair. "I'm coming to the hospital. You're not alone, are you?"

Bonnie sniffed again. "No. Emily's with me. We were shopping, so she brought me as soon as the hospital called." Jeff sighed, thankful that his 30-year-old sister had been on hand when needed. He supposed in all the bustle of the last hour that calling him had been an oversight. *Bonnie's only known for an hour after all. I'm just glad Emily is there.*

"And have you or Emily called Dad and Mom?"

"Emily did when they took John into surgery."

"Then I'm sure they'll be there in a couple of hours, probably a little after ten or so. I'm headed straight over. We'll be there in ten to fifteen minutes, okay?" He heard her blow her nose.

"Okay."

Jeff flipped his phone shut and opened the door to McDonalds.

"Two chocolate milkshakes to go, please." The cashier keyed in the order. "And please hurry."

Brian shot him a puzzled look. "Aren't we eating here?"

Jeff squatted in front of them. "Boys, we're going to go visit Aunt Bonnie and Aunt Emily at the hospital, okay?"

"Why are they at the hospital?" Brandon's wide eyes searched Jeff's face.

"Uncle John's been hurt pretty bad and he's there now." He watched Brian blink back sudden tears. Jeff's heart twisted. His tender one. "But the doctors are going to take good care of him, Brian, okay?"

Brian nodded and Brandon edged closer to Jeff. His lower lip trembled. Jeff wrapped his arms around their shoulders and smoothed back their sandy hair. "Aunt Bonnie needs to stay with Uncle John now and I need to go see what happened. Do you understand?"

"Yes, Dad."

Jeff smiled at them. He straightened and paid the teenage girl behind the counter. She wedged the shakes into a portable cup tray and slid it toward Jeff.

"Have a good evening." She drummed her fingers on the counter.

Too late for that. Jeff nodded politely and ushered the boys out the door.

At the hospital, the glass doors slid open. Jeff and the boys hurried into the lobby. Jeff crossed the expanse of tiled floor to the reception desk.

"Where is the ICU?"

The receptionist looked up and smiled. "2nd floor, sir." The light reflected off her glasses. "Up the elevator, then down the hallway and to the left."

"Thanks."

"No problem."

Jeff herded his boys past her desk to the elevator doors. He punched the up arrow.

The doors opened and Brian and Brandon clambered on. "I want to push the button!" Brandon squeezed in front of Brian and stretched his fingers toward the button panel.

"Brandon." Jeff's reprimand was stern. Brandon's eyes lowered and a blush covered his cheeks.

"Here, I'll lift you." Brian wrapped his arms around Brandon's waist. He strained with all his might until Brandon's finger found the second floor button.

"That was very nice of you, Brian." Jeff smiled his approval. Brian flushed and looked pleased. "Did you say thank you, Brandon?"

"Thanks Brian." The words were whispered. Jeff gave him a reassuring squeeze on his shoulder.

The elevator slowed to a stop and the doors opened. Jeff led the way into the waiting room, holding each son by a hand.

Only Emily rose to greet him. Her eyes were red-rimmed. Her long straight sandy-colored hair framed her tragic expression.

Jeff pulled her into a hug, then released her and sank down on a couch. "Where's Bonnie?"

"She's talking with the nurse. They've been back there about ten minutes."

"Are Mom and Dad on their way?"

"Yeah, Dad started loading the car while I was still on the phone with Mom. They said they'd be here by ten or so. They're heading straight here to the hospital to be with Bonnie."

"Tell me again what happened." Jeff glanced at Brian and Brandon where they fought over a magazine in the corner. "On second thought, don't tell me yet. I want to get the boys to bed first."

Emily looked at her watch. "Well, how about I take the boys to John and Bonnie's house to spend the night? It's two minutes away so we wouldn't have to run the forty-five minutes back to your house. We can switch places tomorrow while you get some rest."

Jeff nodded. "Good. And you can bring Bonnie some necessary stuff from her house when you come in the morning. The boys have extra clothes at their house anyway, so I think that's the best arrangement."

Bonnie appeared around the corner. "Jeff." She ran to hug him.

Jeff wrapped his arms around her, his hand stroking her back. "Shh, it's okay." They had always been close, though more so in the last few years. Jeff had introduced Bonnie to his brother eight years ago. He'd been thrilled to watch them gaze at each other, their love obvious to everyone. Now her expression showed complete devastation. Mascara painted dark trails down her cheeks.

Bonnie pulled away and wiped her face. "I'm okay." She hiccupped. "But John's not doing so well. The doctor said...."

"Bonnie." Emily's voice cut her off. "I'm going to take Jeff's boys to your house to spend the night." She glanced over at Brian and Brandon who now listened to the conversation with wide eyes. "Jeff will be here while I'm gone, and Mom and Dad are coming around ten o'clock."

Bonnie nodded and sniffed. "Thanks, Emily."

Emily rose to go. "If you need anything when I come back in the morning, call my cell." She pointed to a sign above the door to the waiting room. "And don't forget you can't use your cell phone in here." She pushed her abundant hair over her shoulder and bent to pick up her purse.

"Boys, are you ready to go?" Emily smiled at their excited faces.

"Is it really okay, Dad?" Brandon's eyes swiveled to Jeff's for approval.

"Of course." Jeff smiled at his youngest. "Be good." He bent to kiss his sons. "I'll see you in the morning." He ruffled Brandon's hair.

"All right!" Brian raced for the elevator and Brandon tore after him. They both stopped at the doors and impatiently waited for their aunt.

Emily gave Jeff a peck on the cheek. "I'll see you tomorrow." She pulled Bonnie into a hug on her way to the elevator. "I'll be praying for you and John."

"Thanks, Emily."

The elevator doors closed on the trio and Jeff turned back to Bonnie. She returned his look. "Oh, to be that young again. It's so easy for them to put the unexpected behind them." She sighed.

Jeff rubbed her upper arms. "So, what's John's condition?"

"Doctor Lenhart told me he's stabilized, but they have him on oxygen now." She shuddered. "Jeff, he's in a coma." Her eyes welled up again. "The doctor says he was shot at close range because the bullet went completely through his body. It missed his left lung and grazed the vertebrae on the way out. They said if he comes out of this, there is a good possibility that he'll be paralyzed." Bonnie covered her face with both hands. "Jeff, I think he would die of depression if he couldn't ever walk again." Her voice was muffled behind her shaking fingers and she lowered them. "In all honesty, I don't see how either one of us could handle it." She stared at the floor, despair in her eyes.

Jeff's own emotions hovered near the breaking point. He carefully controlled his voice. "Can you tell me again everything that led to this?"

"I got the call from the hospital while Emily and I were in the middle of Penny's, so we left right away and came here. I called the station before I called you. John had left about half an hour before the call reporting the shooting came in. Kyle said that he put someone on it right away."

"John's got some good friends in the force." Jeff's voice was soothing. "They'll take care of him—and you too." He rubbed her back, and then pushed her down onto a couch, taking a seat across from her.

They both fell silent, each engrossed in their own thoughts. There were four other people in the waiting room, but no one spoke. The clock ticked in the stillness.

Jeff rubbed his tired eyes and stretched. "Why the coma? If the bullet went through his body, it wouldn't have put him in a coma, would it?"

Bonnie rose out of her own thoughts with an effort. She cleared her throat. "The doctor said that he suffered some head trauma as well. Somebody hit him on the head several times with a blunt object."

Jeff shook his head. *Why John? And who did this to him?*

CHAPTER 3

"What's up with Jeff, Mom?" Emily unfolded her long tan legs from the couch and adjusted her heavy ponytail.

Her mother stared at the front door, which had just slammed after a stormy 18-year-old Jeff stalked out to the car. Concern clouded her eyes and she sighed. "I don't know, Emily. I think he's going through…" she glanced at the study doorway where her husband sat with his laptop "…a phase." She finished in a whisper.

Emily pushed herself up from the couch. "Well, I hope his phase doesn't have anything to do with Miss Shawna-Shorts-So-Short-You-Can-See-Her-Underwear. She makes me sick and I hate to see Jeff throwing himself away on her."

"Where are you going?" Her mother's voice sounded uncertain.

"Running. I need to vent some frustration because of my dumb brother." She bent to tie her running shoes.

"You and me both." Her mother smiled ruefully. "But, Emily, he's not dumb. Just… confused." She sighed and attacked the burner edges with her steel wool.

Emily pushed her thoughts to the back of her mind. She hadn't allowed herself to think about Jeff's wild days for a long time, but watching his tender care for his sons this evening brought the two parts of his life into striking contrast.

She dropped the car keys onto the kitchen table and turned to face the boys. "Well, boys," Emily said, and rubbed her hands together. "Y'all want bedtime snacks?"

"Yeah!" Brian's enthusiastic response echoed through the hallway. But Brandon looked conscience-stricken. "Dad never lets us have snacks before bed."

Emily squatted to eye-level with the boy. "But this is a special occasion, Brandon. Your dad isn't going to mind just this once."

His eyes lit up. "Okay!"

"Deal." Emily grinned. "You boys go up and get ready for bed. I'll fix some popcorn and then we can watch Veggie Tales or something."

Brandon danced in a circle. "I *love* Veggie Tales!"

Brian wore a superior look. "Well, it's okay for younger children. We can watch it for Brandon, though."

Emily laughed. "Why, how nice of you, Brian, to put your brother first. Next time we'll watch what you want." She turned them both and swatted their behinds. "Go on now; get ready for bed."

The boys stumbled around the corner. "I'll race you to the top!" Brian's shout brought Brandon pelting after him.

Emily smiled and shook her head. She opened the pantry door to pull out the jar of popcorn kernels. Setting it on the counter, she cracked a cabinet door to grab the oil. She turned to the stove to grab a pan.

A man stood in the doorway, gun in hand. Emily stopped short, opening her mouth to scream.

A hand clamped over her lips. She felt a solid body behind her, and the more she struggled, the less she could move.

"Get the lads."

Emily could feel the rumble of the man's voice behind her. *He's got an accent.*

The man with the gun disappeared up the stairs. Emily struggled harder, fearing what he would do to the boys.

"Fighting's not getting you anywhere." The man's snarl reached her ears. "You're not escaping, so pipe down. It'll make this simpler for both of us."

Emily willed herself to relax. She could hear footsteps on the stairs. The boys wheeled around the corner of the kitchen, followed by the man with the gun. Their eyes were huge. Already their mouths were stuffed and gagged.

Emily felt the smooth plastic of a zip tie tighten on her wrists. "Why are you doing this?" She struggled to assure the boys with her eyes. "What have we ever done to you?"

The man ignored her and spoke to his partner. "Did you take care of the snake?"

The other man nodded. "She's ready."

"Right then. Let's get this lot shipped off. We've got a lot yet to do tonight." He pulled a dirty handkerchief from his pocket and crammed it into Emily's mouth, securing it with duct tape from his other pocket.

He jerked Emily forward with him. The man holding the boys stood in the doorway. "Move it, Topper," the man holding Emily impatiently growled. "We don't have all the time in the world."

Topper hustled the boys toward the back sliding door. The larger man pushed Emily around the dining room table after them. A car idled in the grass at the foot of the deck, out of sight of the neighbors' houses. Topper prodded the boys into the back seat and climbed in after them. The man holding Emily pushed her around to the passenger side. "Get in."

She sprawled on the front seat, her arms unable to balance her. He slammed the door shut and headed around to the driver's side. Emily squirmed her way upright and glanced back at the boys. Brandon leaned against Brian and his terrified gaze pleaded with her.

The man settled himself behind the steering wheel. He hit the automatic lock and the car crept up the street.

Emily tried to memorize every detail of where they were going, but the man took back roads. After four hours, Emily was thoroughly lost. The adrenaline running through her body had slowed down and she struggled with sleepiness. She pushed her eyes open and gazed at her captor. *Medium build, dark hair. His nose is hooked and he's got big bags under his eyes. Maybe mid-thirties?*

He caught her eyes on him and chuckled. "Are you trying to memorize me?"

Emily jerked her head away from him. The clock on the dashboard read 1:07. *Does anyone even know we're gone? No one will miss us until tomorrow morning.* A bubble of panic swelled in the pit of her stomach. *No one will know we're missing for at least another six hours.*

The car turned down a long lane. Woods darkened both sides of the road and the headlights of the car reflected off the trunks. Then the trees cleared away and an open field lay spread in front of them.

Emily looked to her right. At the far end of the clearing, the moon glinted off the metallic wings of an airplane. Two vehicles parked close to a runway. Two men stood under the plane next to the landing gear. One had his arms up inside a small hatch beneath the plane. Four more people stood near the two cars. The massive airplane hangar loomed at the end of the runway.

A shiver ran up Emily's spine. *Where are they taking us?* She wanted to scream with fear and frustration, but the rank cloth in her mouth kept her from it. She turned her head to see how the boys were doing. They sat still, their eyes wide with fright. Topper motioned for her to turn around and she reluctantly obeyed. She struggled with the zip tie that bound her wrists, but her hands were numb from lack of circulation.

The driver turned the car toward the hanger. Emily could see lights in the windows of the plane. A door lowered on the side of the plane to the paved runway. The car stopped and Emily looked at the driver.

The man nodded to Topper. "Load them." He touched the automatic locks and Topper pushed the back door open. With a push, the boys stumbled out of the car. Topper followed close behind. The driver turned to Emily with a grin. "Get out. You're going to take a little trip."

Emily stared at him, anger and fear brewing inside her.

"Move!" He opened his car door and stalked around the vehicle. He swung her door open and Emily turned to face him. He reached for her shoulder, but she brought her leg up, hard, kneeing him in the groin. The man grunted in pain, collapsing against the side of the car.

Emily jumped past him, running toward Brian and Brandon. Her bound hands made it difficult to keep her balance. Topper heard her footsteps and turned. "What?"

Emily had no plan. On impulse, she headed straight for Topper, head down. She rammed into his stomach and sent him sprawling. Miraculously, she kept her balance and motioned with her head to her two nephews. The boys took off running after her. Emily could see the tree line several hundred feet in front of her. The gap was closing; maybe they could make it. She could see Brian and Brandon struggling to keep up.

Wham! Something had grabbed her foot and she landed hard on her chest. Her chin hit the ground with a bone-crunching thud. Stars exploded in her vision.

"I've got her." A man panted behind her. "Get the lads."

She twisted to her side and watched one of the airplane mechanics picking himself up off the ground. Another mechanic hustled the two boys back, firm hands grasping their arms. Hopelessness settled in.

They boarded the aircraft, listening to the powerful motors warming up. The boys sat across from Emily, eyes wide as they began their movement down the runway.

A blast of noise made Brandon cringe and the plane left the ground. The momentum pushed Emily back in her seat. She rested her head on the headrest and closed her eyes until they leveled out. The two men who had kidnapped them were nowhere in sight.

"Where's Tweedle-Dee and Tweedle-Dum?" Emily struggled to speak around her dry tongue. The gag and zip ties had been removed from all three of them when they boarded the plane.

"They didn't come." One of the men across the aisle had spoken. He had a wart on the side of his nose and Emily wanted to pinch it. He'd probably scream like a girl.

"Why? Don't they believe in finishing a job?" Sarcasm dripped from Emily's words.

Wart Nose didn't answer. He glanced at the bald man across from him. Both turned their gaze out the window. Emily looked out her own window. The landscape below her was black.

Silence blanketed them. After awhile, Emily laid her head back against her seat. The boys crawled into her luxurious seat and snuggled their heads on her shoulders. She wrapped her arms around them both and prayed.

Emily jerked awake. Sunshine streamed in the windows. Somewhere along the line, her mind numb with worry, she had drifted off. She checked her watch, careful not to wake Brian. Five in the morning. Or it was five in the morning in Virginia. Who knew where they were now? She rotated her head to loosen her tight neck muscles, and then glanced across the aisle at her captors. Both were awake and reading magazines.

"Can't you at least tell me where we're going?" Emily kept her voice soft.

Baldy didn't answer. He glanced at Wart Nose. "Make the call."

Wart Nose pulled an air phone from a pocket next to his seat and punched in a number. "Yes, could I have the Intensive Care Unit, please?" He paused. "I'd like to speak to a Bonnie Siegle. She should be in the waiting room."

A nurse hurried into the waiting room. "I have a telephone call for a Bonnie Siegle." Her clear voice startled Jeff awake and he glanced at the clock on the wall. Just after five in the morning. His parents, who slept on couches across from him, jerked awake. Anita, Jeff's red-haired mother, reached over and shook Bonnie's shoulder. Bonnie lifted her head at once. "I'm coming." She pushed herself off her love seat.

"No need, honey." The nurse pointed to the phone on the wall. "I'll transfer the call to that one and you just pick it up when it rings, okay?"

Bonnie nodded and moved to wait by the telephone. Jeff trailed behind her while his father, Gary, stood nearby, anxiety written across his face. The shrill jingle pierced the silence and Bonnie snatched up the receiver. "Hello?"

She was silent for the space of about thirty seconds. "What?" She shouted into the phone and Jeff jumped. Anita rose, her hand gripping her husband's. Across the room, another family watched with interest.

Bonnie dropped the receiver. It hit the wall with a loud thump and swung on the end of its cord. She leaned helplessly against the wall and slid to the floor with a groan.

"Bonnie!" Jeff squatted next to her. "What happened?"

She stared straight ahead. "I d-don't know who was on the other end." She looked up at Jeff and her eyes filled with tears. "Th-They took... your boys." She gulped. "And they overpowered Emily too. They were all kidnapped."

Suzanne washed the last dish and placed it in the drain rack. She emptied her pans and wiped them, then put them in the cabinet below the sink. She dried her hands and dragged herself into the living room, her hand massaging her lower back. Seven months pregnant, she dealt with back pain a lot now. She lowered herself into the overstuffed recliner and kicked the foot rest up. She pulled the daily paper from the stack and opened it to the crossword section.

She was concentrating so hard on it, she didn't notice her husband standing right next to her. "Frodo's friend is Sam, Suzanne." His finger appeared in front of her as he pointed to three across. She looked up.

"Well, that makes more sense than Sap. Thanks!" She accepted his kiss. "How was work?"

He collapsed on the couch with a grunt. "Mmm."

"That bad, huh?"

"Yeah, it was rough." He sighed.

Suzanne sensed there was more. "Everything okay?"

"No." He pounded a fist into a couch pillow. "John was shot. He stopped at WalMart on his way home and got nailed." He sighed. "That's where they found him and his car anyway." Suzanne gasped. "No! But he's your partner!" The fact was obvious to both of them, but Suzanne didn't know what else to say.

"We've got officers at the scene now. Kyle made me come home though."

"Is John… you know… I mean, is he all right?"

"He's in the ICU at Mission. Bonnie's there with him. The doc says he's in a coma." Troy looked defeated. "I wonder what enemy he's made?"

Suzanne's eyes softened. Life on the police force was dangerous, not just for the officers, but their families too. Neither Troy nor John was in the homicide division and the crimes they dealt with were less invasive. Still, dangerous people didn't only show up in the homicide department.

"Should we go see him?" Suzanne wanted to be sensitive, but she had no idea how to handle this situation.

"Not yet. I don't want to overwhelm Bonnie with visitors right now. I think her brother-in-law is there, so I'm sure she'll be okay."

"I'm sure." Suzanne put down her pencil and leaned her head back. "That's awful." She sighed. "I was talking to Kathy on the phone today. She said she heard that there was a partner at Bradley, Bradley and Dunn downtown that was shot, but she didn't know whether he had been killed or not. Two shootings in one day." She shook her head. "What is this world coming to?" Troy didn't respond. She pushed further. "Were you there for that?"

Troy stood up again and stretched. "Yep, our forensic team was there. Kyle put John and me on that one for whatever reason. He knows I've been wanting to get into homicide."

"So did the lawyer make it?"

"He wasn't as lucky." He sighed. "Maybe I'm too soft for this job, you know?"

Suzanne sensed the weight in his words and pushed her paper to one side.

"I love what I do." He paused before continuing. "But when people are hurt or killed because of a failure in the justice system, I get discouraged. How much can we really do anyway?"

Suzanne folded her hands across her swollen stomach. "Troy, you know as well as anyone that people aren't usually hurt or killed because of a failure in the justice system. People make choices and some of those choices are bad. The person who shot John made a bad choice and needs to be punished for it. The same thing goes for whoever shot the lawyer. You, on the other hand, have made a good choice. You maintain order. You uphold justice. You care enough for the people around you that you protect them at all times. I'd hate to think what would happen to this world if there weren't people like you in it." She pushed down her footrest with a snap and struggled out of the chair. Standing on tiptoe, she cupped her husband's cheeks between her hands. "Don't make the mistake of thinking the work you do doesn't matter." She kissed his lips.

"You're a wise woman, you know that?"

"Oh, I know. You're pretty lucky to have me around." She smiled and turned toward the hallway.

"Lucky?" Troy snorted. "I planned down to the tiniest detail how to court you. You didn't know what hit you."

Suzanne giggled, and then shrieked with laughter when she saw Troy run toward her. She whirled around the doorway to the bedroom and peeked back at him.

"Gotcha!" Troy snatched his wife up in his arms and nuzzled her neck.

"Honey?"

"What?" Troy kissed her ear.

"What if the same guy shot both John and that lawyer?"

"Doubtful." He laid her on the bed.

"It could happen though, right?"

"Mmm, maybe. Suzy?"

"What?"

"Can we not talk about that now?"

And they didn't.

Troy lay wide awake at midnight. Earlier, he hadn't considered his wife's suggestion seriously; but why ever not? And *if* that was the case, how were the two situations linked? His mind rearranged the question for a long time until dreams took over.

The next morning, Troy kissed his sleepy wife and let himself out the side door. He glanced at his watch: 6:47. He was going to be late. He hurried toward his cruiser.

Twenty minutes later, he pulled into the station parking lot. One of his fellow officers noticed him and waved.

Troy pushed his door shut. "Morning, Stan. How are you?"

"I'm fine." Stan waved the greeting aside. "You know Bonnie was with John last night at the ICU, right?"

"Yeah," Troy answered.

"Her brother-in-law, Jeff, was there too, and he had sent his kids home with Emily to John's house."

Troy nodded. John had mentioned his sister frequently.

"Bonnie got a call this morning in the ICU ward. She thought it was Emily, but it wasn't."

Troy detested Stan's habit of prolonging a story. "Where are you going with this, Stan?"

"They were kidnapped. All three of them. Emily and Jeff's two boys."

Troy stared at Stan for a minute, his jaw clenching. Then he turned on his heel and walked toward the building.

Troy stormed into the chief's office. "What, in heaven's name, happened here last night, Kyle?"

"Now, Troy." Kyle wiped his thick fingers free of doughnut powder. "We've got the situation under control. Dorian and Jake took the call and are over there now."

"I'm going over there." Troy turned toward the door.

"Troy." Kyle's voice stopped him short. "I don't want you on this case. You're too close to it." He enunciated each word and his eyes bored into Troy. "Do you understand me?"

"Kyle," Troy said and blew out an exasperated breath. "John is like family to me. I really *need* to do this."

"I realize how close you and John are." Kyle walked around his desk, his gaze fixed on Troy. "But under no circumstances are you to follow up on this case."

"Kyle…" Troy knew he was pushing his luck. Kyle was famous for his volatile temper.

"No. Absolutely not." Kyle grabbed another doughnut. "Now don't you have some paperwork to do?" He stuffed the doughnut in his mouth.

Troy felt his ears redden. He opened his mouth to retort, but Kyle cut in, swallowing his mouthful with difficulty. "Troy, I know you want that promotion, but if you keep pushing this, I guarantee that you won't get it."

Troy's temper was at the breaking point. He quickly turned and stomped down the hall to his workstation. Slumping into his office chair, he pounded his fist on the desk. "Confound it." He pounded again for extra measure. "Blazes! How am I supposed to work?" He gazed absently at a pile of papers in front of him.

Suddenly his eyes widened. The name on the top paper read William C. Bradley, Esquire. Kyle had actually assigned him a homicide.

Suzanne's words floated in his mind. *What if the same guy shot both John and that lawyer?* Troy grinned, his path illuminated. He ejected himself from his chair, grabbed his keys, and ran from the cubicle.

CHAPTER 4

Jill stood frozen and stared at the golden eyes of the serpent. She wanted to run, but her feet wouldn't move. *Wouldn't do any good anyway.*

She reached out a trembling hand to flip the lid shut again, but her nervous fingers missed and the whole basket tumbled over with a thud.

Jill shrieked. The snake lay halfway out of the basket. It began to uncoil. It slowly stretched itself to all six feet of its length. Its tongue flicked out once, twice.

"Jesus, help me." Jill's whisper sounded loud in the stillness. She glanced toward her broom hanging from a peg in the corner and inched her way toward it. As she wrapped her fingers around it, the snake slowly raised its head and began to slide toward her.

A squeal issued from Jill's throat. "No, no, no, no, no! Get back!" She waved the flashlight and broom at it. The snake paid no attention to the threats.

Jill drew a deep breath and blew it out with a huff. "Okay. I *will* handle this." She inched toward the snake and laid her broom handle carefully on the floor in front of it. As the head and neck twisted over the handle, she pulled up on the broom, raising half the snake's body off the ground. Jill gasped. A narrow wire twisted around the snake just below its head. Attached to the wire was a turquoise piece of paper from a sticky pad.

Jill reached her flashlight toward the paper. She tried to snatch the paper with two fingers, but her flashlight slipped. It hit the carpet, and suddenly, she and the snake were blanketed in complete darkness.

Jill stood stock-still. If she moved an inch, she was sure she would feel the scaly body of the snake beneath her bare foot. She still had the broom in hand, but the snake's weight was gone. She put the brush end on the floor and poked in front of her. Nothing. She kept going step by step until she reached the wall. She flipped on the light switch.

The snake slid toward her bedroom door.

"No!" She raced down the hallway and scurried past the snake on tiptoe. She reached her bedroom and flew inside, slamming the door behind her. She sank to the floor and shoved both feet hard against the bottom of the door. *Just in case.* She gasped for breath, staring at the door in front of her. *Who in the world drove all the way out to my house in the wee hours of the morning to drop a snake off on my porch?* She thought again of the note and a shiver ran up her spine. *Maybe whoever killed Bill?* She closed her eyes. *What do I do now?*

Her eyes snapped open again as she felt something tickle her foot. Through the crack beneath the door, the snake's long tongue flicked out and in, out and in. It hit her heel, which was planted on the ground next to the crack. Jill jerked her foot back with a cry and scrubbed frantically at the spot.

Muttering unintelligible words, Jill stalked to the bed and stripped the top sheet off. Spreading it out in front of her door, she straightened and opened the door. The snake glided forward onto the sheet.

Jill grabbed both sides of the sheet and hefted them up around the snake. Half lifting, half dragging, she tugged it down the long hallway into the living room and to the front door. The snake tried several times to wriggle through the hole at the front of the sheet, but Jill kept putting it down and adjusting the sheet so it remained trapped. At the door, she undid the chain and the deadbolt in record time, wrangled the door open, and flipped on the porch light. Still grasping the sheet, she hoisted the whole snake and sheet outside onto the front porch. She let go of the sheet. Pulling large gulps of air into her lungs, she watched the snake glide down the porch steps.

"Oh!" Jill jumped forward and snatched the slip of paper on the snake's neck. It popped off the wire and rested in her hand. She scanned the trees lining her front yard. Nothing suspicious moved, but Jill backed toward her door nevertheless. As soon she stood on her own living room carpet, adrenaline took over. She slammed the door shut. She snapped the chain into place and slid the dead bolt home. She ran into the kitchen and hefted up a heavy oak chair. She carried it to the living room and shoved it hard beneath the doorknob. Finally, she retreated again to her bedroom where she sat trembling on the bed. She looked at the paper still in her hand.

Unfolding it, she glanced at the careful print and her brows arched in confusion. It read:

> *Jack and Jill*
> *Went up a hill*
> *To fetch a pail of water.*
> *Jack fell down*
> *And broke his crown*
> *And Jill came tumbling after.*
> *Most every event ticks by*
> *As journalists attack countless klutzes.*
> *Jamming useless lyrical yarns*
> *Upon one and thirty pages.*
> *Don't you see?*
> *To our worst enemies—retribution!*

The next morning, Jill hit her alarm. She rubbed her bleary eyes. Sliding her feet from under the cool sheets, she shuffled barefooted into the kitchen to brew a cup of coffee. She dumped the last of the coffee grounds into the filter and dropped it into the coffee maker. *Mental note: buy more coffee today.* She pushed the start button and trudged back to take a shower.

Ten minutes later, clean and refreshed and more awake, she opened her closet door and reached for a nice pantsuit. As soon as she had taken it down, she hung it back up. Yellow police tape hung around the firm now. It wouldn't reopen until Monday.

Jill moved to her dresser instead, pulling out khaki shorts and a light blue tank top. She dressed and glanced at herself in the mirror, chewing her bottom lip. The khakis contrasted with her long tan legs. The blue in her shirt and the stone in her necklace brought out the sapphire color of her eyes. She sighed and dropped her gaze, moving quickly away from her reflection. She slid on a pair of sandals, and then headed back to the kitchen.

She grabbed a bagel from the bag by her refrigerator and poured her coffee. Sitting at the kitchen table, she spread the two turquoise post-it notes in front of her. She took a sip of her coffee as she studied them. "Riddles." She massaged her temples. "Why is someone sending me riddles?"

The phone rang. Jill reached for the phone and clicked the talk button. "Hello?" She reread the first line of the nursery rhyme. *What do Jack and Jill have to do with anything? My name's Jill. Who's Jack?*

"Hello, Jill. Edward Bradley here."

"Good morning, Mr. Bradley." Jill sat up straight as she set her coffee down, nearly sloshing it onto the table. She had never gotten to know Edward Bradley; certainly not to the extent that she had known his parents. Since he was her superior at work, she was careful to always use his last name.

"Quite a shock yesterday, wasn't it?" Mr. Bradley cleared his throat.

"Yes, sir, it was."

"You did some fine work for my father."

"Thank you, sir." Jill responded, tracing her finger on the tablecloth. She had always prided herself on her hard work for the firm.

"Yes, well." He seemed nervous. He cleared his throat again. "You'll need to get your things out of the office. We've got a new person ready to move in and the space needs to be empty."

Jill gripped the phone. "Excuse me, sir?"

"Yes—that is—since yesterday's shooting; and since Mr. Bradley was your boss—at any rate, the firm feels that it is in their best interests not to retain your services any longer." Silence.

Jill's arm dropped with a thump onto the table. "But sir, you just said that I had been doing some fine work for your father."

"Jill, please don't make this difficult." His voice was clipped. "We've made new arrangements for your office, so you'll want to clear it out as soon the office opens on Monday. Do I make myself clear?"

Jill could feel the tears below the surface. "Sir, will I be receiving any references?" She made a concentrated effort to keep her voice from quivering.

"Oh, certainly, certainly. As I say, you've done some fine work for us."

"So the reason that I'm being...dismissed?" Jill swallowed past the lump in her throat. "Just to be clear, the reason you're letting me go is because Mr. Bradley is...dead? You couldn't reassign me...somewhere else? Surely you or Mr. Dunn could use another paralegal?"

"I'm sorry, Jill. It's the firm's decision." An awkward pause ensued. Mr. Bradley cleared his throat again. "Well." He drew a deep breath. "Thank you for the services you've rendered the firm."

A click, and then silence. Jill's lifeless fingers dropped the phone onto the table. *What just happened, God?* She raised her eyes toward her ceiling. *Is this your way of refining me? Because it hurts, you know.* She glanced back at the notes in front of her. The tears that she had been holding back finally came. The writing on the notes blurred and she reached for a tissue. Her thoughts returned once again to the shaft of pain in her past.

Soft music coursed from the corner of the restaurant where musicians sat hidden behind palm fronds. Jill gazed into the eyes of the young man across from her.

"Good pasta, huh?" David smiled at her.

"Yes, I'm very impressed." Jill waved her hand around the room. "I've never eaten here before, and nobody could have told me that pasta wasn't just pasta. But this," she pointed with her fork, "is exquisite." She swirled the pasta around her fork and took a dainty bite, tapping her lips with a napkin. She let her left hand lie on the table next to her plate where the soft glow highlighted her empty ring finger.

David reached over and pulled her hand into his. "Want to go for a walk?"

All thoughts of food and hunger immediately left Jill's head. "Sure."

Ten minutes later, they strolled along the moonlit pier, boxes of food stowed under David's arm. Jill inhaled the salty air and let her hand nestle in the crook of David's elbow. A comfortable silence blanketed them both. The only other sound was the waves breaking against the wooden pier supports.

When they reached the end, David set the food boxes down. He held out his hand and helped Jill to sit on the edge. She crossed her arms over the railing in front of her and leaned forward, enjoying the moonlight across the moving water. David slid close to her, his arm lining her back. He leaned in to nuzzle her ear with his mouth, then trailed across her cheek to her lips. Jill smiled, returning his kiss, then pulled back. "Let's talk, David."

"I'd rather kiss." He leaned closer. Jill melted into his arms, losing herself in the pleasure of the moment. His kisses turned more demanding and he slid the strap off her shoulder.

Jill gripped his hand. "David." Her voice came out in a whisper. "Stop. I don't want to do that anymore."

"Why?" David pulled her closer, cradling her head, moving his lips down her neck. "You know you want it."

"David, please, we need to stop."

David ignored her.

"No!" Jill was now struggling. "No, David, let me go."

His arms pinned her to the rough planks of the pier with a fierce grip. "You've wanted this for as long as I have." His hand moved roughly to her side zipper. "You know you have."

Struggle as she might, Jill could not free herself. She squeezed her eyes tight, hoping somehow that blindness would keep it from happening. A tear trickled from under her lids. "Please, no."

It was over in moments and David sat back, anger seething from his body. A furious pause ensued. His voice came at last. "Why didn't you enjoy it?"

Jill stared at him through a blur of tears, shaking her head. Her fingers and toes felt numb and she could hear buzzing. He sounded far away.

David stood up and leaned on the railing, gazing seaward. His jaw clenched and relaxed. He twisted toward her, raising his voice over pounding surf. "You've asked for it every day since we met. What did you expect me to do?"

Jill began to sob. "I've never asked for it! I thought you loved me! I thought we would get married. That's why I let you go as far as I have."

"Married?" David stared at her. "Look, little girl, I'm not marrying anyone. Not now, not ever."

"Well, you sure had me fooled." Jill raised her voice to a shout. "My mom even believed in you!"

"Your mom's a blind fool."

Fury shook Jill. The edges of her vision reddened. "Get out of my sight! I don't ever want to see you again."

"I assure you, the feeling is mutual." With an expletive, David kicked the boxes of food from the edge, sending them with a splash into the surf below. He turned and

stalked toward the shore. Jill, devastated, stared at the sea through pools of tears, her mind reeling in shock and confusion. It's all my fault. She clutched her stomach in self-revulsion and curled into a ball, weeping.

Jill slid into the driver's seat of her car. She held her grocery list in her hand. The two turquoise notes, she had stuffed into her purse. She slammed the car into gear. Her front wheels spitting up gravel, she wheeled down the long lane and out onto the country road, picking up speed. She rolled down her window, letting the cooler morning air brush across her flushed face.

She calmed down a little during her forty minute ride to the city. By the time she pulled into the Food Lion parking lot, she looked more like herself. She flipped down her mirror and checked her eyes. They still sported red rims, but the blue in them looked clear enough.

She slung her purse over her shoulder and walked through the sliding doors. Grabbing a cart, she hurried through the aisles. Milk, bread, coffee. She paused before a Nutella stand and dropped a jar in her cart. She started down the aisle, and then backed up. She put the Nutella jar back. "Good decisions, Jill."

Jill paid for her groceries and wheeled them out to her car. She popped the trunk and hefted both bags in. She'd brought her cooler since she didn't plan to head home immediately. She opened it and pushed the milk inside. She had just shut the lid when she heard her name.

"Ms. Lyon?" She turned. A police officer leaned through the open window of his cruiser. Jill recognized him from the crime scene yesterday.

"Yes?"

"Officer Troy Lane. Just drove by and saw you. I've been wanting to ask you a few more questions if you don't mind.

CHAPTER 5

Jeff swished his damp cloth over the shiny bar of the popular London pub where he worked. For the last eight months, he'd taken pride in his work, admiring the glossy finish of the counter and the way it reflected the overhead lights. At home, his parents forever took credit for the projects he had worked for, but this was his own work. He admitted to himself that he enjoyed it.

"Take these to the bloke at table three." His manager plunked four shots of whiskey down on the counter. "I hope he's getting company. That's a lot of drink for one fellow."

"Gotcha." Jeff picked up the glasses in two agile hands and swung around the counter to deliver the drinks. He returned to the bar and picked up the spray bottle, squirting around the register.

"So why London, Jeff?" His manager carefully wiped glasses and placed them on the shelf behind the counter. "Why not some place in America close to where you're from anyway?"

Jeff had known that the question would eventually present itself. He was only surprised that it hadn't come up earlier.

"It was too close to where I'm from." By the time he had left, his parents had been almost unbearable. They'd demanded to know where he'd been every evening, who he'd been with, curfews, even rent in the end.

Jeff frowned as he scrubbed the counter. When his own thoughts accused him of rebellion, he pushed them away. It's their fault and definitely not mine.

His manager broke into his thoughts. "Sometimes, Jeff, a bloke's family is all that keeps him going. I haven't got much wisdom, but I do know that you should never turn your back on your family."

Jeff threw down his cloth and turned to face his manager. "My shift's over, George." He waved to the clock on the wall. "I'll see you tomorrow evening." He grabbed his jacket and strode out the door, rattling the glass with more force than was necessary.

You just have to learn from your mistakes. Jeff tapped his brakes, turned into his brother's driveway, and switched off the motor. From his pocket, he fished out the key that Bonnie had given him. Bonnie, torn between her need to stay with her husband and her distress for her sister-in-law and nephews, had at last decided to stay at the hospital. Jeff was desperate to check out the situation. He had hugged her and hustled out to his truck.

A white Ford pulled up to the curb and Jeff watched two men step out onto the asphalt. Jeff eyed the men suspiciously, then stepped out of his truck, slamming the door shut behind him. He nodded to them.

The men walked toward him. One of them flashed a badge. Jeff felt a swish of disappointment. He had assured Bonnie he would call the police when he got to the house, more for selfish reasons that anything. He wanted a chance to see the crime scene undisturbed by anyone. He knew John would have scolded him soundly if he knew about it, but that was the way he felt. Maybe it was because he'd always distrusted police, with the exception of John, of course. Bonnie must have called them herself after all. He gritted his teeth in disappointment.

The big police officer spoke first. "I'm Officer Jake Thomas and this is my partner, Officer Dorian Lepkowski." Thomas' voice was clipped and cool and Jeff noticed immediately that he had a strong British accent. "So what's the situation here?"

Misgivings arose inside Jeff. John had never mentioned anything about any of his coworkers being British. It did seem odd. Yet the man had a badge and Jeff remembered John speaking of a Lepkowski that he worked with. It was hard to forget a name like that. Jeff narrowed his eyes, but he explained everything that happened the day before, finishing with events of the previous evening.

"So there was my brother in the ICU and my sister-in-law in hysterics.

I had sent my boys here with my sister, Emily, so they wouldn't have to spend the night in the ICU. The rest of us stayed at the hospital for several hours until the phone call came through. Bonnie thought it was Emily calling, but when she answered, it turned out to be the kidnappers... whoever they were."

Officer Lepkowski dug a flashlight from under the front seat of their car and a notepad from the glove compartment. He began scribbling notes on it.

"What did the kidnappers say?" Officer Thomas glanced at the house as he spoke.

"A man first explained that her sister-in-law and both nephews were being abducted. Then he told her that if she wanted all three of them safe, she wouldn't try to look for them until she received further instructions." He paused and then added as an afterthought. "Oh yes, and Bonnie did say that she heard a steady hum or vibration in the background, like a motor was running. Could be they called from a car or something."

"That's all they said?" Officer Lepkowski looked up at this point.

"That's it." Jeff swallowed.

Officer Lepkowski nodded, his eyes venturing to his partner's. They seemed to communicate something and Jeff looked from one to the other, his misgivings returning. Officer Lepkowski tucked his pen in his pocket and flipped his notebook shut. "Let's have a look."

Jeff fumbled with his keys and unlocked the front door. He reached over to flip on the light switch, but the living room remained black. The pale glow of early morning was the only light filtering into the room. He glanced over his shoulder at the two officers. Officer Thomas pushed Jeff aside and crammed his large frame through the doorway. He grabbed the flashlight from his partner and turned it on full beam. "The flippin' breaker's off." He turned to Jeff. "Would you go reset the breaker?"

"Sure." Jeff turned on his heel and jumped from the top step to the sidewalk below, then jogged around the perimeter of the house to the storage room in the back. *I'm gonna call John's boss as soon as I'm done here and check out those two guys, just to make sure.* He swung open the screen door and felt his way along some utility shelves to the back wall. He had located the panel for the breaker when he heard a rattle, like a metal container of beans shaken together. It was so short and quick, Jeff thought for a minute that he must have imagined it. *It's five-thirty in the morning and I've had little or no sleep all night. Of course I'm hearing things.* He opened the panel and began feeling his way down the row of switches.

The rattle came again. It sounded like the baby rattle his mother had given Brian when he was two months old. Jeff whirled around, his breath hissing in the darkness. His eyes were wide, but without light he could see nothing.

Putting his hand behind him, he found a switch and flipped it. The storage room flooded with light. For a minute the light blinded him. He put his hand over his eyes and the rattle came again, longer this time. He lowered his fingers. Lying atop the deep freeze beside him was curled a very large, very long, very much alive rattlesnake. Its tongue flicked in his direction and its head weaved at the end of its long neck.

"AAH!" Jeff jumped back hard and hit the water heater. The snake followed his movement with its coppery eyes. Jeff pressed back against the utility shelf and edged his way toward the exit. The snake's tail lifted once again and the rattle shot right through him, shocking his muscles into action. He bolted for the door.

Hitting the screen running, the door didn't stand a chance against Jeff's 6'2" football frame. It gave way, hinges and all, and Jeff somersaulted into the grass. Rolling onto his feet again, he sprinted around the house toward the front.

He could hear both officers arguing about something. One of them was saying, "I'm telling you, I got the rest of it. No one's going to find...."

"Help!" Jeff threw caution to the wind. The snake's two coppery eyes glittered in his vision. His stomach rolled. The officers abruptly stopped talking and they emerged from the front door at the same time.

Jeff pointed back toward the storage room. "Snake." He put his hands on his knees, his head toward the ground, and began to vomit.

Jake Thomas sprinted around the house. Jeff wiped his mouth. "Snakes always did make me sick." He spat on the ground, and then looked up at the stars. He filled his lungs with air and took a step to follow Jake.

Lepkowski tugged his shirt. "If snakes make you sick, you'd better wait till Jake finishes it off."

Jeff stared at him a moment, then nodded. Lepkowski turned and walked around the corner of the house. Jeff took several more deep breaths, and then followed. By the time he reached the storage room, Jake had loaded the remains of the snake in a black plastic garbage bag. The only evidence of a struggle was a shovel leaning against the house and trampled grass. Apparently the snake was in pieces in the bag.

Lepkowski emerged from the storage room, making his way toward Jeff. "It seems that John knew something that someone didn't want him to know."

"Why do you say that?"

"Take a look." Lepkowski handed Jeff a sheet of notebook paper. "This paper was underneath the snake. It curled up on top of it."

Jeff glanced down at the paper, looking up once to find Lepkowski's close-set eyes fixed on him. A chill ran up his spine. He returned his gaze to the note. The morning light was stronger now. Jeff could read without difficulty.

Jack fell down and broke his crown, tut tut.
We consider it meet that the same thing should occur in John's scenario.
If he breathes a word of anything outside the weather and sports,
don't you know,
His tower will topple.
His crown will not remain whole for much longer,
Though it have on it seven jewels, a grand portfolio,
And the young ones of
Ages six, and eight, and one thirty, all
Will perish for naught, O!
And will never return.
Let us all hope that you would not wish this of the brood.
Even so,
Remember all these things until we meet again.

"Huh." Jeff ran his fingers through the hair at the back of his neck. *What the...?*

"What's going on over here?" Jake headed toward them. He had thrown a large garbage bag over his shoulder, having wrapped the leftover carcass of the snake in it.

Jeff handed him the note. Thomas read it over, then glanced significantly at Lepkowski.

"Mr. Siegle," Thomas said spreading out the note, "obviously this note is addressed to you, and I'm sure you'll want to keep it; however, we should keep a copy of it to take back to the station for further examination. In the meantime, we'll keep our eyes open for any clues as to your children's whereabouts." He smiled a smile that was meant to be reassuring, but fell short of the mark. "It won't be long 'till they're back with their father."

Jeff nodded. "Thanks." His eyes were back on the house.

"No problem, mate. Anything we can do to help." He grabbed the notepad that Lepkowski held in his hand and flipped it open. Glancing back and forth between the note and his notepad, he scrawled the message out onto his page. When he was finished, he flipped the pad shut again, then folded the original and handed it to Jeff. "Here you are, mate."

Jeff nodded. "Okay, thanks guys." He turned toward his truck, swung open the door and climbed in. Backing out of the driveway, he gave a last quick glance at the policemen, now deep in conversation. His foot hit the accelerator and he sped down the street turning right onto the next block. Pulling to the curb, he flipped on the dome light.

He glanced in his rearview mirror, then opened the note again and scanned it. It didn't make a lot of sense, other than the veiled threat that John would get hurt. What was the reference to the Jack and Jill rhyme?

Jeff chewed on his bottom lip. Brian and Brandon's faces swam in his vision. He was tempted to curl into a ball and cry like a little boy. *Come on, Jeff. The boys need your help, so figure this out!*

He pushed the note away from him and pulled away from the curb. On impulse, he decided to drive back by his brother's house one more time. It was very light now and he could see the house and yard much better. The white Ford had disappeared. Jeff could still distinguish the tracks in the dew. He pulled the truck into the driveway once again and got out.

Shoving his hands into his pockets, he strolled around the opposite side of the house, glancing about to see if he had missed anything at all. Finding nothing, he rounded the back of the house to the storage room.

The shovel leaned against the house, so Jeff picked it up and returned it to its holder in the storage room. Coming back out, Jeff bent over and hefted up the top edge of the screen door he had destroyed. He leaned it against the house to fix when he got a chance.

Turning around, he noticed an object in the grass. He leaned closer to it, but recoiled as he recognized a large chunk of what had been the snake. His stomach twisted and he turned his back for a moment. Taking some deep breaths, he grabbed a nearby stick and poked at it. It rolled over. Black print covered the white underside. He leaned close again and his mouth dropped open. He glanced up and around, grabbed the chunk of snake and jogged to his truck.

Climbing back into the driver's seat, he held the snake piece in front of him. His mind worked to figure out all the possibilities. The dark print read: "Made in Japan."

Jeff's head pounded as the full potential of the situation swarmed through his brain. He knew he had seen a real live snake in the storage shed. And yet there was no denying that what he held in his hand was a rubber chunk of a fake snake.

Jeff's suspicions were confirmed. Those men were obviously not cops. A cold chill ran down his spine. Who were they then? What of the note? Did they mean for him to have it and why? Was there a message in it? Jeff pulled out his cell phone to make the call he should have made an hour ago. He punched in 911 on the number pad.

"Hello? Yes, I have a situation to report."

CHAPTER 6

Jill stared in disbelief at the moist strip lying on her bathroom counter. The double line glared a brilliant pink and her knees turned to jelly. She sank down onto the toilet lid. "I can't be pregnant." She gripped the towel rack next to her. "It'll mess up everything." Two tears leaked out of the corners of her eyes. "Why did I trust David?"

A tiny voice inside her head spoke. He was the perfect gentleman for three months. He could have fooled anyone.

Jill heaved a sigh. It's all my fault. If only I had stopped him sooner....

The voice spoke again. When are you going to tell your mother?

Jill shook her head fiercely. "She doesn't need to know. It would kill her. She's already sick enough from the cancer."

She's going to find out eventually. You can't hide a baby forever.

"Jill?" She heard her mother's voice outside the door. "Are you talking to yourself in there?"

"Of course." Jill worked to keep her voice light. "Who else would I be talking to?" She listened to her mother's soft laugh and her footsteps as they echoed down the hallway.

Jill snatched the pregnancy test strip from the counter and wrapped it in coils of toilet paper. She stuffed it deep in the trashcan, then wrapped her arms around her stomach. She rocked backward and forward on the toilet seat, tears flowing freely down her cheeks. I can't tell her. I can't. I can't.

♣♣♣

Troy hurried out to the parking lot in the early morning light, his mind wrestling with William Bradley's murder. He planned first to look through the crime scene again. Then he wanted to find Jill Lyon, the primary witness, and question her some more before he did anything else. He headed toward his cruiser at the same time as Jake Thomas and Dorian Lepkowski moved toward theirs.

"Hey guys." Troy waved in their direction. "You heading out to John's house?"

"Yeah." Jake dug in his pocket for his keys. "The call came in a little bit ago."

"Can you let me know if you find out anything?"

"We'll keep you posted." Jake inserted his key into the lock. "Not sure what we'll find over there." He paused. "You know these things take time, Troy. But honestly, we'll try to put your mind at ease."

Troy nodded. He still fumed about Kyle's decision to keep him off the case, but he understood the policy. It didn't mean that he liked it though. "Thanks, guys." He slid into the driver's seat.

He drove slowly through the streets, heading toward the law firm. As he passed Food Lion, he did a double take. Jill Lyon pulled her trunk lid up and hefted two bags of groceries into the space.

Great. I'll talk to Jill before I go see the crime scene. Troy made a quick turn left, pulled back into traffic, then turned left again into the parking lot. Jill slammed the trunk lid shut. Troy stopped right behind her and leaned out the window. "Ms. Lyon?"

Jill jerked her head up. "Yes?" She smiled as she recognized the officer from the day before. He had been very kind.

"Officer Troy Lane. Just drove by and saw you. I've been wanting to ask you a few more questions if you don't mind. Do you have a few minutes?"

Jill sighed. "I apparently have all the time in the world now. My boss laid me off this morning."

Troy paused. "Wow, I'm sorry to hear that."

Jill nodded. "I've already had a good cry and that's helped some. I'll be fine by tomorrow. Type up some new resumes and all that."

"Good for you." Troy's smile was encouraging. "Hey, you want to go for a bite to eat? I haven't had breakfast yet and was going to run over to K&T Diner. I could ask you my questions there if you like."

Jill nodded. "Sure."

"My treat. Would you like a ride?" He motioned to the passenger seat. "I can drop you back by here on my way to the firm after we're done."

Jill hesitated. "Why not?" She pushed her cart to the cart return, pulled her purse over her shoulder and walked to the passenger door. Troy leaned across and opened it from the inside.

"Thanks." Jill settled herself in and bit her lip.

"I should have asked. Do you like K&T?"

"Oh yes." She laughed. "The manager usually slips in an extra pancake for me."

Troy pulled out of the parking lot. "I wanted to go over with you again what happened yesterday."

Jill stopped him. "Officer Lane, I've told my story to you and one other officer several times over. It's traumatic for me to replay it in my mind. Do I really have to tell it again?"

"Call me Troy." He grinned at her as he turned left at the light. "And can I call you Jill?"

She nodded and Troy continued. "I appreciate your honesty. I actually wanted to ask you about a couple of new angles that have cropped up in the case. No replaying the murder scene, I promise."

Jill hesitated. "Okay, shoot."

Troy was already turning into the parking lot of the diner. "Let's get our food first."

The bell jingled as the two walked in.

"Morning, Jill." The waitress slid her rag off the counter. "Your table's free."

Jill laughed. "So are all the other tables, Bess. Thanks. I'll take my usual." She led the way to a corner table and slid into the booth.

"And for you, sir?" Bess caught Troy in her gaze. "Eggs over easy, tater tots and bacon, please."

"Comin' right up."

Troy slid in the booth across from Jill. Bess soon returned, bringing back a large tray piled with pancakes on one plate and eggs, tater tots and bacon on the other. She placed a half empty bottle of ketchup and a sticky jar of syrup on the table between them.

Jill bowed her head to pray. When she looked up, she found Troy watching her carefully. "You a Christian?"

"Yes." She directed her full attention on him.

"My partner on the force was—uh—*is* a Christian." Troy popped a tater tot in his mouth. "I used to tease him that I'd starve to death by the time he got done saying his prayers."

"You used to?"

"Yeah, long story." He didn't elaborate. He glanced down at Jill's necklace. "Jill, that's a beautiful ring. Where did you get it?"

Jill pulled her necklace up to study it. The gold ring hung from a matching chain. The ring was intricately engraved. A flawless sapphire rested in the center of the setting and Jill knew it brought out the blue in her eyes. "It's been in my family for generations. I've always liked sapphires, so I had it put on a necklace to wear. My mom gave it to me when I was eighteen. It's been a tradition in our family—to give this ring to the oldest son or daughter on his or her eighteenth birthday."

Troy leaned in for a closer look. "What's that print around the outside of the stone?"

Jill squinted to read. "It's Latin and says *Veritas Unum*. It means *One Truth*."

Troy popped the ketchup bottle open and smothered his tater tots with the red sauce. "So do you know of any enemies that Mr. Bradley may have had? Any irritable clients with unstable personalities?"

Jill swallowed a bite of pancakes and patted her mouth with a napkin before answering. "No. I mean, there's always the client that complains about an exorbitant bill or something, but no hostility really from anybody. He was well known as a nice and generous man. I don't see how anyone could have done this to him." She took a swallow of orange juice, then picked up her fork again to cut off another section of pancakes.

"Was your own relationship with Mr. Bradley a pleasant one?"

Jill stopped chewing and stared at him. "I didn't kill him, Troy."

"I'm not suggesting you did." His eyes were serious. "I just need to see the big picture."

"Okay." Relief filled her. "I'm still in shock. He was like a dad to me in a way. My own dad was killed in a trucking accident when I was just eleven years old, and then my mother died of cancer three years ago. Bill and Maggie went to my church and they kind of adopted me. I spent a lot of time with him and his wife off work hours when Maggie was still alive. He kept up with me after she died last year. We were pretty close." Her eyes welled up. She blinked rapidly and looked out the window.

"It's okay to cry, Jill."

"I know." Jill dabbed at her eyes. "But I only let go when I'm by myself."

"There's a term for that."

"What? Reclusive?"

"No. Subconsciously withdrawn."

"Whatever." Jill's mouth quirked into a half grin. Then she sighed and twisted her napkin into a wad. She looked back up at Troy.

"Something wrong?" Troy's concerned gaze swept her face.

Jill wiped her hand on her shorts and reached in her pocket. Pulling out two turquoise sticky notes, she spread them on the table. "Troy, yesterday some strange stuff happened. I—well, I find it hard to trust many people, so I wasn't going to tell you. But I will, because I'm working on trusting more and quite frankly, I'm out of options. Don't take that as an insult."

Troy grinned. "Thanks, Jill. No offense taken." He gulped from his glass of milk. "So what strange stuff happened yesterday?"

She reiterated the story of the phone call and the snake in the middle of the night.

"Jill!" Troy exploded, pounding his fist on the wobbly table. "You weren't going to tell anyone about this?"

She shrugged lamely. "Like I say, I have a hard time trusting people. I know it's not an excuse though." She handed him one of the notes. "Anyway, that's the note that I found on the snake's neck."

Troy quickly scanned the note. "Huh." He scratched his head.

Jill continued when Troy glanced up. "And then I found this other note in my office yesterday afternoon before I went home. The paper was stuck to the base of my chair." She paused. "Obviously, the note's addressed to me, but I have no idea what the note is supposed to mean or who would have left it for me."

Troy took the scrap and scanned that one as well. "Who is Wolsey?"

Jill shrugged. "I don't know. I had decided I was going to head to the library to do some research before you intercepted me." She grinned. "And type up a new resume."

Troy stared at the paper again. "Could I take this back to the station with me?"

"Sure." Jill took a sip of orange juice. "But I'd like a copy of it if I could."

Troy hesitated. "Actually, we don't let anyone take evidence or even copies of evidence till it's been to the lab and been tested. I'll see what I can do though after I send this to the lab." He paused. "I'm sorry, Jill."

"That's okay." She smiled at him. "No big deal. I've read it so often I've got it memorized anyway."

"Okay, well, thanks for answering some of my questions." Troy swung his legs out of the booth. "I have to run for now. I need to get over to the firm and check up on progress there, and then I wanted to go make a few house calls to some other firm employees—see what else I can dig up." He glanced down at the slips of paper now in his hands. "But this is good stuff. Thanks for being honest with me, Jill."

"Sure." Jill stood up and scooted the leftover food items into the middle of the table. "I'm going to walk back to my car. It's right down the street and I need the exercise. I believe you have my phone number? Call me if you need anything."

Troy stood as well. They shook hands. "I'll get the check." He smiled. "Hope it goes well at the library. I'll be in touch."

"Thanks. See you, Bess." Jill pushed open the front door and slipped out into the muggy July heat.

She walked the three blocks to the Food Lion parking lot and cut across the lot to her car. Unlocking it, she switched on the motor and blasted the air conditioning. She opened her glove compartment and pulled out a writing pad and a pen. Glancing out the window, she quickly wrote the words engraved on her mind in letters of fire.

Emily clenched John's arm as she stared at the envelope in her mother's trembling hand. Tears gathered in the corner of their father's eyes. "Open it." His voice was

gentle.

"You. I—I can't." Anita thrust the envelope at her husband.

Gary took it, his own fingers shaking. "It's been a year and a half. I wonder what he's got to say." He flipped the envelope to the stamped side. "Apparently he's in London. That's where it's postmarked from." He tucked his thumb under the flap and ripped it open.

Emily, John and Anita listened wide-eyed as Gary read the letter's one line.

"Gary & Anita, please sign over the CD that you had saved for me and is in your name. Send it to the address attached. I need the money. Thanks, Jeff."

Anita promptly burst into tears. Gary's face was chalk white, his eyes dazed. John growled, his hand gripping the kitchen counter he leaned against. "What a...." He stopped at a look from his father.

Emily swallowed hard and stepped forward to pull her mother into a hug. Anita continued to sob. "He—he didn't even call me Mom." She pulled back to grab a tissue.

Emily pushed her anger to the back of her mind. Right now, she needed to be there for her parents. Why was her brother acting like such a jerk? If he even was her brother anymore. Apparently, he was disclaiming the family on top of his extended absence and lack of communication. At least, that's what it felt like.

Emily sat with a rigid spine on a cold stone floor urging her thoughts back to the present. Jeff's history affected the family with a strength that still existed to the present, particularly in Jeff's relationship with Gary. The strain was evident whenever the two were together. Emily sighed. She didn't like thinking about it.

Brian and Brandon huddled close to her, shivering in the damp air. Emily pulled them closer, rubbing their arms to keep them warm. The room was dark, though a dim light flickered from a torch by the huge oak door. No windows graced the walls, only dingy stone slabs.

Emily gritted her teeth, struggling against the hate that threatened to consume her. *Hate of what, though? I don't even know who's doing this to us.* She looked upward. *Help us, God.* She had prayed the same prayer countless times in the last 24 hours since their plane had landed and they had been escorted to this stone dungeon. They had been blindfolded, of course. It wouldn't do for them to recognize their surroundings. *I don't even know where in the world we are. South America? A Russian prison? Europe?* Her imagination began to go wild as she remembered World War II history lessons. She saw German soldiers in the corner, their faces rigid, their torture chambers ready. She gulped.

Soft footsteps from the outer corridor interrupted her tumultuous thoughts. A key clicked in the lock and the door swung open with a deep groan. Brian and Brandon sat up straight, their eyes wide in fright.

"Hello, Americans." A sultry female voice greeted them. A tall, curvaceous woman stood before them with a—was that a *snake* wound around her neck? Emily blinked to clear her vision. "I hope you are comfortable?" A dimple appeared in the woman's rosy cheek.

"Obviously not." Emily glared at her. "But I hope you are because it won't last. You're going to rust in jail for this, you know."

A soft chuckle followed Emily's heated comment. The woman lifted the head of the snake with her left hand. Her right hand stroked the top of its scaly head. "Did you hear that, my darling? Rust in jail? So plebian."

The soft insult was meant to bring a retort, Emily was sure. She rebelliously clamped her teeth hard on her bottom lip.

The woman approached the threesome slowly, bending when she reached them to look each individual deep in the eye. The snake, five or six feet in length Emily guessed, had arranged itself around its mistress' neck, its head finding its way down her arm. The head of the snake explored the space off the end of the woman's hand. Brandon tried to scramble behind Emily when the woman came too close. She reached her arm in front of Brandon, shielding him from the snake, and glared at the woman. "Don't you have anything better to do?"

The woman's gaze centered on Emily and she straightened. A smirk covered her face. "I didn't intend to bring you with the boys. Did you know? But I think it does work better this way."

"Why?" Emily's frustration finally burst out of her. "Why does it work better this way? Why are we even here in the first place?"

"I wish to see your brother of course." The reply came quickly as if the woman had expected her to ask. Emily bit her lip again. *Which brother?*

"The more I have of his precious family, the more incentive he will have to come." The woman trod softly toward the door, her slippered feet making little or no noise on the stones. In the faint light of the torch, she turned to face them once more. "His children don't favor him greatly." Her voice was low and controlled as she answered Emily's silent question. "They must take after their *mother*." She spat the last word as if it was distasteful and looked down at her scaly pet. "Shall we go, my love? I promise to let you visit with them later, yes?

CHAPTER 7

Jeff drove aimlessly down first one street, then another. He took a deep shuddering breath and tried to smash the bubble of panic that tied his stomach in knots. "God, I need your help to find them." *Where are they?*

He turned on his blinker to head east on route 33. "It's not going to do any good to hope I stumble across them." He needed to come up with a strategy. Outwit whomever the kidnappers were. He slammed his fist against the wheel. *Just a small lead, please, God?* "I know, I know, you're asking me to trust you in this. All I'm saying is that I'm panicking here!" A car changed lanes in front of him and Jeff hit the brakes a little too hard. His knuckles whitened as he gripped the steering wheel. "Come on, Jeff, think!" He slowed down to allow more space between them.

"I meet fake cops. The snake was hiding a note about Jack and Jill. John was shot. Emily, Brian and Brandon are missing."

He glanced at his blind spot as he eased over to the left lane. He sighed in frustration. "God, I need a sign. I don't mean to be like Gideon or anything, but I really need something to go on here." He waited. The only sound was the vibration of the motor and the intermittent thump of his tires as they hit various potholes in the road.

The large buildings of downtown rose slowly around him. Glancing down at the note beside him, he reread the first words. "Jack breaks his crown. I wonder if that's a threat for John? Or me? It sure talks about his crown a lot." He stopped for a stoplight and tapped his fingers on the steering wheel. Glancing to his right, he saw a sign reading "Shenandoah

Regional Library." The light turned green and Jeff started to go, but at the last second, cut sharply across the right lane and turned into the library's small parking lot. Jeff stepped out of the car. "Okay, God, I'm ready for that sign any time now." He grabbed the note and shoved it into his pocket. Snatching his pen from the glove compartment, he headed into the library.

Jeff walked toward the counter. "Could I use one of your computers?"

"Sure, son." A tiny elderly woman looked up from a book she was reading. "We've got two in the back and one over there on the side." The air blew in a whistle through her front teeth every time she said an *s*. "They just came in two weeks ago. We kept pounding the city council until we got a grant to buy those computers." The *s* squealed loudly on the last word. "Got to keep up with the times, you know." She stared seriously at him over her bifocals.

"Yes, ma'am. Thank you, ma'am." Jeff backed up a few steps, turned and headed back toward the rear of the library, careful not to laugh out loud. At the end of a long row of dusty reference volumes, Jeff found two small computers. Though certainly not the latest models, they at least looked functional. Seating himself in front of one, he typed in the first search engine he could think of.

Stretching his hands high above his head, he yawned immensely, then brought his fingers down to type "Jack and Jill." Clicking his mouse over the search button, he felt his eyelids droop.

A website for Mother Goose rhymes slowly appeared. Jeff nodded sleepily as he waited. As if in a dream, he pulled the note from his pocket and spread it out carefully next to the keyboard. Looking back at the computer, the words appearing on the screen began to haze and then criss-cross.

Mmm, just a short power nap. Jeff drowsily laid his head on his arm. *Good thing I'm so far from the front of the library. Gopher lady might kick me out.* Then he was out.

Jeff's dreams were distorted at first, shadowy images that flitted through his semi-conscious brain and then left again. Before long, however, memory took over and he once again lived his past.

Jeff glanced around the dimly lit clearing at several members of the coven. He had attended similar meetings twice before and by this point he knew what would happen. A large pentagram of carefully placed stones occupied the center of the clearing. Tiki-torches circled the area creating dancing shadows on the ground.

As yet, there were only seven members there. Five more were to arrive and then Jeff's membership initiation ritual was to begin.

"Nervous?"

Jeff turned to look at the tall woman next to him. Her robe hung open over a low-cut green blouse and plenty of cleavage was available for inspection. Jeff's heart skipped a beat then hurried on at double-quick march.

"Some." Unbidden, a memory of his father reading the Bible at the table after dinner one night came to mind. The acts of the sinful nature are obvious: sexual immorality, impurity and debauchery; idolatry and witchcraft.... Jeff ruthlessly shoved the thoughts to the back of his mind.

"You'll like it. We're a community, and everyone here leans on everyone else." Her voice was clear and musical. Jeff found himself hoping she would say something else so he could hear it again.

"Communities are nice." Jeff's voice sounded inane in his own ears. He glanced at her neckline again. She followed the direction of his glance, then met his eyes and gave him a slow smile.

"So is communion." She stepped forward. "One—between—another." She punctuated each word with a warm moist breath against his cheek, then brushed her lips against his just enough to tease him. She pulled back, sending her beautiful smile in his direction, then strolled to the other side of the clearing. Jeff watched her go, his blood pounding in his ears.

When Jeff awoke half an hour later, his brain was still fuzzy and he could feel moisture trailing along his cheek. He sat up quickly, realizing he had drooled on the computer desk. He pulled several tissues from the box next to his desk and wiped up the mess. The nursery rhyme note shifted over in the process, but Jeff was so busy cleaning up that he didn't notice.

The woman at the computer next to him smiled. "Sleep well?" Her blue eyes brimmed with amusement.

"Great." Jeff grimaced. "Almost as good as a real bed." The woman's hair gleamed a brilliant gold in the light from the windows.

"That's good." Turning her attention back to her computer, she began typing again. Jeff did likewise, but he found himself glancing repeatedly at the woman out of the corner of his eye. *I bet her hair is really soft.*

He shook his head slightly, leaning closer to the screen. *Focus, Jeff. Think of your boys.* With these thoughts in mind, Jeff stared at the window that had popped up before he fell asleep. *Nursery rhymes. Hmm.* Jeff scrolled down the screen until he came to the J's. Clicking on "Jack and Jill" he read the poem twice through. He glanced furtively back at the woman. She was gazing intently at him, her eyes huge.

"Sorry, I couldn't help but notice." She pointed discreetly toward Jeff's nursery rhyme message. "I know I shouldn't have looked." She shrugged slightly. "But it's hard to miss." Indeed, the paper was nearly underneath her keyboard.

She leaned forward. "I was wondering if anything strange has happened to you in the last day in relation to this note?" She glanced behind her as if expecting someone to jump out from one of the many bookshelves.

Jeff stared into her blue eyes, his mind working. *Trust her? Or not? Help me, Lord.* He heard the echo of a whisper. *You asked for a sign.* He rubbed the back of his neck. "Yes. Why?"

The blond pulled out two pieces of paper from her pocket. She twisted them in her fingers for a minute, appearing to be deep in thought. "Let me start by introducing myself." She talked fast, almost incoherently. "My name is Jill Lyon and up until this morning, I worked in the law firm of Bradley, Bradley and Dunn. I wasn't sure whether to ask you about this note, but I trust you because I saw your T-shirt. I think that I'm supposed to talk to you because I've been praying and asking for a sign. I don't really know where to go from here, but you showed up and I saw your note, so I felt like God was telling me to ask you about these." She held up the pieces of paper in her hand.

Jeff stared at her, his own prayers he had uttered in the car now echoing through his head, and then glanced down at his shirt. It was a T-shirt that he had bought two years ago at a church retreat. Large bold letters on the back proclaimed, "I am crucified with Christ. Now I no longer live, but Christ lives in me."

Jeff looked back up at Jill and smiled. He found it difficult not to when he so fully appreciated blond hair and blue eyes. "Hi, Jill. I'm Jeff." He extended his hand. "Now tell me what's going on."

Jill's voice dropped to a whisper. "Yesterday, I overheard a conversation at work—some sort of plot to murder somebody." Jill's whisper sank so low that Jeff could hardly hear her words. "And then when I got back to my boss' office, he was dead. Shot between the eyes. The police questioned me and sent me home. Last night, the phone rang in the middle of the night. A man with a British accent told me to look at something on my front porch. When I brought the basket in, there was a huge snake in it."

"A snake!" Jeff leaned closer. "Interesting. Go on."

"I managed to get the horrible thing out of my house, but before I did, I found a note attached to a wire around the snake's neck." She handed him one of the papers in her hand. "And that's why I'm talking to you now. Because I think there might be a connection from my note to yours."

Jeff scanned the note quickly. "So both your note and mine are in reference to Jack and Jill. That's odd." He looked up. "I was just looking that up on the Internet." He waved his hand toward the screen. "But it didn't give me much information."

"What were the strange things that happened to you with your note? If you want to say, that is."

"Where should I start?" Jeff sat back. "Let's just say my brother was shot and is now in a coma, my sister-in-law is in hysterics, my sister and my two sons were kidnapped, nobody has any idea where they are, the two cops sent to investigate the crime scene were fake cops, and I had my own snake experience as well."

"What?" Jill's eyes widened.

Jeff quickly went through the events of the last evening and night in more detail. "And you've already seen my note." He motioned toward the paper.

"Hmm." Jill rubbed her hand over her forehead. She glanced at Jeff's computer. "Scroll down for a minute. I want to see if there are any footnotes."

Jeff obliged. As the screen moved down, three or four more paragraphs appeared beneath the nursery rhyme.

"Well, would you look at that." Jeff's scanned the words. "So Jill was not originally supposed to be a girl? It says the original poem was Jack and Gill. That's interesting."

"No, look!" Jill's finger pointed at the screen. "Look at that!"

Jeff's gaze followed her finger. "Who was Wolsey?"

"That's what I was trying to find! Look, it says that Wolsey and Tarbes failed in their peacekeeping attempts between Britain and France, and the poem was written in reference to those two men. That's why Jill is actually Gill. It's for two men. And they "broke their crowns" because Wolsey failed in what he had set out to do." She read it through again.

"I still don't understand how Wolsey relates to what's going on with us." Jeff rubbed his temples. Jill leaned so far over to see the computer screen that her hair brushed his shoulder. *Her hair smells like flowers. Lilacs maybe?*

"Oh, I forgot." She unfolded her second piece of paper and eagerly handed it to him. "I found this in my office the same afternoon I found—well, found the body." Still leaning close, she looked up at him to see his expression.

Jeff dragged his eyes away from hers and read the note. "So what does Wolsey and his failure to keep the peace have to do with us today? And for sure, what connection does he have with whoever it is that killed your boss, shot my brother, and kidnapped my boys and sister?" He looked back up at Jill. "And how do they know where we live and work?"

She shivered slightly. "I don't know, but I don't feel very safe." She glanced behind her again.

Jeff snagged his note and stuffed it back in the pocket of his jeans. "Well, I have to get back to the hospital and let my sister-in-law and my parents know everything that's going on." He paused. "You want to come? We could work on this thing together."

Jill nodded decisively. "Of course I'll come. I want to know what this is all about." Her mouth twisted. "And it's not like I have a job to get back to."

"My foreman's covering for me till I can get back. Thankfully,

I remembered to call him after the snake incident this morning." He yawned. "I have to get sleep some time. Maybe at the hospital. You'll follow me over?"

Jill nodded. "I'll be right behind you."

With a nod at the gap-toothed librarian, they exited the building.

CHAPTER 8

Troy headed back to the station, turned into the parking lot and switched off the motor. He grabbed the notes that Jill had given him and hurried in through the glass doors and over to his cubicle. Spreading both notes in front of him, he studied them intensely. From all appearances, the print seemed to be the same—a handwritten set of characters that were large and precisely formed as if a child just learning his letters had written them.

Troy sighed. Jill had already had her hands all over the papers and, of course, he had too, so there wasn't much use in sending them to the lab for a fingerprint examination; but the lab might be able to find something he was missing. Pulling a zip-lock bag from his desk, he pushed the papers carefully inside and zipped it shut.

"Find yourself some evidence, did you?"

Troy looked up, startled. "Lee." His greeting was less than enthusiastic. "What could possibly bring you by my desk today?" He smoothed the bag carefully. "I'm sure it wasn't my winning personality that drew you in?"

"Just wondering what you paid Kyle to give you the Bradley case." Lee held a coffee mug in his hand and casually stirred his straw through it. His eyes were down, but Troy heard the steel in his voice.

"Kyle assigned it to me, Lee, so that's what I'm working on."

Lee set his mug down suddenly on Troy's desk and leaned both hands on the edge. "Oh yeah? And why would he pick a cop not even in the homicide department to work on a murder case, Troy? Answer me that."

He gritted his teeth. "I should have gotten that case and you know it."

"Just what is your problem, Lee? Why are you so offended that I got the case and you didn't? Because it's high profile? Is that it? You think you'll get a raise if you manage to take out the person who did this?"

Lee bored a hole through him with his eyes. "That's not your business; but yes, I should have gotten the case."

"Yes, well." Troy stood up. "As much fun as I am having discussing this with you, I have work to do, so I better get on with it." He grabbed his zip-lock bag and brushed past Lee.

"Not so fast, Lane." Lee's gravelly voice trailed him. "You know that promotion you've been after?" Troy stopped and Lee stood toe to toe with him.

Troy sighed. "What about it?"

Lee suddenly relaxed and glanced around the room. "I hear rumors that the big chief himself has *me* in mind for the position." He flicked an imaginary fleck of lint from his sleeve and smirked at Troy.

Troy stopped. "What makes you so sure?"

"I heard that bout you had with Kyle this morning about working on John's case. You don't think it'd be very hard to convince him that you've been following some little rabbit trails, do you? Maybe some rabbit trails leading right up to John's hospital room?"

"Lee, I have not done anything of the sort." Troy's face reddened, mostly because he'd planned to visit John as soon as he left the station. He started to walk again. Lee scurried after him.

"Or you could let me help you work on this homicide case and let's say we forget about the fact that I would get the position." He paused. "You can have it."

Troy stopped once more and stared at him. "Lee, why is this so important to you?"

"Will you take the reason that I think you're going to blow it and homicide is going to end up with a mess to clean up after you're done with it?"

"No."

"That's too bad, because that, my friend, is the only answer I'm going to give you for now."

"If you're trying to make me like you any better, Lee, it isn't working,"

Troy turned on his heel.

"Reckon I'll go have a talk with Kyle then." Lee turned as well, this time in the direction of Kyle's office.

"Hold it." Troy laid a heavy hand on Lee's shoulder. He sighed. "There's a remote possibility that you could prove to be helpful. So I will let you tag along for the investigation." He turned to continue down the hall. "And Lee." He called back to him over his shoulder. "I call the shots. You can come with me tomorrow, not before. You got that?" He strode through the lobby doorway.

His ears barely registered Lee's mumbled reply. "Well, we'll have to see about that, won't we?"

Troy pulled away from the lab, fuming. "I Can't believe I let Lee blackmail me. I can do this investigation myself." He chewed his lip as he glanced in the rearview mirror at the car behind him. "But I *am* following up on John and if word gets back to Kyle, I'm busted. *And* I don't get promoted." He sighed. "And with the baby coming, I sure could use that promotion." He looked both ways as he pulled into traffic.

Turning into the parking garage at the hospital, Troy spotted a space close to the door. He strode to the reception desk. "Where is the ICU?"

"Second floor." The receptionist turned back to her computer, her long French manicures rapidly clicking the keys.

Troy thanked her and made his way to the elevator. Punching the arrow pointing up, he glanced around the lobby. People milled through in a busy crowd, looking in the gift shop, opening and closing the front doors and checking in at the reception desk. Troy didn't know why, but for some reason the skin on the back of his neck crawled. *It's all in my imagination, but it sure feels like there's a pair of eyes looking right at me.*

The elevator doors opened and Troy stepped in, sighing in relief. He glanced back at the lobby. The crowd still stirred noisily. Troy couldn't pick out any one person staring at him, but the creepy feeling didn't leave him until the doors had shut fully.

Walking out onto the second floor, Troy followed the signs for the waiting room. Rounding a corner, he stopped short. "Jill! What are you doing here?"

Jill sat on a chair in the small waiting room. Across from her sat Bonnie, John's wife, and another man. An older couple completed the group, sitting on a sofa to one side. The woman's head lay limply on the man's shoulder. She raised her head and turned to look at Troy. Jill looked up and smiled pleasantly. "Hello, Troy. What are *you* doing here?"

"Came to check up on my partner—see how he's doing." He sat down on a nearby chair. "How are you holding up, Bonnie?"

Bonnie smiled wearily. "Okay, I guess." She had dark circles under her eyes. "Not much improvement so far. The doctors have done everything they can. They said right now it's just a waiting game." She twisted a handkerchief in her hands. "Jeff and Gary and Anita have been great, staying with me all this time." She motioned to the younger man sitting next to her and the older couple. She cleared her throat. "Two officers from your division came to the hospital and asked a bunch of questions. They didn't give me much info about the kids though. Do you know anything?" Her eyes pled with him.

"Bonnie, we still don't know a whole lot." Troy took her hand and squeezed it. "But we're definitely making headway bit by bit. We'll get them back. I promise." He struggled to make his voice sound reassuring. "Jake and Dorian are good guys. I know them well, and they're letting me know what's happening as it happens."

At this, the young man suddenly leaned forward, his eyes intent. "Officer, there's something you should know about Jake Thomas and Dorian Lepkowski."

Troy swiveled his head to look at him. "What's that?"

"There are two men claiming to be Jake Thomas and Dorian Lepkowski who really are not."

Troy narrowed his eyes. "How do you know this?"

"I was at John and Bonnie's house early this morning to check out the situation when two men pulled up in an unmarked car and identified themselves as Investigator Jake Thomas and Officer Dorian Lepkowski. They went through the house while I went to flip the breaker, which was off. When I turned it back on, the light in the storage shed was already on and someone had planted a rattlesnake on the freezer." He paused and shivered slightly.

"I—well, I get really sick when it comes to snakes, so I hit the door running. One of the men killed the snake. When I came back to the scene, the other one showed me a note that was hidden under the snake. They gave me the original note, then said they had to make a copy for their records. So the one guy wrote down the note, then gave me the original. I left at that point – maybe I was suspicious then. I'm not sure." He blew out a breath and glanced at Jill.

"Anyway, after I drove away, I went back on impulse to see if we had missed anything. I hadn't had much of a chance to look at the rest of the house. When I got there, I found a chunk of snake in the grass that the man had missed. It was part of a fake snake. It said 'Made in Japan.'" He blew out his breath. "I don't know what's going on, but I thought you should know."

Troy stared at him. "All that happened this morning?"

"Yes, sir."

Troy paused. "How are you related to the Siegles?"

"I'm sorry, I should have said at the beginning. I'm Jeff Siegle, John's brother." He held out his hand. Troy shook it firmly.

"Did you call our department then after you discovered the snake piece?"

"I called 911 and the real Jake Thomas and Dorian Lepkowski showed up in answer to that call, along with the fire squad and the ambulance. So now I've met them and know who they are. I—uh—didn't tell them about the note though. I wanted to keep it for a little bit to analyze it myself."

Troy's mouth twitched at one corner. "You sound like Jill. She didn't want to tell the police about her notes either."

Jill smiled ruefully at him from her place on the chair. "So did you get it analyzed?" He turned his attention back to Jeff.

Jeff shook his head sheepishly. "No. The message makes no sense really. It just says that I shouldn't look for my kids or my sister. And if John ever gets out of his coma and talks, then beware. Of *course* I'm going to look for my kids. But the note doesn't even leave me any clue of where to start. I guess I'm at a loss."

"So," Troy said and sat back. "Two snakes, one for each of you." He scratched his neck. "One major mistake those two so-called cops made this morning was giving you the original of that note. They must not have known about that rule. Did they have badges?"

Jeff nodded. "They weren't wearing uniforms though." There was silence for a moment.

Jeff spoke up again. "They also had British accents."

Troy sat up, suddenly alert. "Jill, didn't you say the two guys you overheard in the hallway at the firm had accents?"

Jill nodded, her eyes widening. She glanced from Troy's face to Jeff's. "Show him your note, Jeff."

Jeff quickly dug in his pocket. "Here's the note that was under the snake." He handed it to Troy. "What I don't understand is why the guys freely let me have the information that was on the note. Seems like they wouldn't have let me see it, much less take it with me."

"Maybe they're trying to bait you." Anita spoke for the first time. "You know, lure you somewhere."

"That's comforting." Jill looked at Troy, raising her eyebrows.

Troy sighed. "Jill, I just sent your notes to the lab for tests, but do you remember word for word what they said?"

Jill nodded sheepishly. Reaching in her pocket, she pulled out two slips of paper. "Here." She handed them to Troy. "I wrote them down as soon as I got back to my car this morning. I doubt I'll ever forget the words again, but I thought I should write them down just in case."

Troy chuckled. "I guess it works out then." He spread all three notes carefully on the coffee table in front of him. He leaned his elbows on his knees and studied them.

Jeff yawned. "I think I might snag a nap while I can. I need to be able to think, but right now, my brain feels like it's under water." He got up and wandered over to a full-length couch and collapsed on it, almost immediately snoring lightly. No one else said anything and silence blanketed the group.

Troy glanced about at the occupants of the waiting room once more before returning his attention to the notes. There had to be some clue buried within.

CHAPTER 9

Two men sat quietly in the lobby of Mission Hospital, one calmly reading *Newsweek* and the other one fidgeting and glancing around furtively.

"Do you think they'll get it put together, Elliot?" The fidgeting one's clipped British tones mirrored the tension evident on his face.

"I don't know, Topper." Elliot licked his index finger and slowly turned a page. "And do you know that's the fourth time you've asked me that question?"

Topper nodded, his knee bouncing. "Sorry, Elliot." He chewed a hangnail. "I mean, she knows what she's doing. We're just here to make sure that it gets done."

"Mm-hmm." The magazine rustled as Elliot turned another page.

Topper studied his bleeding hangnail. "Why she ever teamed up with that bloke, I'll never know. He'll probably be the ruin of everything. But with any luck, we can still get away with it. After all, England is a long way from here, and they'd have a hard time proving that she's a...."

"Topper!" Elliot jerked the magazine down as an elderly lady sat down on the couch across from them. Her cheeks wrinkled as she gave them a fragile smile and reached for the most recent copy of *Good Housekeeping*.

Topper nodded curtly in her direction and Elliot flipped his magazine shut with a snap. He stood up, stretched his long, thick legs, and then strode toward the gift shop. Topper stared after him, his teeth gnawing on his thumbnail.

The woman peered over her magazine at him. "It's a beautiful day, isn't it?" Her thin voice trembled.

Topper nodded absently, his eyes darting around the room.

"I thought maybe I'd plant my petunias this morning. The soil is just perfect from the rains we've had lately and they're such pretty flowers."

Topper didn't even bother to nod this time. He stared at the people in the lobby, glancing every now and then in the direction of the gift shop where Elliot pulled a 20-ounce bottle of Dr. Pepper from the glass case.

"I didn't get the petunias done after all." The old lady's blue eyes pooled. Topper glanced at her uncomfortably. He hated tears, particularly when a woman shed them.

"But my husband had some indigestion, so we had to bring him in here."

"Is that so?" Topper edged further away from the woman and scanned the room once again.

"Yes. Oh!" She clapped her hands in delight. "You must be from England. I'd know that accent anywhere. My husband is British."

Oops. Topper's jaw locked. If he and Elliot weren't careful, they'd be leaving a trail of evidence based solely on their accents.

The lady seemed to have forgotten the accent immediately. "Such a pity about my husband's indigestion." She sighed. "This is only the second time it's acted up since he died two years ago. The doctors told him then that he shouldn't have too much trouble anymore. It's so curious that it's bothering him again."

Topper's head swiveled and he gawked at the woman. He rose immediately and began backing away. "I'm sorry to hear that," he said and stumbled over the corner of a chair, frantically gripping the back of it to regain his balance.

"Oh, are you? Such a nice young man." She fumbled with a handkerchief and dabbed at her eyes. "You remind me of my grandson. God rest his soul." She wiped her nose and laid her handkerchief on her lap. "He drowned in a well when he was about your age." She glanced airily at the magazine for a moment before continuing. "He was going to come with my husband today, but decided to stay at home and have supper ready when we return. Such a good boy." Her blue eyes hazed as she stared back up at him, then her gaze drifted as she looked through him and to the window behind him. Seeming to suddenly forget he was there, she turned the page in her magazine and returned to her reading.

Topper turned and moved quickly toward the gift shop, glancing over his shoulder at the elderly lady. He collided with a large body.

"Blimey! Watch it, Topper." Irritation filled Elliot's voice. Topper glanced down at the open bottle of Dr. Pepper in his partner's hand. Half the liquid had splashed onto Elliot's shirt and pants. Most of it puddled on the floor.

"Oh, sorry, Elliot." He grabbed his partner's arm and pulled him to the men's restroom nearby. Inside, he grabbed a handful of paper towels and fumbled to wipe his partner's hands.

Elliot shoved him away and snatched the towels himself, muttering under his breath. He wiped fruitlessly at the dark stains. At last, he savagely stuffed the towels in the trash can. "You tosser!" He turned squarely to face Topper. "As if we needed one more thing to make us stand out!" He motioned to the stains covering his clothes.

Topper shrugged helplessly. "I'll go mop up the puddle." He grabbed some more towels and swung out the door. He wiped up the rest of the mess, and then hurried back into the bathroom. He threw away the handful of towels as Elliot finished cleaning himself up.

"Sorry about that, Elliot. That old crone sitting near us was as batty as they come. Said her husband was in hospital today, but that he'd died two years ago. And her dead son stayed at home to cook supper. Absolutely daft." He took the used tissues Elliot handed him, twisted them together in his hand and threw them into a trashcan.

"So you came running for old Dad?" Elliot looked at him condescendingly. "Come on, Topper. Stiffen your spine once in a while."

"I'll let her tell you the story. See if you think she's as loopy as I do." Topper pointed back to the couch where the elderly lady had been, but the couch was empty. "Huh." He glanced around. "She was there just a few minutes ago."

"Maybe she left to go find her dead husband." Elliot shrugged, unconcerned. He led the way back to the chairs. Topper sank back down and picked up a magazine while Elliot moved to the huge panes of glass and looked out at the parking lot. After a minute, Topper glanced up. Elliot's furious eyes were fixed on him. "W–what?"

"His car is gone." Elliot's voice was quiet, but Topper didn't miss the steel behind his words. "Because of your little stunt with the drink, we missed his exit."

Topper tried to defend himself. "We couldn't have missed more than five minutes or so."

"Topper, must I open up your pea-sized brain and write in a language that you understand that five minutes, or so, of time can elapse before that policeman *and* Jeff *and* Jill can stroll from the lift to the front door and be out of our sight before we even miss them?" His finger pointed rigidly at the front door. "That's the second muff you've had in two days. I'm going upstairs now to see if, for some daft reason, they're still there. You will stay here and if they're gone, she's going to expect an explanation. You'd better come up with one quickly." He turned on his heels and strode to the elevator.

Topper looked after him in utter dismay. "No." He felt his knees begin to tremble and sank down onto his chair. "Please no."

Jeff had not slept more than ten minutes before he felt a hand shaking his shoulder.

"Jeff, wake up," Troy's voice urged. Jeff's eyes opened and he blinked, his vision hazy. "I have an idea, but I need you and Jill to come with me."

With a grunt, Jeff rolled off the couch, the heels of his hands rubbing his eyes. Jill was already on her feet, her purse slung over her shoulder. Her eyes met his and she smiled. Jeff's heart skipped a beat.

Gary gently moved his sleeping wife from his shoulder and stood. He stretched with a groan. "Jeff, would you like me to ride along with you? Or do you prefer to have us stay here with John? We're here for both you and Bonnie, you know."

Jeff smiled appreciatively. "Thanks, Dad. I'm glad both of you are here, but I think Bonnie and Mom need you more at this point. I'm not sure exactly what Troy's got in mind, but it's probably easier to get more running done with less people."

"Okay, son. Just so you know we're here for you." Gary clapped Jeff's shoulder and then pulled him roughly into a hug. "We'll be praying that you find Emily and the boys. You are all so important to us."

Jeff nodded against his father's shoulder and when he pulled back, he swiped at the tears on his cheeks. "That means a lot, Dad. And I'll let you and Mom know any new developments as we find them."

Troy stuffed the three notes into his shirt pocket and leaned over Bonnie's still sleeping form. "Bonnie," he said quietly. She opened one eye. "We're going to follow up on an idea I have. Do you want to stay here or come with us?"

Her eye shut for a minute. "I'll stay here. I want to be here when John wakes up." She reached her hand up to grasp Troy's. "You will let me know, though, just as soon as there are any leads?"

"You bet. The info might come through Jake or Dorian, but I'll definitely keep following up on it."

She nodded, curling both hands under her cheek. "Thanks, Troy." Her eyes closed again.

Jeff and Jill followed Troy out of the room. Jill glanced over her shoulder. Gary went to stand by the window, his hands clasped behind his back and his lips moving silently. Anita and Bonnie lay quietly on two couches. More people waited in various seats and Jill's heart melted again. *All of these people in here are waiting for a loved one—to know whether he or she is going to live or die.* Her eyes welled up with tears again and she impatiently brushed them away.

Troy punched the down button on the elevator and the doors opened almost immediately. "So what's your idea, Troy?" Jeff entered first and turned to face the officer.

"I'll tell you about it in the car."

Jill felt the elevator shift and moments later, a soft ding sounded. The doors slid open, and the three of them walked to the front door and out into the late afternoon.

"Well, that's good." Troy lead the way to his cruiser.

"What?" Jill glanced up at him.

"When I went in the first time, I could have sworn that somebody was watching me. Didn't get that feeling coming out though."

Jill wrapped her arms around her waist, uncertainty filling her. She looked up at Jeff. "It sends shivers up my spine. What in the world have we ever done that someone is getting revenge for?"

"Beats me." Jeff shrugged. "I intend to find out though."

Troy unlocked the cruiser and Jill climbed in the front seat. She turned to look at Jeff as he slid into the back behind the sliding window. He grinned. "Never thought I'd be riding in the *back* of a police car. Isn't that supposed to be reserved for criminals?"

Troy chuckled. "Something like that, but you, my friend, have the advantage of no handcuffs. You're pretty lucky." He put the car in reverse and backed up.

"That's what they tell me, but after yesterday and today, I'm not so sure."

"You're still alive, aren't you?" Troy gunned the car forward and turned a sharp left onto the main road.

"Yes, but are my boys and my sister?"

Jill chewed on her bottom lip and gazed sympathetically at Jeff before turning to face the front.

The elevator doors slid open on the second floor of Mission Hospital and Elliot stepped out. He stood still for a moment, looking around. The nurses' station to his left buzzed with activity.

Elliot followed the signs for the waiting room at the far end of the hall. He cautiously peered around the corner, knowing that if Jeff Siegle caught a glimpse of him, there would be trouble. But just as he had guessed, Jill, Jeff and the cop were long gone. *That idiot she's assigned me to work with just let them walk out. Now we haven't the foggiest notion where they're going.* He turned on his heel and strode back toward the elevator.

"Can we help you, sir?" One of the nurses at the station looked up as he marched down the hall.

"No." He pressed the down arrow and the doors slid smoothly open.

He stepped in, his anger building until the blood pounded in his ears. As soon as the doors opened again, Elliot walked into the sunlit lobby. Topper jumped up immediately.

"Were they there?"

Elliot pulled his phone out of his pocket. "I'm putting in a call to her. You've got to be replaced."

"No, Elliot." Topper's voice sank into a whine. "Please, I'll do anything. Anything you want. Please, please don't make that call." His desperate fingers reached toward the phone in Elliot's hand but didn't touch it.

Elliot eyed him in disgust. His thumb had already dialed the first several numbers, but he paused and considered the matter. At last, he slid the phone back into his pocket.

"Fine. I won't make the call—for now. Just remember though, if you mess up again, I show no mercy. And you know that *she* doesn't believe in mercy."

"Y-yes." Topper's face showed his relief.

"Good. You just keep remembering that. I'll think of some way sooner or later for you to repay me."

CHAPTER 10

"Mom, what can I do for you right now?" Jill rubbed her mother's back as the older woman lay gasping next to the toilet. *"Do you think you can hold any tea down?"*

"No." Irene weakly pushed herself back to lean against the wall. *"Jill, you've got to call the hospital. This has been going on for too long."*

"But chemo usually makes you throw up."

"Not this much. This time, it's worse. I think they need to see me."

Jill's heart plunged to the pit of her stomach where her baby stirred. *"Mom, you can't go yet. I still need you here."*

"I've got to go, Jill." Irene raised her pale face to meet Jill's gaze.

"I don't mean the hospital, Mom."

"I know and I don't either." She clutched her stomach in pain. *"Jill, I want more than anything to stay here with you. But we both know the prospect is bleak—and the pain is worse—and I do so want to see your father again."* Tears filled her eyes.

"I know, Mom." Jill sniffed, tears falling down her own cheeks. *"But I'm— pregnant."* The words slipped out before she could snatch them back.

"What?"

Jill swallowed hard and nodded.

"David," Irene said weakly, pushing herself further up the wall and staring up at her daughter. *"Is that what happened between you two?"*

"He—he raped me." She shut her eyes against the wave of pain that passed over her mother's face. *"It was my fault. I let the situation get out of control."*

"Come here, my girl." Irene held out a trembling hand. Jill did as she was told. Irene stroked the back of her daughter's hand. Jill noted the blue veins where they

threaded her mother's gaunt muscles. "No matter what anyone tells you, including yourself, it's not your fault. David had a responsibility to respect you. He blew it." She smoothed a strand of Jill's hair behind her daughter's ear. "And Jill?"

"Yes?"

"You're right. You do need me here. So I promise I'll stay around as long as I possibly can."

Jill dropped to her knees, pulling her mother into an embrace as both of them cried. "Thank you, Mom."

Jill shook her head, blowing out her breath in a huff and blinking back tears.

"You okay?" Troy glanced over at her from the opposite side of the car.

"Yeah, just thinking." Jill straightened and turned to face him. "So, Troy, tell us about your idea."

Troy checked his mirrors as he merged onto I-81 North. "I've got a hunch that both of those notes are a code of some sort." He squinted into his rear view mirror.

"Really?" Jeff leaned forward to hear better.

"Yeah. I tried a couple of things and couldn't make any sense out of it, but I have a friend who is a cryptologist. He's done a lot of work for the force."

Jill chewed on her lip. "But why would they try to cover up their messages in codes? Why couldn't they just tell us straight out what they want?" She hooked a strand of hair behind her ear. "What's the name of the cryptologist, Troy?"

"Zachary Mayfield."

"Do you think he'll be able to decode the notes right away?"

"It's hard to say, Jill. It depends on how complicated the code is. He's taken several weeks sometimes for some things we've brought him and only a few hours at other times."

Jeff cleared his throat. "Well I think it's pretty obvious that John found out something that nobody wanted him to know. The note I got said as much. But if these notes *are* hidden messages, then Mom's probably right, too. They're luring us somewhere, giving us clues where to go."

Jill huffed. "But what really irritates me is that we have no idea who *they* are."

"And it's my job to figure that out." A muscle jumped in Troy's jaw. Traffic around the car lessened and the high rise buildings of downtown melted behind them. "I'd better call Zach before we get too far in case he's not there." He took his phone from his belt and punched in the numbers.

"Zachary? Yeah, this is Troy Lane. I need a favor if you'll be around. I'm working on a case, and I've got a couple people with me. We're heading to your house right now. You going to be home? Yeah, two of them. I'll explain it when I get there. You sure that's okay? Good, we'll see you in about an hour then." He slid the phone back into his belt. "Well, that's that. I guess we'll see what he's got to say."

"Sounds good to me." Jill heard Jeff settle back into his seat. His breathing evened out quickly as his tired body relaxed. Jill stared at passing vehicles and it wasn't long before her eyes grew heavy as well. Her lids slid shut and she succumbed to the monotonous rhythm of the highway.

Troy's tires bumped over white gravel as he pulled into a long driveway. He stopped next to a large white farmhouse, abundantly lined with lilac bushes, and turned off the motor. "We're here, guys."

Jeff's voice was gravelly from sleep. He cleared his throat. "This is Zachary Mayfield's house?"

"Yep." Troy climbed from the driver's seat. "Looks like he came out to greet us."

A large black man stood out on the front porch. He was completely bald and his eyebrows were shaved to match the rest of his head. Jill thought he looked intimidating until he broke into a huge smile and waved to them.

"Zach, good to see you again." Troy bounded up the porch steps. The two men shook hands.

Zachary's voice boomed. "How you doing, brother?"

Troy nodded at Jeff and Jill as they followed more slowly. "This is Jeff Siegle and Jill Lyon. They're each deeply involved with some of the work I need you to do, so I thought it best to bring them along."

Zach grinned at them. "Good to meet you both." He shook Jeff's hand and then turned to Jill. "My, my, what do we have here, pretty lady?" His white teeth sparkled. "You spoken for, honey?" Jill felt her cheeks go hot as his large hand engulfed her slim fingers.

Jeff cleared his throat. "Beautiful land out here." He pointed to the mountain ranges in the distance, somehow managing to place himself between Jill and Zachary. "You've got some gorgeous views."

"Thank you, brother. I do enjoy my home." He swung open the screen door. "Why don't you all come on in and make yourselves comfortable?"

When they were all seated in Zachary's living room, Troy reached into his shirt pocket and pulled out the three slips of paper. "These two are only copies of the originals, Zach." Troy laid them carefully on the coffee table in front of Zachary. "Jeff's is the original. I couldn't get Jill's originals from the lab before we headed up here." He laid the third note next to the first two.

Zachary stared hard at the pieces of paper. "I'm going to need some background." He rubbed his forefinger relentlessly over his thumb cuticle.

Jill jumped in without waiting for Troy. She pointed to one of her notes. "I found this one on a snake's neck at my house early this morning. I think it was around four or five o'clock. The snake had been left on my front porch in a basket. *I* think it has some connection with my boss' murder yesterday. He was shot to death in the office next to mine."

Zachary nodded. "Heard about that. It was all over the papers this morning."

Jill glanced at Troy. He motioned for her to continue. "This one I found in my office yesterday morning just after I discovered my boss' body." She pointed to the second note. "It was stuck to the base of my office chair." She hooked her hair behind her ear and sat back. "Then one of the partners called me this morning and laid me off from my job."

Zachary nodded again. "And you think the notes are in some way connected to your layoff?"

"Well, yes, I suppose. I've always worked hard for the firm and I couldn't think of any other reason that they would lay me off. Mr. Bradley did say that the reason was because my boss was dead and they no longer had the position open for me. But since I've been there for three years, which is more than most of the other secretaries, I felt that I had some seniority. So I thought it was strange that I was let go at the same time as I found these notes."

Zachary steepled his fingers and rested his chin on his fingertips. Troy motioned to Jeff, signaling him to give his story.

"I found my note early this morning underneath another snake, a rattler. I had spent the night at the hospital, because my brother, Troy's partner, was shot and is in the ICU ward now in a coma. I was there with my sister-in-law and my parents when Bonnie got a call letting her know that my sister and my two sons were kidnapped."

"Any idea why they told your sister-in-law instead of you?" Zachary broke into the narrative. "They must have known you'd be at the hospital with her."

"I don't know. I had sent my boys to John's house with Emily for her to look after them while I was at the hospital with Bonnie." Jeff paused. "My wife died over a year ago, which is why she wasn't there to take care of the boys."

Zachary nodded, motioning for him to continue.

"After we got the news, I went to check out the situation. When I got there, I met two men acting as cops. They'd copied the identities of two cops in Troy's unit and got badges and everything with the new names on them. You know," Jeff said slowly, turning to stare at Troy, "they were impersonating the two cops that were actually assigned to John's case, right? How would they have known that?"

Troy's jaw hardened. "Good point, Jeff. Somehow they got inside information. I wonder if we have a leak?" He massaged his temples.

Zachary tapped the coffee table. "Please continue, Jeff."

Jeff turned back to him. "Anyway, they checked over the house while I went to flip the breaker. That's where I found the snake, in the storage shed. One of the guys killed the snake, or I guess pretended to, because later I found a rubber chunk of snake left in the grass with the words

"Made in Japan" imprinted on it. I'm pretty sure they carried the real snake out in a garbage bag."

Jeff pointed to the note. "This was the note that the snake had been curled up on. They gave me the note and I showed it to Troy after I found out his connection with the case."

Zachary nodded again, staring at the notes. "Troy?"

Troy blew out his breath. "I was assigned to investigate William Bradley's murder. I wanted to work on John's case, but Kyle shot down that idea. Still, I have an idea that somehow the two cases are related. So I started snooping around anyway and found these two." He nodded to Jeff and Jill. "Their stories strengthen a lot of my theories." He blew out a breath. "My latest theory is that these notes are coded messages, but I've been scratching my head all day to try to figure out what they could mean. That's where you come in."

Zachary rubbed a hand along the back of his neck, massaging knotted muscles in his shoulder. Abruptly, he looked up. "You all want any supper? I've got apples, cheese and bread in the kitchen. Soup in the pantry. Help yourselves." He picked up the notes, walked into an adjoining room and shut the door gently with his foot.

"His office." Troy pulled his phone from his belt. "He usually tries to give us a little something to go on before we leave." He dialed some numbers.

Jill pushed herself off the couch and went into the kitchen, intending to start supper. Spotting some apples in a fruit basket, Jill found a small paring knife in a drawer and began cutting apples.

Jeff entered the kitchen behind her. He untwisted a bread bag that was resting on the counter. "So when your world isn't upside-down and spinning out of control, what do you do?" His tone was a study in casualness.

Jill glanced at him from the corner of her eye and smiled. "Throw the world into complete confusion again." Jeff flashed a grin, then shook his head and sighed.

Jill slid her knife into an apple. "It's okay, Jeff. I know your tendency is to let guilt consume you if you feel happy while your sons are missing, but you are allowed to smile. Go to your happy place." She rested the knife on the counter and leaned a hip against the wood as she gazed up at him.

Jeff's mouth turned up at the corners. "And where exactly is that?"

"Oh you know, where general good feelings reign in abundance, where one occasionally teases another, where the corners of one's mouth turn up instead of down." She smiled and found a plate in the cabinet. She began arranging the apples halves on it.

"Thanks, Jill." Jeff's voice was sincere. "I needed that."

She continued. "So to return to your question, besides working at the firm, I have always loved horses and I enjoy working with kids. So I've been volunteering at a local farm for the last eight months. They have horses, and they use the horses for therapy. During the evenings and weekends, they have disabled children come out and they let the kids help take care of the horses. It's a small-scale operation at the moment, but the owner is hoping to expand as more interest is generated in the Valley."

"Does that actually work?" Jeff neatly sliced the bread in diagonals and stacked the pieces on a plate. "I mean, does it help the kids overcome their disabilities?"

"Usually, over a long period of time. Not right away. Time coupled with love is the best doctor in a lot of these cases. But it's interesting to watch the kids and the horses relate to each other. The horses, oddly enough, seem to sense that the kids need to be able to connect with something. They really can't connect very normally in our world. So the kids connect with the horses. It's one of the neatest things I've ever seen."

"It's obvious you love the kids." His voice was quiet and Jill realized he was studying her face.

"I've always loved kids." She lowered her eyes, feeling the blood rush to her cheeks again. *Why do I blush so easily?* She carried the plate of apples to the table. "So what do you do when you're not worrying about kidnappings, shootings and snakes?"

Jeff dug in the drawer for a can opener then crossed the kitchen to the pantry to pull out two cans of vegetable soup. "I'm a general contractor for a housing company. I build houses in four counties so I'm on the road a lot. The kids play in the community soccer and basketball leagues, so I stay busy practicing with them, too."

Jill lifted the plate of bread triangles, carried it to the table and placed it next to the apples. "You're a good dad. And I think your sons must appreciate the time you spend with them."

"Yes." He sighed. "I'd give anything to know where they are right now. Or even just to know that they're okay." He sniffed and brushed the back of his fist over his eyes.

Jill's eyes pooled with moisture, and she blinked it away. She went to the fridge, pulled some cheese from it and began slicing through the large orange block. "Jeff," she said and then hesitated, "you mentioned to Zachary that your wife has been gone for a year. If you don't mind me asking, what happened to her?" She heard the soup-covered spoon clink as Jeff set it down on the stove. He picked up the pot and swished it quickly in a circle, the contents swirling around the edges. He set it back on the burner and picked up the spoon again.

"She died just over a year ago from cancer."

Jill's knife paused in mid-air. "I'm sorry."

She saw a muscle in his jaw jump, then relax. "I know." He paused. "It was hard to let her go—probably the hardest thing I've ever done. And it was hard on my boys. They'd wake up crying for her for months." He swallowed. "It's hard to be strong—strong for Cindy when she was still alive and strong now for Brian and Brandon."

"Hey, supper ready yet?" Troy came around the corner.

Jill threw an apple at him across the kitchen and continued slicing. "Sit. Eat."

"You hear that, Jeff? She's got those dog-training methods down pat. Give the dog a command and then a treat if he obeys." He tossed the apple from one hand to the other with a grin and took a huge bite.

Jeff snorted. "You calling yourself a dog?"

Jill deftly arranged the cheese slices on another plate and set it on the table. "That's because I've always wanted a dog and read up on all the training methods while I begged my mom to let me have one. But she never gave in, so I never got to practice." Her lips spread into a grin as she grabbed some napkins and dropped them on the table and sat down.

Jeff brought the soup from the stove and set it on a potholder. He sat next to Jill at the head of the table. "Let's pray."

Troy stopped chewing momentarily, his cheeks flushing. Jill and Jeff bowed their heads. "Jesus, thank you for this food and our many blessings. Please be with my boys and Emily. Help us to find them quickly. Help us to figure out the puzzle we're finding ourselves in. Guide our steps and protect us. In Your name we pray, Amen."

"Guess I should have figured you'd be a Christian, too." Troy reached for a piece of bread. "John was always good at praying."

Jeff nodded. "John's always been a great example to me. Hope he comes around soon so I can thank him for it."

The meal passed pleasantly enough and Jill sat back at last, her stomach satisfied. Two apple halves remained on the plate.

Jeff glanced at his watch. "Wonder if Zach's gotten anywhere in all this time?"

"It's only been a solid hour and a half." Troy pushed his plate back. "Give the guy time."

No sooner had he spoken than they heard footsteps. Zachary rounded the corner into the kitchen. He looked pleased with himself and snatched an apple half and stuffed it in his mouth. He winked at Jill and pulled out a chair.

"Well, then, down to business." He drummed his fingers on the table. "I have some good news, Troy. Your gut instincts were right. These notes are encoded messages.

CHAPTER 11

The phone rang and a man's soft fingers curled around the receiver. "Hello?"

"The deal hasn't been completed yet." The voice was resonant.

The man's fingers trembled and he glanced around the shadowy hallway behind him. "What do you mean?" He jerked his gaze to the open window, but black stillness lay beyond the fluttering curtains.

"She needs you here. Now."

"Now? You mean, tonight?"

"Yes. Her plans are not yet complete and she wants you here."

"But it's a long flight from here. How am I going to get there in time?"

"She expects you tomorrow morning. One of her jets is waiting for you at the airstrip."

The man glanced over his shoulder again and his voice dropped to a whisper. "What if you tell her I don't feel like coming? That I've decided to stay here?"

"That would be unwise." The voice chilled him. "You've killed a man."

The man nodded reluctantly, then remembered to answer. "I understand. I'll be there."

"Good. We will meet you when you arrive. We'll give you instructions then." The phone clicked into silence. He dropped the receiver back into its cradle and slumped against the wall.

"Really?" Troy leaned forward to view the notes that Zachary was spreading across the table. "What did you find out?"

Zachary smoothed out the note closest to Jeff. "Let's start with Jeff's note." He glanced up at him.

"So this is the hidden message." He paused. "'Meet outside the tower on July thirty-first for return of children.'"

Jill gasped. "What?! How did you get that out of it?" She stared at Zach in amazement. Troy looked speculative.

"A lot of trial and error, actually." Zachary tapped the note with a pencil. "But my final guess is confirmed by one of Jill's notes, so I know I'm right. I'll get to that in a minute though." He pushed the note to the middle of the table and leaned over it.

"I've seen work like this before." Zachary paused. "When people try to leave hidden messages in notes such as this one, a lot of times they will have keywords to look out for. Since the sentence structure is so strange, I started looking for a keyword on each line. This is what I came up with." He pulled his pencil from his shirt pocket and quickly circled the words for them. When he was done, the note read:

Jack fell down and broke his crown, tut tut.
We consider it **meet** *that the same thing should occur in John's scenario.*
But if he breathes a word of anything **outside the** *weather and sports,*
don't you know,
His **tower** *will topple.*
His crown will not remain whole for much longer,
Though it have **on** *it* **seven** *jewels, a grand portfolio,*
And the young ones of
Ages six, and eight, and **one thirty,** *all*
Will perish **for** *naught, O!*
And will never **return.**
Let us all hope that you would not wish this **of** *the brood.*
If you want your **children** *safe, even so,*
Remember all these things until we meet again.

"Wow," Jill said twisting the paper for a better view. "That's amazing. How did you know which keywords to pick? Couldn't you pick a lot of others and come up with a totally different message?"

"Technically, yes. Like I said, it's trial and error. And since the notes cross-reference each other, I confirmed this message when I figured out those." He paused. "It also helps that the authors didn't try real hard to hide the subtle meanings. They used some very common keywords."

Jeff leaned closer for a better look. "Where is the thirty-first then?"

"When they were listing the ages." Zachary pointed. "One thirty, or in other words, thirty one."

Jeff appeared to be thinking hard. "What tower do they mean? There are a lot of towers around here." He looked puzzled. "It could be the silo next door and we wouldn't know."

"I'm glad you asked, Jeff, because it's really so simple." Zachary gripped his pencil again and at the end of each line, he rewrote the last letter of that line with a hyphen next to the sentence. The note now read:

Jack fell down and broke his crown, tut tut. - T
*We consider it **meet** that the same thing should occur in John's scenario.* - O
*But if he breathes anything **outside the** weather and sports, don't you know,* - W
*His **tower** will topple.* - E
His crown will not remain whole for much longer, - R
*Though it have **on** it **seven** jewels, a grand portfolio,* - O
And the young ones of - F
*Ages six, and eight, and **one thirty**, all* - L
*Will perish **for** naught, O!* - O
*And will never **return**.* - N
*Let us all hope that you would not wish this **of** the brood.* - D
*If you want your **children** safe, even so,* - O
Remember all these things until we meet again. - N

Jill's eyes were huge. "The Tower of London!"

"It's a big tourist trap now." Jeff sat back in his seat. "I wonder where outside the Tower they want to meet us."

"My guess is that they'll find you." Zachary glanced at Troy. "You probably won't even need to worry about finding them. Saves you a lot of trouble in the long run."

Jill stared at the note. Suddenly she looked up. "It's July 27th today!" Her wide eyes stared at Jeff first, then Troy. "We've got to get plane tickets." She started to push herself up from the table.

"Give us a minute, Jill." Troy laid a calming hand on her arm. "Right now, let's see what Zach figured out about the other two notes."

"Right." Zach spread out the next note. "This is the one you took off the snake, correct?" Jill nodded.

Zach pointed. "This one was coded differently from Jeff's, but it still has some similarities. The message is still hidden in the text, but instead of actual words, they chose the first letter of several words to make a word in code. Look." He once again took his pencil and circled letters in the note. It now read:

Jack and Jill went up a hill
To fetch a pail of water.
Jack fell down and broke his crown
And Jill came tumbling after.

Most **e**very **e**vent **t**icks by
As **J**ournalists **a**ttack **c**ountless **k**lutzes.
Jamming **u**seless **l**yrical **y**arns
Upon one and thirty pages.

Don't you see?
To **o**ur **w**orst **e**nemies - **r**etribution!

"But there's no message in the nursery rhyme itself." Troy looked at Zach for clarification.

Zachary sat back in his chair. "Do you know any of the history behind this nursery rhyme?" He pointed his pencil at the note.

"Yes." Jill nodded. "I actually met Jeff in the library when we were looking up that very thing. The footnote said that Jill was originally Gill in the poem and Jack and Gill were two men. They were supposed to be in reference to a Cardinal Wolsey and a Frenchman named Tarbes, who tried to set up a peace treaty between Britain and France, but failed to do so. So the poem meant that when Jack and Jill tumbled back down the hill, they had actually failed in the mission they had set out to do."

"Excellent, Jill!" Zach slapped the table in delight. "Couldn't have said it better myself. Cardinal Wolsey was Lord Chancellor of England during Henry VIII's reign. This treaty between Britain and France was Wolsey's first failure apparently. As it turned out, Henry VIII used the failure for his popularity because he then went on to defeat France in the Battle of the Spurs in 1513." Zach finished with a grin.

"Wow, Zach." Troy chuckled. "You're quite the historian."

"My favorite classes in high school and college," he explained with a grin. He went on. "Something else you might find interesting: Cardinal Wolsey, after that first failure for Henry the VIII, didn't win any popularity contests with the king or his first wife, Catharine. He couldn't get a divorce pushed through the Roman Catholic Church for Henry from Catharine. Henry really wanted the divorce because Catharine couldn't produce a male heir. So chop chop and snip snip, Henry got illegally divorced and Wolsey was stripped of his title. The only thing he had left was the archbishopric of York. Soon after that, the king arrested him on charges of treason. He was on his way to prison, but he got sick before they arrived. He ended up being so sick that they never moved him from where they stopped, and he died there. And guess what his prison destination was supposed to be?"

Jeff guessed. "The Tower of London."

"Correct you are, my friend." Zach laughed.

Jill spoke up. "So you said that this note confirmed the date in Jeff's note? It only says 'Meet Jack, July, tower.' I guess the 'one and thirty' isn't coded. It's just blatant." She gnawed on her bottom lip.

"Yes." Zach winked at her. "It is pretty blatant."

Jill blushed. "So this message for me to meet Jack, does that mean that I am to meet Cardinal Wolsey?" She chewed a fingernail. "But it obviously can't mean that. He's been dead a long time."

Zachary smiled at her and unfolded the third note. "This might clear up things a little; or it might complicate things even more. Look here." He tapped the note with his pencil. It read:

Jill,
Both kings and commoners all alike
Use this device much as a tool,
The commoners to send a note to post,
The kings to make a rule
(859) 185-1919
218-9147
(251) 521-1819 5111
Don't let what happened to Wolsey happen to you.

"I looked and looked for a hidden message in the text itself, but didn't find anything that made any sense." He glanced around. "So I think this is a riddle."

"Huh." Troy tapped his fingers on the table. "That's interesting."

Jeff agreed. "Very. Anybody any good at guessing riddles?"

"Not really, but I'll try." Jill sat back and looked at her hands.

Zach smiled encouragingly. "Take your best shot."

"Well, since it's something that both kings and commoners used, it's not something extremely rare. Sending a note to post, I guess, would be something like a stamp, but they didn't have stamps back then, so I'm not sure what it means exactly. Plus kings can't make a rule with a stamp."

Zach shook his head. "Not with postage stamps. But what about an actual stamp, or as it's better known, a crest or a seal?"

Jeff looked puzzled. "A seal? Why are they telling us about a seal now?"

"And what are the phone numbers at the bottom?" Troy looked curiously at Zach.

"They're phone numbers for you to call so you can figure out the codes in these notes." All three stared at him.

Jill found her voice. "You're not serious."

"No, I'm not," Zach said grinning, "but it was a funny thought." He pointed to the numbers. "What I did for this one was count which number corresponded to which letter, starting with A as one, and B as two and so on. It's a pretty common way of decoding number passages so that was my first thought when I saw the figures. Some of them," he said, circling a 1 and an 8, "are in the double digits, so it made it a little more confusing, but when you decode the whole thing, it makes sense." He leaned over and began writing the letters above the corresponding numbers. When he was done, the paper read:

H E I R E S S
(8 5 9) 18 5 - 19 19

B R I N G
2 18 - 9 14 7

Y O U R S E A L
(25 1)5 21 - 18 19 5 1 11

"So it *is* a seal in the riddle." Jill's eyes gleamed. "But who is the heiress? What do they mean by that?"

Jeff stood and stretched his hands above his head. "Well, Jill, since you're the only female at the table and the note is addressed to you, it's most likely you."

"But I don't have a seal." Her eyebrows crinkled in confusion. She looked around the table. "How can I bring a seal if I don't even know what they're talking about?"

Zachary noted the confusion on each face, but felt helpless to come up with an answer. While the decoding had been relatively easy, the motive had him completely stumped.

"I don't know, Jill." Troy finally broke the silence. "But maybe if we go, whoever *they* are will be able to give us a hint as to what they mean. And if it's important enough, they can come back and get it, I guess."

Jeff nodded. "I guess that'll have to do. I hope they're not too cranky about it though." He smiled faintly.

"Don't we all," Troy muttered.

Jill was silent for a minute and Troy and Jeff looked at her. "What's up, Jill?" Jeff eased himself back into his seat.

"Are we for sure going then? I mean, this is a huge risk. We don't know anything about who these people are or how dangerous they are."

Troy and Jeff exchanged glances. Zachary watched from his place at the end of the table, not wanting to interrupt a tense moment between the three players in a twisted play.

Jeff sighed. "All I know is that I have to do everything necessary to get my boys and my sister back safely. And if that means that they come out unharmed and I don't…." He slid back in his chair, his eyes hooded. "Well, so be it." Then he leaned forward again. "But Jill, this is me, what I feel. If you're hesitant to come along, then by all means, stay here. Not one of us would blame you a bit."

Jill sighed heavily. "No, Jeff, for some reason they want me along or they wouldn't have given me the notes, killed my boss or any of the other things that have happened. If I didn't come along, who knows what they would do to your boys as a result?" She gave a determined nod, smiled with an effort, and glanced around at the group. "So tomorrow I'll get tickets to London?"

CHAPTER 12

The sun had crested the mountain range the next morning when Troy pulled into the police department parking lot. He swung his door open and hurried to the double glass doors.

"Good morning, partner."

Troy stopped. His fingers tightened around the door handle. Slowly, he let go and forced a smile on his face.

"Good morning, Lee." He worked at loosening his rigid shoulders and turned.

"Oh, come on now, Troy. Good mornings don't sound so good if you can't stop gritting those teeth of yours. Tsk tsk." He swung easily past Troy and opened the door himself.

Troy followed him in. He sighed. "Lee, I really can't see you and me working together on this case. I'll just handle it from here, eh?" He tried to sound persuasive.

Lee headed over to his cubicle. "Nice day yesterday, huh? I thought so anyway. It was a great day for hospital visits."

"Lee." Troy's jaw locked once again. "There is nothing in policy against going to see about my partner's health."

"Really?" Lee's gray eyes stared at him unswervingly. "Then I happen to know that you did not even visit that partner of yours. You were there for about ten minutes in conversation with five other people. I also happen to know that you have been on Jake and Dorian's tail about any information you can get out of the kidnapping case." He paused, clicking his fingernails on his desk. "Nurses make great friends, you know? Am

I right?"

Troy sighed. "Looks that way. Though for your information, the only tidbits I'm getting from Jake and Dorian are just because I'm concerned about John." He turned toward his own cubicle. "You coming with me today then?"

"Well, well." Lee snickered. "I thought you said you didn't want to work with me on this."

Troy forced some choice words back. "I'm leaving in ten minutes. If you're coming, be at my cruiser by then, or I leave without you."

Troy, with Lee in tow, pulled up next to the parking meter in front of Bradley, Bradley and Dunn, PLC. It was barely 8 a.m., but the sun was already shining with intense heat. Troy glanced up the winding staircase then over at his new partner.

Lee frowned at him. "What now?"

"Nothing." Troy held up his hands defensively. "I'm just going in to check over the crime scene again and we'll go from there." He unbuckled and eased himself out, not really caring if Lee followed him or not. He heard the passenger side door slam, so he knew his partner was on his heels.

Troy fumbled with the unfamiliar key and then pushed open the front door. He circled the main reception desk to reach the foot of the stairs. Bounding up the steps, he jogged down the hallway to the back of the building. He stopped in front of Jill's door and peered through the window.

Lee leaned against the wall behind him and folded his arms. "I'm waiting in eager anticipation to see your brilliant mind at work on this visit, though I bet Bradburn and Randall have already gotten all the evidence. Wouldn't surprise me though; they *usually* work with the homicide cops."

"Lee, that comment doesn't even deserve a response, so I'll just pretend you didn't say it."

"Pretend away, Lane."

Troy gripped the doorknob harder than necessary and swung it open. Officer Bradburn slipped into Jill's office from Mr. Bradley's, bags under his eyes. "Hey, Lane."

"Bradburn, you still here?" Troy chuckled at his haggard appearance.

"Yeah, I've been here most of the night. I didn't get all the sketches done yesterday and Randall's been switching off with me, doing more fingerprinting. Don't know what he thinks he's going to find though. Seems like every idiot in the place brushed over it with their fingers before we could get here."

Troy smiled. "Go home, Joey. I'm going to finish up here and they can reopen this place on Monday."

Bradburn nodded wearily, folding his sketch pad over and tucking it under his arm. "I'll drop this by the station on my way home, but I've got to get some sleep."

He nodded briefly to Lee and ducked under the police tape to exit the room. Troy slapped him on the shoulder on the way past, then swung under the tape. He stood in the center of the office, swiveling his head to take everything in at once.

Lee came to stand beside him. "Murderer enter through the window?"

"That's what the preliminary report says, but I wanted to make sure. I personally didn't inspect it when we were in here day before yesterday." Troy walked to the window and looked out. The office was on the second floor and there was no piping or any kind of a roof for someone to climb up. Troy rubbed the back of his neck. He reached down and wiped a thin blanket of dust from the windowsill. Walking back around to the front of the desk, he stared hard out the window and then at the chair behind the desk. His eyes suddenly pinpointed the window again and he rounded the desk quickly.

Troy grunted as he pulled upward on the window. "Sometimes I think the police force is a bunch of idiots." The window didn't open. "See?"

"I do." Lee rounded the desk to inspect the window. "The window locks on the inside and since the crime scene was left exactly the way it was when we—uh, sorry—when *you* were called to the scene, the murderer had to have left the scene from the inside."

Troy turned back around to gaze at the desk. "Not only that, but I think the murderer never entered through the window, even *if* Mr. Bradley did have the window open. I think he or she entered from this door right here." He pointed to the door adjoining Jill's office.

"Why is that, oh wise one?"

Troy shot Lee a withering glance. "Trust me."

He ducked under the police tape into Jill's office, jerked the outer door of her office open and plucked something off the wall in the hallway beside her door.

"First of all, that dust on the window sill hasn't been touched; certainly not today and probably not for a week or more." He ducked back under the police tape and came to stand beside William Bradley's ornate cherry desk.

"I just now figured this out." He held up a small, lined turquoise sticky-note pad. It had been hanging on a mold on the wall just outside Jill's door, obviously for anyone to leave messages for her if the need arose. A pencil rested in the holder next to it.

Troy began thinking out loud. "I've seen these post-it notes before— with a message written on them, addressed to Jill Lyon, Mr. Bradley's secretary.

"Now time wise, the murderer could not have come out into the hall, grabbed a piece of paper, the pencil too, written his or her message, which would have taken a slice of time, ran it back into the office and put it on Jill's chair base." Troy's voice was rising as quickly as his excitement.

"Jill left her desk to go to the restroom at 2:10. She remembered looking at William Bradley's clock before she walked out. She stayed there five minutes, during which time she overheard the conversation in the hallway. Immediately after that, she returned to her office, around 2:15 or 2:16, according to the report.

"The murderer could not have stayed in this office with her in the adjoining one. He or she would have had to actually write the message before they even entered the office and shot Mr. Bradley. The characters on the note were detail oriented and precise, probably to avoid handwriting similarities. They obviously took some time with it. After they shot the attorney, they would have placed the note on the foot of Jill's chair."

Lee rubbed his chin. "Maybe Jill took her time in the restroom. Those two men she overheard could have returned to the office and finished the job that they messed up the first time."

"No, Jill said she returned to her office as soon as the men disappeared.

The shooting had already happened while she was listening to them. Besides, the nature of the conversation indicated that it was someone else." Troy paced the length of the office. He stopped.

"You know, the report says that Mr. Bradley was shot from the front. If someone had come in by the window, he would have heard if they had waited to shoot until they could circle to the front of him. The way he was positioned when Jill found him was facing full front and completely slumped over the desk. They couldn't have shot him unless they were standing right in front of him—in the doorway."

He looked back at the pad of paper in his hand. "I think we're looking at an inside job."

For the second time in two days, Jeff found himself back at the Shenandoah Regional Library, counting off the minutes until the librarian would unlock and open the doors. "It's 9:56 now. Maybe we should knock." Because it was Saturday, the library didn't open until 10 o'clock and both felt keenly the passing minutes.

Jeff leaned against the wall of the library, eyeing Jill appreciatively. She looked refreshed this morning without the scared-rabbit look that had haunted her blue eyes yesterday. Jill had been too afraid to go back and spend the night in her house, so Jeff had taken her back to the hospital and told Bonnie and his parents to go home and sleep.

Jeff felt much better himself. As he had prayed before drifting off, a deep peace had stolen over him. He had sunk into a dreamless sleep that lasted until early morning. Then he had picked up Jill at the hospital and per her request, drove her to her house for a shower and change of clothes.

"Shadows and boogieman seem so much more real when it's dark, don't you think?" Jill's grin had lit up her face. "But it's not nearly so bad when it's daylight and you're here to keep the boogieman away."

Jeff had laughed. "I'll do my best."

Now Jeff watched Jill twist her hair up into a pony tail, outlining her figure and showing the firm muscle tone in her arms. His mouth suddenly went dry and he straightened, peering through the double glass doors.

"It'd be a whole lot easier to buy tickets online if I actually had Web service at home." Jill glanced at her watch. "I've always had it at work, so I never felt like I needed to spend the money for service at home."

Jeff nodded. "Cindy and I never bothered with it. We didn't want our boys to have hours to surf the Web and not get outside and play sports and learn to be creative."

The librarian was visible now through the doors and she shuffled over with a ring of keys. She eased the doors open and stared at them. "It sure is nice when I see people coming back here two days in a row." Each *s* sound whistled shrilly. "People just don't appreciate the written word anymore." She narrowed her eyes as if suspecting that they were guilty of just such a sin. "Come in."

Jill flashed a smile and eased past the lady. "Thanks."

Jeff nodded politely to her and followed Jill back to one of the computers. It wasn't yet turned on and Jeff leaned over to hit the switch. A steady hum filled the air.

Jill sat in the waiting room of the clinic, her mind numb.

'You really want to go through with this?' The small voice sounded sad. 'You know your mom wouldn't have wanted it this way.'

"I can't take care of a baby—not at this point in my life." Jill shifted restlessly. "Besides, it wasn't supposed to happen. It was all David's fault."

'How about trusting that God will provide for you and your baby? Ever think of that?'

"God let me down as far as I'm concerned and I'm pretty ticked at Him right now."

'God doesn't let people down, you know. He just doesn't always work the way we think He should work.'

Jill sighed impatiently and shoved the voice aside. "I'm going through with this— it's what is best for me." She swallowed hard, then added, "And I'm sure Mom would have understood if she had lived." A tear pooled in the corner of her eye and she impatiently wiped it away.

The door to the waiting room opened. "Jill Lyon?" A white-clad woman smiled into the room.

Jill sighed and typed in the Web browser, shaking herself free from the holds of her past. She scrolled down through the options appearing on the Web page. "Hmm. It's all pretty expensive." She pointed at the screen and glanced up at Jeff. "The cheapest is $1200 round trip to Heathrow."

Jeff leaned closer, the scent of his aftershave drifting over Jill. She tried to concentrate. "Since it's so last-minute, there are no good deals left."

"Well, we don't have a lot of options. I say go for it. They have three seats?"

"Yeah." She clicked on the 'Choose This Departure' icon and began working her way through the information. At length she turned. "Okay, we're leaving from Dulles International tomorrow the 29th at 7:30 p.m. They're supposed to send a confirmation e-mail once we pay for it."

"I'm glad we're getting there a day early." Jeff leaned back in his seat. "It won't hurt anything to get there a day before they said. With any luck, maybe we can surprise them and find Emily and the boys ourselves."

"Luck doesn't have anything to do with it, Jeff."

"I know." He smiled at her.

"Do you think the London police will be handling our accommodations, hotel, etc?"

"I don't know. Troy's working everything out with Scotland Yard, so we'll have to check with him. "

Jill pulled out her credit card and entered the information for the tickets. Jeff's cell phone rang and he jumped up to answer it. "Hello?"

Jill turned to look at him, hoping for some new information. He shook his head at her unasked question. He listened for a minute, then nodded. "Okay, I'll see what I can do, but yes, I'll try to be there in about an hour." He flipped his phone shut. "Jill, I've got to meet my foreman pretty soon and I can't get out of it. Can I drop you back by the hospital so you can do whatever you need to this afternoon?"

Jill nodded. "Sure."

"Okay." Jeff stood up and stretched, his fingertips reaching for the ceiling. "Well, my building site is almost an hour north, so I guess we'd better get going."

"Right." Jill exited the Web browser. She slid her purse over her shoulder and led the way past the checkout counter and out the front doors. The librarian peered over her bifocals as they passed. "See you later," the words whistled through her teeth.

CHAPTER 13

Jill pulled out of the hospital parking garage and looked both ways before turning left. Her goal now was to head home and do some packing for the trip.

Stopping at a red light, she glanced in her rear view mirror and brushed back some strands of hair that had escaped her ponytail. A small smile played around her lips.

Jeff had seemed reluctant to leave her in the garage. He had opened her car door for her, and when she got in, he had draped himself over it, making small talk. *Okay, admit it. You like him. It's been three years since David...not thinking about David. Jeff is for real.*

The light turned green, and Jill repositioned her mirror as she accelerated. *Of course, it's up to you, God. But I'm just letting you know my wish list once again.* She suddenly brought her mental processes to a screeching halt. *But now's not the time to think about that anyway. He's just lost his two sons, for crying out loud, and here I am planning our wedding.* She turned left onto Route 33, resolutely focusing on the road in front of her and planning what she needed to take with her to London.

Jill lived a good distance from the city and she always enjoyed her drive home. Fields and forests interspersed mountains and valleys. The sun blazed overhead and fluffy white clouds threw small shadows across the mountain ranges. Jill could not have asked for a more gorgeous day.

The wind whipped strands of hair across her face. For just a few minutes, she allowed herself to forget about Bill's murder, about the snake, the notes, London. The road changed to two lanes and the speed limit jumped to 55 miles an hour. Jill pressed the accelerator and her car flew down the road.

She checked her mirror again and noticed a white Ford riding her tail. She tapped her brakes as a warning, but the Ford didn't slow down. Instead, it just crept closer.

Jill gripped the steering wheel in frustration. "Okay, morons, brake check coming your way." Her jaw clamped. She slid her right foot over and hit the brakes harder this time. The Ford's tires squealed as its driver slammed on his brakes. The white car jerked violently to the left, but it wasn't enough. The front right bumper hit Jill's left brake light with just enough force to throw off her car's direction. She over-adjusted, her tires lost traction and she swerved wildly.

Her car spun off the right side of the road, down a steep hill and into a gully. Tree branches slapped her windshield, and a crack shot across it. Her front left tire hit a boulder and her whole car jumped, twisted sideways and landed hard on its right side.

Jill's white knuckles gripped the steering wheel, her eyes wide. Her airbags had deployed and hung limply from the wheel. She dangled from her driver's seat by her seat belt. *Thank you, God.* Her hands began to shake. *I'm still alive.*

She sniffed. *Smoke.* Jill started thrashing like a caged animal.

Frantically searching for her seat-belt release button, she finally thrust the button into its hole. Her seat belt gave way and she tumbled against the door below her. Standing up, she reached above her and unlatched her door. Crouching on her consul, she pushed upward. Using the strength in her legs, she heaved with all her might. The door flipped open. Her purse was wedged between the two front seats. With a moment of clarity, she snatched it and threw it out the door, then scrambled her way out. As soon as her feet hit the ground, she started running. Before she had covered a hundred feet, she heard a deafening explosion. She was thrown to her knees, her hands breaking her fall.

Jill twisted sideways, staring back at the wreck that had once been her car. Flames licked at blackened, twisted metal. A few branches on the surrounding trees burned, then turned slowly into smoke. Jill gawked, her mind numb with shock.

She licked her dry lips. *I need to call Jeff.* She picked herself up off the ground and stumbled back toward the car. Her purse had landed in a thicket about fifteen feet away. She pulled it loose and carried it to a tree. She sank to the ground and her hands fumbled with the snap on her purse. Her fingers rummaged through the purse.

"Cell phone. Where is it?" She pulled out her billfold and her glasses case. Shuffling the hodgepodge of items, she finally lost patience and dumped all the items on the ground. No cell phone lay in the pile. In a flash of memory, Jill saw herself falling against the passenger side door. Her cell phone lay wedged in the door handle next to her feet. Her eyes returned to the blackened, smoking metal heap. She swallowed.

"I guess I need to start walking." Her tongue felt thick and her mind reeled like an out-of-control spool. She slowly picked up the items from her purse and put them back in, the methodical movements calming her.

"Jill?" A voice called through the woods. "Jill? Where are you?"

She froze. Through the trees, she could see two figures moving down the hill from the roadside toward her car. Jill began edging toward the road again, stepping quietly and careful to stay behind trees.

"There she is." One of the figures jogged toward her. Jill walked faster toward the edge of the trees and the hill up to the road.

"Wait, lady." The man caught up with her. She turned to face him, her back to the road. Her eyes narrowed suspiciously. After glancing at her apprehensive face, he stuffed one hand in his pants pocket and pulled out a badge.

"Officer Jake Thomas here. Saw your car go off the road and wanted to see if there were any survivors." He motioned toward the wreck. "Looks pretty bad."

"You don't look like a cop." Jill knew she sounded rude, but at the moment, she didn't care.

"Plainclothesman, ma'am. That's my partner over there, Officer Dorian Lepkowski."

Jill's mind whirled. Through her shock and daze, she vaguely remembered Jeff telling about the two fake cops at his brother's house. Were these real or not? What had Jeff said about accents? This man did seem to have one. She shook her head slowly as if to clear it. A thought suddenly exploded in her brain. Her mouth had trouble forming the words as terror seized her.

"How did you know my name?"

"Uh…." Jill saw Officer Thomas' eyes flicker to the right, then come back to land on her face. "Someone called in your car tags as they saw you run off the road. We traced it through that–oi, wait!"

Jill bolted. She ran through the rest of the trees and straight up the hill, her purse swinging wildly over her shoulder.

"Get her!" She heard footsteps close behind her as the two men scrambled up the hill. She saw the roof of the white Ford at the top of the hill and she headed for it, her breath coming in short gasps. She risked a glance behind her and saw the big guy almost on top of her.

With a huge adrenaline boost, she kicked up sprays of dust as her long legs carried her to the top. Her lips murmured a desperate prayer. She angled toward the driver's side door of the car and flipped the handle. Relief spiraled through her as she saw the keys that still dangled from the ignition switch. She flung open the door and jumped in the drivers' seat, flipping the automatic door locks as she did so. All four locks went down at once, just as the first man reached the door.

"Open up, Jill!" He swung his fist at the driver's side window. The window jarred, but didn't shatter. "Wait! You don't understand! I've got to take you with me." The ignition flared up with a roar and Jill slammed the accelerator to the floor. The car fish-tailed in the gravel, spitting rocks in the air behind it, then hit pavement and was gone.

The smaller man cleared the crest of the hill, panting hard. "Elliot, what are we gonna do? We can't lose her, and now she's got the…."

"Shut up, Topper! You think I don't realize that?" He kicked a clod of dirt with a vengeance, an expletive spewing from his mouth, and then he stood looking after the disappearing car for a moment. Suddenly, he dug in his pocket for his phone.

"What are you going to do?" Topper looked curiously at the phone.

"We're going to call in a stolen vehicle, Topper. We paid for it legally and that's not her car." He punched in the numbers.

Jill glanced repeatedly in her rear view mirror as she struggled hard to keep her attention on the road. Tears rolled down her cheeks and she prayed desperately. "Help me, God, please help." Her breath came in quick, shallow bursts, her head felt light, and she realized suddenly that she was in the midst of a panic attack. She drove further out into the country, turning onto random roads, trying to get her bearings again.

"How can I go home? They know where I live. Are they there?" Her lips moved wordlessly, the tears coming faster and thicker as the situation finally set in. She eventually pulled over to the side of the road. Collapsing her forehead onto her hands, she abandoned all restraint and sobbed.

I will never leave you nor will I forsake you.

Jill looked up and glanced around. "Huh?" She sniffed.

Fear not. I have redeemed you. I have called you by name. You are mine.

Jill wiped the tears from her cheeks. She drew in a deep breath and let it out slowly. "Okay." She drew in a shaky breath. "I'm yours, God. I know you're protecting me. That means that even though I don't understand why all this is happening, you've got me in your grasp. So God, I'm…I'm trying really hard to trust you right now, but I need a little extra help." The sobs started again.

Don't lean on your own understanding. You've acknowledged me and now I will show you the way to go. Just trust.

"Okay." Jill swallowed hard. "I choose to trust you, God." Her panic lessened and calm descended. She could breathe easier now. She reached into her purse and pulled out a pack of tissues. She blew hard and wiped her cheeks and eyes dry, then put the car back in drive and pulled slowly out onto the road.

She glanced around her. "I don't even know where I am." A knot tightened in the base of her stomach. The trees were getting denser, and she had completely lost her sense of direction. She turned right onto the next road, then on impulse, swung into a graveled driveway to turn around. She shifted the car into reverse and started to back up when she looked in her rear view mirror. A little girl skipped across the driveway behind her. She slammed on the brakes, jerking the car to a rocking stop.

An older boy ran to scoop the girl up in his arms. "Sorry 'bout that, ma'am." He wore overalls and a straw hat, which he tipped in her direction. "Laura's blind. She don't watch where she's going." He seemed oblivious to the irony in his words.

Jill stepped out of the car. "That's okay. I'm just glad I saw her." She looked around, and then licked her lips. "Uh, excuse me, but I think maybe I'm lost. I need to get back to route 33 and then back into town from there."

The boy's freckled cheeks stretched into a grin. "Lemme go get my mom or dad. They're better with directions than I could ever get." He placed Laura carefully on her feet again, not caring or not realizing that he had simply left her in the presence of a complete stranger, and ran toward the house.

"Hello." Laura's big brown eyes turned toward Jill's soft greeting. A smile lit up her face. *Six? Maybe seven years old?*

"Hi." Laura's voice was high and soft.

"Laura is a beautiful name."

"My mommy thinks so, too."

"Then your mommy's a wise woman."

"Are you a wise woman?"

The question caught Jill off guard. She paused and then laughed. "I try to be. But sometimes I'm not very good at it."

"You have a nice laugh. Can I show you my rocks?" Laura held out her hands. "Lemme show 'em to you."

"Okay." Jill walked to the little girl and took her hand.

"You have skinny fingers. My mama has skinny fingers, too."

Jill laughed again. "Thanks, I think."

Laura pulled one hand free. She unzipped a small pouch she had clipped around her waist and pulled a pine cone from it. "I'll tell you where I found it," she whispered, "but you can't tell. It's a secret."

"I won't tell," Jill whispered back.

"I found this behind the sunset." Laura fingered the pine cone. "I went there once and it was so pretty. And these were everywhere. I asked the Mistress-of-all-Sunset-Things if I could take one back with me and she gave this to me."

Jill smiled and nodded, then remembered that Laura couldn't see her.

"It's very intricate."

Laura nodded. "Int'rkit." She reached back into her bag and pulled out a bundle wrapped in a red handkerchief. "This one, Ariana the Elf Princess gave to me." She gravely unfolded the cloth surrounding a miniature acorn. It was attached on one end to another identical acorn. "I was crying one night 'cause I thought the acorn might have been lonely without another acorn to keep it company. And Ariana came and danced under the tree where I found it. She gave me another one and attached them two together so they would never get lonely again."

Jill chuckled. "She sounds like a nice elf." Jill sensed that little Laura would be offended if she patted her on the head and told her that she had a vivid imagination.

"And this one is the last one I have." She pulled one more thing from the pouch. "This one, Jesus gave to me one night. He told me that when I get scared 'cause I can't see, that I can hold this rock and 'member that He's right there." She paused. "It's my favorite." She held out a pressed rose to Jill.

Jill's eyes filled with tears. "It's beautiful," she whispered, her heart crying. This little girl trusted so deeply in something she couldn't see. Or perhaps she *could* see. *Why is it so hard for me to trust you, God?*

Jill took the rose kindly. "Why do you call them rocks?"

"Because they're what keep me steady. If I didn't have my rocks, I wouldn't have anything to imagine or think about."

"I see." Jill dabbed at the corner of her eye. "I think the rock Jesus gave you is my favorite one, too."

"You got any rocks?" Laura's shining eyes searched in her direction.

"My rocks aren't the same as yours, but yes, I have some."

"What's your favorite?"

"Well, my mama's Bible, I guess."

"Can I feel it?"

Jill hesitated, realizing that Laura was asking to "see" it. "It's at home." Jill felt chagrined as Laura's face drooped. "Oh."

"But I do have my second favorite rock with me. Do you want to feel that one?"

"Yes! What is it?"

Jill removed the necklace from her neck and dropped it into the girl's outstretched hand. Her fingers deftly moved over the ring, tracing each bend and shape in it. "It feels pretty." Her voice was wistful.

"Yes, I think so. My mama gave that to me when I was eighteen. It was kind of a tradition in our family."

"Tr'dishun." Laura giggled. "Mommy, here's a pretty ring." She held it up high.

Jill stood quickly and turned around.

A middle-aged woman watched the scene with a smile on her lips. "You got a way with her. Laura don't open up much to strangers. Takes mostly to family and that's it."

"She's beautiful." Jill glanced back down at the small girl.

The woman chuckled. "Now that is her daddy's fault. Never was a handsomer man." She unfolded her arms and wiped them on her apron. Reaching out to shake Jill's hand, she said, "Viney Miller. You lost?"

"I guess so," Jill answered. "I ran into a bit of trouble back on route 33 and then kept driving till I was calmed down. Must have made a few wrong turns somewhere."

"What kind of trouble?"

"My car ran off the road and blew up."

The woman looked at the Ford, then back at Jill.

"Two men followed me, and—well, it's a long story, but I know that they're not good guys, so I ran away from them, got in their car and drove away." Her voice trembled, more from exhaustion than anything else.

"Honey, sounds to me like you need more than just directions." She walked over and wrapped her arm around Jill's waist. "You come on in and sit a spell. I've just got cornbread out of the oven and you can put your feet up and make a few phone calls if you need to."

Now Jill did cry. "Thank you." She swiped at the rivulets running down her cheeks. "God does care, doesn't he?"

"He sure does, honey. He sure does. You just keep trusting Him." She guided her to the door, Laura following behind, playing happily with Jill's necklace.

CHAPTER 14

Jeff grinned down at the bubbly girl in front of him. She coyly dropped her lashes, her green eyes dancing merrily. Of course he knew the girl was flirting with him. He glanced around the room full of people. Celia would have a fit if she knew he was encouraging it. She hadn't been able to come to this party, citing a gathering of Parliament. They had had a huge row. There wasn't any particular reason for the fight. He supposed they were starting to grate on each other's nerves. He knew it irritated her that he wouldn't come to live with her, though why he didn't, he couldn't say. Maybe he still had too much of his parents' influence ingrained in him.

His sister's face floated in his mind's eye as he watched the quirky grin of the green-eyed girl. He frowned abruptly and stalked toward the snack table.

"Jeff." A deep, booming voice hit his eardrum as a hand clapped his back.

"Oh, hi, Jim." Jeff's spirit deflated some more. He tried to head for the door.

"Are you well, lad?" The man circled around to the front of him, forcing him to either stop or run him over. Jeff opted for the first choice.

"I'm okay, I guess."

"How's that job of yours going?"

"Dandy." Jeff kept his tone discouraging. This man had dogged his steps for the last three months.

"Jeff, do you think this Sunday it might work for you to come to church with my wife and myself? We'd love to have you."

If he'd come to church. Not again.

"Sorry, Jim, but I have to work this Sunday. I have to work pretty much every Sunday. I've told you that."

"Aye, you've said that. I meant Sunday evening. We're having revival meetings for

a whole week, and the first one is this Sunday."

Jeff opened his mouth to offer the same excuse but Jim stopped him. "I've checked with your employer, too. He's not making you work Sunday evening."

Jeff blew out his breath in exasperation. "Jim, I'm not interested. Not interested in God nor anything to do with Him." If he thought his rude answer would make Jim back off, he was wrong.

"Why, Jeff?" Jim's voice lowered, his look compassionate. Jeff's stomach started to roll. "What's happened to make you turn your back on the only One who can give you true love?"

Jeff pulled in his breath, but Jim went on. "Because you can't tell me that what you get from the Duchess is true love. Your parents and sister and brother are all praying for you—pouring out their hearts for someone who turned away from them three years ago. The Duchess probably wouldn't give you a second thought if you walked away from her, except to be angry that you jilted her."

Jeff stared at him, stunned. "How do you know about my family?"

Jim put a hand on his shoulder. "Connections, lad. Give Sunday some thought. I'll be here for awhile and you come find me if you decide you'll go." He nodded at Jeff and wandered toward the punch table.

Memories of his parents and siblings floated in full color before his eyes. No matter how hard he pushed, he couldn't rid himself of them. Rebellion bubbled up inside.

'Come on, Jeff.' He squared his shoulders. 'You've learned magic. You've come a long way. Now use what you've got and get yourself out of this.' His anger burned against the man who had brought his family back to his mind. With a whispered hex, he put his anger to rest and waited expectantly for his justification to come.

Instead of the expected result, however, pain hit his windpipe. What the...? He clutched at his throat. The air he attempted to draw in was slow in coming. He gagged and choked. The air flow stopped completely. He fell to his knees, his eyes dimly taking in the staring people around him. Blackness closed in from the edges of his vision.

From far away, he heard a voice. 'In the name of Jesus Christ!' Suddenly, his windpipe released. Air rushed in. He blinked and the darkness receded, rushing from the room. He shook his head slowly from side to side, heedless of the people gawking at him. Jim stood over him, hand extended. "Need a hand up, laddie?"

Jeff brushed his thoughts away like dusty cobwebs, old and unwanted. He climbed into his truck, pulling onto 81 South. As distracted and upset as he was about his boys, there was also a tense excitement in him as he thought about his flight to London the following morning. It felt good to be *doing* something, even if he didn't know what exactly he *was* doing.

Troy called his cell phone. The London officials were expecting their arrival. Because of the nature of the instructions in the mysterious notes, though, Jill and Jeff would be "bait." Troy and Scotland Yard would remain inconspicuous and keep their eyes open. Jeff's adventurous nature was starting to blossom. It had been a long time since he had been in London.

Jeff shook his head, clearing his thoughts. He had enjoyed London itself, but his regret for the mistakes he had made there, the rebellion and denial of his family, threatened to return when he thought of its crowded streets. *I'm sorry, Lord.* How many countless times had he said that?

He punched a button on his phone. "Bonnie Siegle, please."

After a long pause, Bonnie's voice answered. "Bonnie Siegle."

"Bonnie, Jeff here."

"Hi, Jeff."

"Have you gotten any rest?"

"I've been dozing off and on for the last couple of hours. Brought some books from the house last night, so I've been trying to read some. Gary said he needs to return to work in the next couple of days, so they're not sure how much longer they'll be able to be here. But they did say they'd stay as long as possible."

"That's good. Tell them I'll call them a little later."

"Sure." She sighed.

"What's up?"

"I keep thinking about Emily and your boys."

"I know." Jeff nodded even though she couldn't see him. He clenched his jaw against the pain in his heart and emotions. "I'm trying really hard *not* to think too much about them. It's the only way I'm making it."

"I guess you're right."

"How was the house? I mean, was it still messed up from the

kidnapping?"

"It was empty," Bonnie answered. "The police have finished with the inside. There's an officer parked on the street around the clock though, in case anyone returns, I guess." She paused. "You coming over?"

"No, I have to meet Troy at the police station. Jill will meet us there, too, along with Troy's wife, Suzanne, and then we're all going to spend the night at your house. Although I guess I really should have asked. Is that okay?"

"No problem." She coughed. "But why the slumber party?"

"We're flying to London tomorrow evening."

"What?" Bonnie's voice shot up.

"Yeah, guess I should have told you that, too." He grinned as he checked his mirrors.

"Yes, you should have. Why London?"

"Long story short, we found some clues that are leading us straight to the Tower of London."

"Jeff, that's a prison!"

"Not for years, Bonnie." Jeff realized that he sounded impatient and adjusted his voice. "It's a tourist trap now. There'll be lots of people around, and we've got London police working with us on this."

Silence. Jeff tapped his fingers on the steering wheel. "Any sign of improvement in John?"

"Nothing yet. We'll see though. Keep praying."

"I am. And Bonnie?"

"Yeah."

"Tell me right away if he says anything, anything at all, even a grunt. Even if I'm in London."

"Got it. Tell Jeff. Words and grunts. From John."

"I'm serious, Bonnie."

"I know you are, and I am, too. I'll let you know."

"Okay, gotta run. I'm almost back to town now."

"Take care. I'll be praying for you."

"Me, too. Bye."

"Bye."

Jeff slid his phone in his belt and it immediately rang. He pulled it back out and answered as he signaled to exit the highway.

"Hello?"

"Jeff, Troy here."

"Hey, what's up?"

"Have you tried calling Jill lately?"

"Was thinking about it. I haven't gotten a chance to yet, though. Why?"

"She's not answering."

"Maybe she's on with somebody else."

"Could be, but I thought I'd let you know. You almost here?"

"I just got off the interstate. I'll be there in ten."

"Alright, see ya. And let me know if you hear from Jill between now and then."

"Gotcha." Jeff hung up. "Where is that girl?" He frowned. "Please keep her safe, Lord." He checked his mirrors before gazing at the road in front of him again.

He dialed her number. An operator came on immediately, informing him that the party in question was not available. Would he like to leave a message? No, he wouldn't. His foot pressed the accelerator harder and his truck sped toward the police station.

"Kyle?" Troy knocked quietly on the chief's open door. "You got a minute?"

Kyle unfolded his bulky frame from his chair in front of the computer and grabbed his coffee mug. "What's on your mind, Lane?" He walked to the counter and poured himself another steaming mug.

Troy eased himself inside the office and shut the door softly.

"Kyle, I've been working on the Bradley murder."

Kyle turned slowly, stirred his coffee and took a noisy sip. "That's a good thing, Lane, 'cause that's exactly what I assigned to you." He narrowed his eyes.

"What I wanted to say, sir, is that in tracking down evidence and clues to solve the case, I stumbled on some evidence that connects this case with my partner, John. It was completely by accident, sir, but I wanted to let you know about it." Troy realized he was talking fast. He could see his hopes of promotion slowly ebb as he watched Kyle's eyebrows lower. Kyle took another sip of coffee.

He probably wants to have a moist mouth to say, 'You're fired.' Troy mentally pictured his own abject face as he went to tell his pregnant wife. In his mind's eye, he could see Lee dancing with glee.

"Let's see the evidence."

Troy's eyebrows rose. After an infinite second, he fumbled in his uniform pocket. "Yes sir." He eagerly pulled out the three slips of paper he had taken from Zachary Mayfield's house the night before.

He spread the papers out on the counter next to the chief, smoothing the corners so all the words could be seen.

"These are the **two** notes associated with the murder." He pointed to the nursery rhyme and the one with numbers plastered across the bottom. "They were sent at different times to the primary witness in the case."

"Miss Lyon?"

Troy looked up in surprise. "Yes, sir."

"I've been reading over your report, Lane. It's good, thorough work." He nodded approvingly, and then waited for Troy to continue.

"Thank you, sir." Troy swallowed and continued. "But here's what I didn't include in the report yet. This is the third note, found at John Siegle's house, but directed to John's brother, Jeff. It's a long story how I managed to find the two people that these notes are connected to, and I'll cover that extensively in my report. But these notes—at least the originals in the lab—all have the same block letter print."

Kyle nodded thoughtfully.

Troy went on. "Also, I had a hunch that these were codes of some sort and we used Mayfield to decipher them. All three notes link together with their hidden messages. Whoever the author is wants to meet both Jill Lyon and Jeff Siegle on the 31st of July." He paused. "In London."

Kyle sighed. "Troy, as you know, it's against policy for you to work so closely on an incident involving your partner's life."

"But sir…."

Kyle held up a hand. "But as you've done most of the research leading up to this point and have connected two very high profile cases, I'm going to let you finish the matter." He smiled reluctantly.

Troy was speechless. At the least, he had expected to be let off with a warning and a reprimand and the evidence given to someone else.

After a moment, he remembered his words. "Thank you, sir."

Kyle returned to his chair. "Get going. You have a flight to get ready for." He took another sip of coffee, then rotated his chair to face the computer.

"Yes, sir." Troy nodded, then quickly folded the notes again, hurrying from the chief's office.

Jill's belly comfortably digested homemade cornbread. The terror of the morning had subsided somewhat under the family's calming influence. She was now curled up on their couch, a telephone receiver in her hand, trailing a twisted cord across the living room floor into the kitchen. No such thing as cordless handsets here. Laura sat on the floor near Jill's head, playing with a dolly.

Jill dialed Jeff's number and he answered almost immediately.

"Jill?"

"Hi, Jeff." Relief flooded her at the sound of his voice.

"Where are you, Jill? We've been worried about you."

"I know and I'm sorry I couldn't call you sooner. It's a long story."

"First of all, are you okay?"

"Yes." She closed her eyes and tears seeped through. "Now I am."

"Okay." There was a pause. "Go ahead and tell me the story."

"You know those two guys that were at your brother's house, claiming to be police officers?"

"Yeah?"

"They followed me when I was heading home. I didn't know who they were then, obviously, but they were tailgating me and I got mad. It's a pet peeve of mine." Jeff chuckled, and Jill continued. "Don't laugh. I know I need to work on that. Anyway, I gave them a brake check. They caught my bumper and sent me off the road into a gully, where my car got banged up and ended up on its side. Then I smelled smoke, so I got out as fast as I could. I got my purse, but my cell phone stayed in the car, which is why you couldn't call me. I started running and the car blew up behind me. All I could think of was that I needed to call you. That's when I realized I didn't have my phone in my purse."

Stunned silence. After a minute, Jeff found his voice. "Jill, you—I'm just glad you're okay. What about the two guys though?"

"Well, they had stopped at the top and then walked down to find me. I was still in shock. They were calling my name, and I didn't realize that they should have had no idea what my name was. But the big guy walked up to me and showed me his badge, trying to reassure me, I guess. He said his name was Jake Thomas. The name rang a bell from when you told your story. That's when I realized that they had been calling my name. So I ran. They ran after me and I headed toward their car because I know I couldn't have outrun them for long. I prayed really hard that the car was unlocked and the keys were in it. It was, and they were, and I took off."

A tear rolled off the end of her nose and she swiped at it. "I took some wrong turns, but it's okay because God led me to this wonderful family. I hadn't been trusting God, not really. When I prayed, he answered it in the form of these wonderful people." She sniffed and grabbed a tissue from the stand next to the couch.

"Who are you with, Jill?" Jeff sounded tentative.

"Jeb and Viney Miller. Hold on a second, Jeff." Viney was making waving motions at her. Jill put her hand over the mouthpiece. "Did you need something?"

Viney nodded. "Honey, Jeb and I were just talking." She nodded to her husband who was still seated at the table. "From what you've told us, you wouldn't be safe going back to your house tonight. Would you like to stay here tonight and then head back into town tomorrow to meet up with your friends? We'd be pleased to have you, but no pressure either. Just whatever you feel comfortable doing."

Jill smiled in relief, emotion washing through her. She felt so safe here and she dreaded leaving, heading back into the danger she knew waited for her.

She nodded. "I'd be pleased to stay. Thank you so much. You've all been more than helpful."

Viney wiped her hands briskly on her apron. "It's settled then. No one is going to hurt you here. I'll go get our spare room ready." She bustled down the hallway.

Jill put the phone back to her ear. "Jeff, Jeb and Viney just invited me to stay overnight here instead of heading back into town. You and Troy don't need me before tomorrow, do you?"

Jeff sounded concerned. "Do you trust them, Jill? Are they alright?"

"Oh, yes. This place has been an oasis for me, Jeff. It'll give me a much needed rest from what's going on before heading full-tilt to London tomorrow evening."

"Alright then." Jeff sounded only slightly mollified. "But call me before you leave to come to town tomorrow so I'll know when to watch for you."

Jill's mouth quirked into a smile. "Yes, papa."

"Jill, I'm serious. You've been almost kidnapped in the last few hours and my sister and boys *have* been kidnapped. For goodness' sake, Jill, you were almost killed! Just be careful, okay?"

"I will, and I'm sorry for teasing." Jill touched a strand of Laura's hair, combing through it with her fingers. Laura looked in her direction with a smile. Her eyes fixed just above Jill's head, her expression radiant.

"Don't apologize. I'm just tense right now." Jeff paused. "Hey, Jill, what's your username and password for your email? Troy was going to check and see if ticket confirmations were in yet."

"Two like the number, capital T, small r-u-s-t." She chuckled. "Can you tell what I've been working on lately?"

"Yeah, God's got a way of throwing you in the water sometimes to see if you can swim. Hey, by the way, do you have a current passport? Because if you don't, we have a problem.

"It's still current. I went to Nicaragua for a mission trip with my church last summer."

"Good. Troy and I have current passports as well, so one less thing to worry about. Okay, I'll see you tomorrow then. Hey, Jill?"

"Yeah."

"I am not your papa, and I do *not* view you as a daughter."

Jill's mouth curved upward at the edges. "Take care, Jeff."

"You too."

Jill hung up the phone and looked down at Laura, the small girl's beautiful face ablaze with delight. "You're staying overnight!"

Jill chuckled. "Yes, I am." She smoothed a stray curl behind Laura's ear.

Jeff hung up the phone. "She's okay." He blew out a gusty sigh.

Troy looked up from his desk and chuckled. "You like her, don't you?"

Jeff bent and retied one of his shoes. After a couple of seconds, he straightened, not quite meeting Troy's gaze. "Of course I like her. You like her too, don't you?"

Troy worked to keep the grin from floating to the surface. "Sure, sure."

Jeff shifted in his chair. He picked up Troy's paperweight and tossed it between his hands. "I mean, who wouldn't like her? She's... well, she's got guts." He tossed the paperweight up and tried to catch it. "And I really admire that about her. I still can hardly believe she's coming to London with us." He dropped the paperweight on the floor and dove after it.

Troy let the grin surface.

Jeff's face appeared above the edge of the desk. "Fine." Jeff thumped the paperweight back in front of Troy. "I do like her. Satisfied?"

"Okay, buddy." Troy held up his hands. "Just giving you a hard time. Somebody has to."

Jeff still looked grumpy. "Okay, but not in front of her. We've only known each other for—uh—two days?" He looked startled. "Is that allowed? I mean, to like somebody after that short of a time?"

"Anything's allowed, Jeff. You just have to decide what's right. I proposed to Suzanne the same weekend I met her." Jeff's eyes widened. Troy took a sip of coffee. "Six months and eleven proposals later, she finally said yes."

Troy typed in Jill's username and password. He drummed his fingers on the mouse pad as the computer rumbled under the desk. "It'll be the world's fastest record if we get that ticket confirmation in time. I've flown a lot in my life and I've never once gotten the ticket confirmation before a week's gone by."

"You probably also bought the tickets way in advance, too."

"That might have something to do with it."

A box popped up reading that a new message was waiting. Troy clicked on it.

"Good." He took a deep breath. "Well, that's it. Take-off is tomorrow evening at 7:35 p.m. You said your sister okayed us using her house until we have to leave for the airport?"

"Yeah, she did. Although I guess it'll just be you, Suzanne and me spending the night tonight. In fact, if Jill's not staying, you probably wouldn't even need to bring Suzanne if she didn't want to come."

Troy shook his head. "Suzanne's going to drive the car back from the airport. She's already got her things packed to come over. Jill can meet us in town tomorrow and we can head back to the house for a late lunch before we leave for the airport. We probably should head out around 3 o'clock so we're there in good time to get to the gate."

Jeff nodded and scuffed his toe against the vinyl rug cover next to Troy's desk. "Troy, do you think we're just walking into a trap here? I mean, we're following their instructions to the letter almost. They told us to wait outside the Tower of London and so we are; though I guess since Jill doesn't know what seal they're referring to, she can't follow those instructions."

"We don't know enough about the situation, Jeff. We *have* to play by their rules for now. If we knew more, we could call the shots." He pressed print on the ticket confirmation page, then looked intently at Jeff. "I know that you and Jill are in some danger. If you pull out, okay. We'll try to come up with a plan B. But for right now, I think this is the best thing we can do to make it work."

"Hello, Troy." Lee made his way across the room, weaving between desks.

Troy's shoulders sagged. "What do you want, Lee?" He consciously relaxed his jaw.

Lee ignored the question. "Well, well. Look who's here visiting. Why, it's Jeff Siegle. Now, Jeff, you wouldn't be any relation to one John Siegle in the ICU ward at Mission now, would you?"

Jeff looked confused. "Yes, he's my brother."

"Look at that, Troy." Lee's voice rose into a sarcastic whine. "His brother. And you said you were keeping off the kidnapping case?" He snorted. "I knew you didn't have it in you to stay away. And now I'm going to see that you're busted. Where's Kyle?"

"Go find him, Lee, if you want." Troy couldn't quite suppress the snide note in his voice. "I just had a nice chat with him this morning. He agrees with me that there's enough evidence in my case now to connect it with the kidnapping case. So I'm free to investigate all I want." Troy finished, trying hard to keep the I-told-you-so look from his face.

A thundercloud formed on Lee's forehead during this speech. He opened his mouth to speak, then abruptly shut it and stalked away.

"What was that all about?" Jeff gazed after him.

Troy chuckled. "Don't ask. I'm just glad it was a short partnership."

CHAPTER 15

Jill finished a luxurious breakfast with all the Millers except Jeb, who was finishing chores at the neighbor's farm. After helping Viney do the dishes, Jill stood reluctantly by the phone, one finger pointing to the scrawled phone number in her wallet and the other one slowly punching in Jeff's number.

"Hello?"

"Good morning, Jeff."

"Hey, Sunshine. You coming in now?"

"Soon. Where do you want me to meet you?"

"Let's meet at the police station. Troy's doing a few last minute things, and I need to grab some toothpaste at the store before we head out. What time do you think you'll be here?"

"Nine o'clock at the latest, I think." Jill glanced at her watch. "I'm on my way out the door."

"Okay. I'll see you then. You need anything? I can pick up something for you before you get here."

"You don't have to pick up anything." Jill twisted a strand of hair around her finger. "I do need some things, but I'll get it all when I get back into town. I'm going to get some clothes at the store, too. I haven't had a chance to go back to my house and pack, and honestly, I'm terrified to go there now. I'd rather wait till this whole thing is resolved."

"Hey, Jill, Bonnie's about your size. When we go to her house to eat before we leave, maybe we can grab some of her clothes for you."

"If that's okay with her, that's fine by me."

"I'll check with her." Jeff paused. "See you in a little bit."

Jill hung up the phone with a click.

Half an hour later, with hugs from Viney, Laura and Sam, she sat in the white Ford and backed slowly out of the driveway. She felt refreshed and was able to think more clearly after hours of normal conversation that didn't have to do with snakes, kidnappings or mysterious riddles. Laura had reluctantly handed back Jill's necklace and Jill had hunched down to the little girl's level to speak in her ear. "Next time I'll bring it again for you to play with, and I'll also bring my favorite rock, my mama's Bible." The family exchanged phone numbers with her and she left amid promises of coming again for dinner sometime.

Jill spread the hand-drawn map on the seat beside her as she drove away. Following it turn for turn, she eventually found herself once again on Route 33. She knew she was about 35 minutes from town, and if she hurried, she would reach the station by 9 o'clock. She pressed the accelerator harder.

She flew by a sign that flashed "Left Lane Closed." Jill moaned. All she wanted at this point was to get back to the station and see Jeff. She wondered about the intensity of the feeling. "I've just had a rough couple of days." She moved her foot over to cover the brake.

Traffic inched along in the right lane. The Toyota in front of her kept his brakes firmly pressed. She sighed impatiently and glanced at her watch. 9:03.

I'm still a long way from town and I told Jeff 9 o'clock at the latest. He's going to be worried, and I don't have a phone to let him know. She tapped her nails on the steering wheel. Looking to her left, she drove slowly past the scene where her car had left the road and she shuddered. The skid marks where she had swerved still shone vivid and black on the pavement. Jeff had told Troy about the accident and he had sent someone out to take care of it.

She glanced at her gas tank. The needle pointed to the red mark just below the E. Great. It would be just her luck to run out of gas now.

She craned her neck and saw the last of the orange and white barrels. Traffic began to pick up again and she glanced at her watch: 9:38. Now they really were going to be worried.

As soon as the right lane opened back up, Jill gunned it. Weaving in and out of cars, she headed toward the city. The buildings were sprouting up around her and she dodged through some of the main streets. Two more blocks to go. Traffic lined the curb and the lane narrowed. An oncoming car drove dangerously close to the middle line. She jerked the wheel to the right. She missed the front bumper of the black Dodge Neon but she scared herself in the process. The driver honked as he sailed harmlessly past.

She blew out her breath and gripped the steering wheel.

Blue lights flashed in her rear view mirror. "Oh, no." Her heart dropped to her toes. "Not right now." She craned her neck to check her blind spot, flipped her blinker and edged from the flow of traffic to the curb. She felt her wheels scrape the sidewalk edge and she glanced nervously at the narrow lane remaining. A truck roared by. It rocked her car with its force and shifted Jill's hair in its hot whirlwind.

The cop stepped onto the pavement. He adjusted the belt line of his uniform and strutted in her direction. "License and registration please." Sweat soaked his collar and he stuck a finger inside the neck of his shirt to loosen it.

"Sir, I'm so sorry. I'm running late to meet some close friends and I know they're worried sick by now." Jill's chagrined face didn't faze the officer.

"Ma'am, I need your license and registration." His tone was firm. "You'll need to leave earlier to give yourself more time."

Jill sighed and flipped open her billfold. Handing him her license, she rifled in the glove compartment and found what looked like the registration. She thrust them both into his outstretched hand. As he walked back to his car, she chewed on her pinkie nail while she watched him in her rear view mirror.

Jill gave up on the fingernail and twisted her watchband around and around her arm. The morning sun glinted off the face of the watch and hurt her eyes so she hung her arm over the steering wheel with a sigh. Abruptly, she leaned to shut the open glove compartment when she noticed familiar block letters, not as neat as what had been written on her notes, but bearing a strong resemblance.

She snatched the pad of paper resting in the glove compartment and stared at it. It was written in journal style with each heading dated. Her eyes skimmed the words and her mouth opened in astonishment.

The first entry was dated about two months previously and detailed the author's arrival in America. His task was to search out one Jill Lyon, employee at Bradley Bradley & Dunn in Northern Virginia.

She flipped ahead. Each entry ended with the sentence, *I will send my report to you the first of the week.* It was signed with a five-point star and a circle connecting the points.

Jill's eyes froze on the name, Jeff Siegle, in an entry dated June 28th.

I have located Jeff Siegle according to your instructions. He is a building contractor in this area. We have followed him extensively when Jill is at work or home. He is currently a widower with two young sons. I am still working on following up on his extended family per your request. I will send my report to you the first of the week.

It was signed, like all the other entries, with the five-point star again and the circle connecting the star's points.

Jill looked up, her wide eyes staring blankly ahead. So there had been someone following them both for almost two months! She shivered.

A movement in her rear view mirror caught her eye. Jill quickly slipped the pad of paper into her purse and buttoned it. The officer approached her car swiftly, his face intent. "Ma'am, I'm going to have to ask you to come with me."

Jill's eyes widened. "What happened?"

"Well, it appears that you are driving a stolen vehicle. I've got to read your rights." He pulled a small card out of his pocket. "You have the right to remain silent...."

"I know what my rights are." Jill sighed, a sheen of tears obscuring her vision. "Can you please just take me to the station? I promise I'll answer any and all questions there. My friends, I know, are frantic by now."

The officer stared at her, appearing to contemplate the request. "Ma'am, how did it come about that you are driving a stolen vehicle?"

"Please, sir, I'll explain it all at the station, but I've simply *got* to get there."

At last he nodded. "Okay. I'll take you there." He turned to survey the busy traffic, then faced her again. "Who are your friends?"

"Troy Lane and Jeff Siegle."

The officer nodded, squinting his eyes against the sun. "Troy's my commanding officer, so maybe once we get back to the station, we can get this mess figured out."

Jill snatched her purse, unbuckled, and stepped from the car, following the officer to his cruiser. He touched the radio on his shoulder, requesting a tow-truck for the Ford. The radio crackled as the dispatcher took his request. He circled to the side of the cruiser away from traffic and opened the back door for Jill. She sank gracefully into the seat and thanked him politely. He circled the car and slid into the drivers' side. He turned on his signal and pulled smoothly into traffic. The ride was a short and silent one. They passed through two green lights and turned right into the station parking lot.

The officer blandly reopened Jill's door for her and she climbed out onto the asphalt. She had taken three steps toward the front doors with the officer when Jeff and Troy catapulted out. "Jill!" Jeff ran toward her, Troy on his heels. Stopping short in front of her, he grasped her upper arms. "Are you okay?"

"I was just arrested for driving a stolen car." She glanced sideways at the officer escorting her, a smile playing on her lips. She could relax now that she was back with Troy and Jeff.

Jeff looked accusingly at the officer.

Troy stepped in. "Alright, Steve, before Jeff throws a punch at you, let me tell you that Jill is not a thief, did not steal a car—though she may have borrowed it—and that I've already got a handle on this case."

Steve nodded. "Okay, lieutenant. Whatever you say." He paused, and then turned to Jill. "But I did pull you over in the first place for a speeding ticket, didn't I?"

Jill's eyes widened and she felt the smile slide from her face.

"But since Lane will probably string me up if I give you one, I'll just forget about it." For the first time, his lips turned upward in a smile and he walked toward the station.

Jill breathed a sigh of relief. "Thanks, officer!" He turned and tipped his hat to her. "Welcome."

Jeff still had not released her arms and she looked up into his wide eyes now. "I'm really okay, Jeff."

He rubbed his thumbs along her shoulders. "Okay." He finally nodded. With no warning, he pulled her forward and hugged her fiercely.

"I'm glad you're okay." Jill could feel his chin resting on the top of her head. She felt warm and protected and she didn't want it to end.

Troy stood by, a grin on his face. "Well, I guess I'll wait in the station then if you don't need me. Sure you don't need me? Okay then." He turned toward the building.

"Wait, you goofball." Jeff released Jill and laughed. "We're coming, too."

Troy assigned an officer to run a report on the Ford to see what they could find out. With those orders, the three took their leave. An hour later, after a brief shopping trip for supplies and last minute details at the police station, they headed over to John and Bonnie's house to eat lunch. Jeff bounded up the porch steps to unlock the door. Jill pulled a duffel bag from the trunk that she had purchased on their shopping trip. She had already stuffed it with various articles of clothing, two tubes of toothpaste, shampoo and conditioner, floss, makeup, and other assorted items.

As she had cruised around the store, Jeff and Troy had watched her with amusement. "You staying for a month?" Troy picked up a 40-ounce bottle of lotion and pointedly held it up for Jeff to see.

"No." Jill felt a frown covering her face. "I just want to be ready for whatever comes." She snatched the bottle from Troy's hand, threw it back in the basket and stomped off, but not before she saw Troy and Jeff struggling to hide their grins. They both immediately sobered, however, when they saw her brush a tear from her cheek. The ride to the house was subdued.

Jeff flipped open the living room blinds, then went directly to the thermostat. "It's hotter than blazes in here."

Troy emerged from the brightness outside. "Suzanne's on her way over." He slipped his phone into his belt.

"Oh, good. I'm looking forward to meeting her." Jill's voice floated into the living room from behind him. "But I'd also like to get inside, too." Her jovial mood had clearly returned.

Troy grinned but didn't move. "Pushy women. What can you do with 'em?"

Jill's head appeared over Troy's shoulder. "I'll have you know that I am never pushy. Now let me in or face the consequences."

"Yes, ma'am." Troy scrambled to one side.

Jeff headed for the door. "I need to grab my carry-on, too. Have to add a few things."

"I'll get it." Jill dropped her bag and immediately wheeled back out the door.

Jill reached inside the trunk for Jeff's duffel bag. "Hang on, Jill." His hand closed around hers. He hadn't done that before. Jill's breath caught in her throat. Mutely, she stood back while he grabbed his duffel bag. He swung it easily over one shoulder. But instead of turning for the house, he slipped his free hand around her empty one. His thumb brushed the back of it gently and he stared at her.

The sun was brilliant and Jill watched the light play on his sandy hair. Her heart beat unsteadily.

He spoke. "I like you a lot, Jill, and I expect my feelings will probably get deeper the longer we spend together."

He paused and Jill spoke, the corners of her mouth curled upward. "I like you too, Jeff."

Jeff looked down at her hand and turned it palm upward. He traced the lines in her skin and his voice came out in a whisper. "It seems like forever since Cindy—and my boys need someone." He swallowed. "You don't know everything about me, Jill, and there's some stuff that you'll need to know before you get too attached."

Jill nodded, her wide blue eyes glistening. "Okay, when you feel ready."

Jeff pulled her hand to his mouth and kissed the palm. "When I feel ready. Thank you, Jill." He curled her fingers closed, sealing his kiss. Together, they turned and walked toward the house.

Troy looked up from his spot on the couch when they walked in. "You two get lost out there?" He looked irritatingly innocent.

Jill picked up a pillow from the love seat and threw it at him.

"Hey, I'm an innocent bystander!"

"Innocent is debatable." Jill rounded the couch to stand in front of him. "You're less innocent than I was driving a stolen car."

"But you were innocent of the stolen car, so that makes me only a *slightly* suspicious bystander."

"Y'all don't make any sense." Jeff laughed as he set down his duffel bag and collapsed into an easy chair.

"*Oh!*" Jill clapped both hands to her cheeks.

Jeff sat up straight. "What?"

Both of the men stared at her.

"I completely forgot." She squatted down next to her purse and pulled it open. Snatching a notepad from it, she waved it in the air. "I found it!"

Troy cocked an eyebrow.

She stared at him for a second before comprehension dawned. "I never mentioned it, did I?" She shook her head. "Oh, Jill."

Jeff snickered. She pinned him with her eyes and he sobered immediately.

She cleared her throat. "I found this in the Ford. It was in the glove compartment. It's a journal, detailing the work for the last two months of the 'them' that we've been wondering about."

"What!?" Jeff jumped from his seat.

"Let me see it." Troy came off the couch in one smooth motion and reached for the pad.

Jill handed it to him.

Jeff looked over his shoulder and scanned the contents.

"Interesting." Troy scratched his chin.

"What's that symbol?" Jill pointed to one of the stars dotting the pages.

"It's a pentagram. Many people use it, though in particular, it's thought of as a Wiccan symbol." Jeff's voice was grave. His past rose before him like a specter. A boulder came to rest in the pit of his stomach.

"As in witches?"

He nodded.

Jill's eyes rounded, her pupils filling up her irises until there was hardly any blue left. "Jeff, why would witches be interested in us?"

CHAPTER 16

A brief knock sounded on the screen door and Jeff, who was standing nearest the door, opened it. "Welcome."

The pregnant woman on the doorstep carried a paper bag. "Hello, everyone."

Troy vaulted over the love seat and wrapped his wife in his arms. "Hello, sweetheart." He bent his head to kiss her. "Come in and meet my friends."

Suzanne set down the paper bag and followed her husband to the center of the room. She held out her hand to Jill who shook it warmly. "I'm glad to meet you, Suzanne. Troy keeps mentioning you."

"All good, I hope." Suzanne laughed. She turned to Jeff. "So this is John's brother." She held out her hand to him as well. "Any new word on him?"

"Still in a coma." Jeff squeezed her hand and nodded. "Bonnie's going to let me know the minute there's any change in him, though."

"I need to call her. I wanted to make her a couple of meals so she doesn't have to cook during some of this time."

"That's sweet, Suzanne. Thanks." Jeff felt the smile cover his face.

There was a pause in the conversation. Suzanne retrieved her bag from behind the couch. "Anyone want to eat? I brought stuff for taco salad."

"Aw, honey, you're too good to me." Troy tugged his wife's hair. "How am I going to do without your good home cooking for days on end?"

"Incentive for you to come back." She pecked him on the cheek as she sailed past him into the kitchen.

Troy broke off into a tuneless rendition of "Ain't No mountain High Enough" as he followed her. Silence fell for a minute, then Troy came back to the couch, the notepad still in hand. "I need to look this over some more."

Jill nodded and went to the kitchen to help Suzanne. Jeff grabbed his duffel bag and carried it to one side of the room. He picked up the cordless phone and dialed his parents to give them more details of the trip to London.

"Hey, Dad."

Gary's voice carried clearly into the room. "Hey, son. Bonnie told us you're heading to London."

"Yeah." Silence. "Dad, I know it's been awhile, but I'd like to think I've earned back yours and Mom's trust since—well, since I was so young." He slipped off his sandals and curled his toes into the thick carpet.

"I know, Jeff, and your mother and I do feel that you've come a long way. But are you sure that London is necessary?"

Jeff sighed. "We're sure." He paused. "The notes clearly indicate that we're to meet the kidnappers there. I honestly don't see any other way to get Emily and the boys back to safety."

"I understand. And Jeff?"

"Yeah, Dad?"

"We do trust you—to do what's right. We're praying for you, too. I know we never really talked about this. You got back from London and we just sort of smoothed things over. It probably wasn't the wisest decision, but we felt at the time that it was best. But I wanted you to know that your mother and I have put that part of your life behind us. We've learned from it and we've moved on. We love you, son, more than we can say."

Jeff sniffed, moved beyond words.

"Thanks, Dad." His voice cracked. "I love you both, too."

Silence again.

"When is your flight?" The older man's voice gave a tell-tale quiver.

"7:30-ish this evening. We'll leave for Dulles in a couple of hours to give us plenty of time."

"Well, we wish both you and Jill well."

"Thanks, Dad. Tell Mom hi for me."

"Will do. Take care now."

"Love you. Bye."

Jeff glanced at Troy. The man had put down his notepad and was studying him closely. "Everything work out with your dad?"

"Yeah." Jeff nodded, smiling easily and blowing out a deep breath. He felt as if an eight-ton brick had just been lifted from his heart. "It's surprising how many years you can let things fester. Don't ever do that."

Troy chuckled as his cell phone rang. "Hello?" He flipped the pages of the notepad back and forth. "What? No way." He absently set down the notebook. Jeff leaned his elbows on the back of the couch and raised his eyebrows questioningly. "Uh huh. Uh huh." Troy looked at Jeff, a frown now covering his face. "Okay, I'll keep on the lookout. I tell you, Greg, I'll be glad when this is all over." He shook his head and tossed the phone on the couch beside him.

"What was that?"

"The Ford's gone—the car Jill was driving." Troy glared at the notebook in his hand.

"What? Who took it?"

"I'm guessing the two guys who chased her earlier."

"But how would they have stolen it from the impound? I mean, wasn't it locked up?"

"Yeah, that's what no one can figure out. It was there one second and then the next, it was gone."

"Should we tell Jill?" Jeff looked over his shoulder toward the kitchen.

"No. At least not yet. She's got enough on her plate at the moment. Who knows, if those guys have their car back, they might come sneaking around here."

"I'll keep my eyes peeled, but I'm kind of glad we're leaving the country tonight."

Troy lifted an eyebrow and stared at Jeff. "Only problem is, I'm pretty sure they'll be coming with us." He shook his head and sighed. "I doubt it'll be on our same plane, but if they've been tracking you for two months, they're not just going to stay here while we go flying off somewhere. I can just about guarantee you that we'll see them in London."

Jill set the table and the four of them sat down to taco salad. Jeff and Jill bowed their heads and the other two waited quietly until they were done.

As soon as everyone began helping themselves to the assortment of chips, meat, and fresh vegetables on the table, Jill started the conversation. "What I'm trying to figure out is how this Wicca star is supposed to relate to all the stuff we've been finding out about Henry the VIII and Cardinal Wolsey and all that. Zachary sure knew a lot. I wonder if he would know why this popped up."

"I don't know." Troy's mouth was full and his reply muffled. Suzanne pinched his elbow and he sheepishly swallowed. "It puts a new spin on the case. You know anything about this stuff, Jeff?"

Jeff's head stayed down and he shoved the food around on his plate. For a minute he didn't answer and Jill met Troy's glance over the table.

"I know some." Jeff looked up finally and his eyes met Jill's. "I used to be part of it. I was a member of a coven in London when I lived there before."

Jill's eyes widened and she sucked in her breath.

Jeff sighed and explained. "I practiced what I considered to be 'white magic,' never imagining that the powers I thought I controlled could ever control me. I got really good at simple spells and soon people started to respect me—called me really good at what I did." He glanced again at Jill. Her shock was fading quickly, and he must have been encouraged by her expression. He grabbed a handful of chips and crushed them onto his plate.

"But before much time had gone by, my spells stopped doing exactly what I wanted them to do and started taking on darker and more dangerous symptoms. I refused to acknowledge this until one of my spells nearly killed me." He paused, stirring his taco salad aimlessly with his fork.

"I followed the Wiccan Rede to a point—practicing my spells only on inanimate objects and for other people's good. Inside me, though, was a thirst for power. The more power and respect I gained as I practiced my magic, the more I wanted. At that point, though, I never would have admitted that as my goal." He sighed and set down his fork. He glanced again at Jill and she nodded.

"One night, I was in a group of people at a party. I didn't really want to go, but I did, and I wasn't sure why at the time. A man, a customer at the pub where I worked, showed up. He had stopped in several times to visit me over the past few months, and he never stopped inviting me to go to church with him. I mean, the guy *never stopped.* Of course I wouldn't hear of it. He confronted me about how I had turned my back on my family. That made me incredibly angry because I had ruthlessly torn them from my life and was shoving my guilt into a deep, dark corner." Jeff absently began folding his napkin into small triangles.

"All rational thought flew out of my head. As he walked away, I put a hex on him. I had gotten pretty consistent results with my hexes before and this one, I thought, was a harmless one. It was supposed to scare him just enough that he would leave and everything would go back to normal for me. I don't even remember what the hex was now, but I do remember being incredibly surprised when, instead of the usual result I got with my spells, the room got visibly darker. All at once, something like a vise gripped my throat. My windpipe shut and I couldn't breathe. I struggled and remember falling to the ground. Everything started to go black, but by the grace of God, this man realized what was happening." Jeff paused.

"Go on." Jill heard the words slip out before she could stop them.

Jeff shot her a half smile and continued. "I lay struggling to breathe on the ground. The man called upon the name of Jesus Christ, and just like that, I was free. I could breathe again and the darkness faded instantly. He gave me a hand up and he showed me how to find Christ that night." Jeff's voice faded here and a tear trickled from his eye. "I realized how chained up I was in my hatred. But when I asked Jesus to set me right again...." He paused and drew a deep breath. "I never felt so free."

Jill's wiped the tears away with one hand and gripped Jeff's hand with her other. "God's grace is amazing, Jeff."

Troy and Suzanne remained quiet. Jill was thankful for the respect they showed, though she knew they didn't share the same convictions.

"Turns out that Jim Higgins, the man I tried to hex, was actually a friend of my family. They had discovered that I was in London and had written him, asking him if he would try to reach out to me. If I had known about that before my conversion, I would have been really angry. After I became a Christian, though, I was thankful that I had a family that cared so much." Jeff's hand still gripped Jill's and he rubbed his thumb along the back of it.

"After that, I had it in my head that I was going to be an evangelist like Billy Graham. I was determined to go to seminary, but Jim sat down and looked me in the eye. 'Jeff, your gifts are not there. Yes, God will work in your life in amazing ways, but evangelism is not one of them.' I realized he was right when I tried preaching a sermon one night at the church I started attending. All but eight of the people were nodding off by the end." Jeff chuckled.

"I came back to the States and my family accepted me back as though nothing had gone wrong." He stopped and swallowed hard. "We didn't talk about my London experience for years. It was so painful for all of us. Just half an hour ago, I talked to my dad on the phone. The reality of what we're getting ready to do gripped us both. My dad told me for the first time since all that happened that he loved me." Jeff's voice broke.

No one spoke and after a minute, Jeff was able to go on. "When I came back, I went into business for myself as a building contractor. I met Cindy soon after and we got married. I have two incredible kids that are now in the hands of the same people I used to rub elbows with every day. Quite frankly, I'm scared to death." Tense silence blanketed the group.

Troy finally shifted in his chair and broke the quiet. "Jeff, it's obvious that your experience has been pretty traumatic. But would you be open to providing us with an inside look at this religion? I think if you can handle it, it could be very helpful to our investigation."

Jeff nodded. "I won't say that the past doesn't bring pain, because I'm still horribly ashamed of the way I lived. But I know God's grace has covered all of that." He smiled at Jill. "So yes, I will do anything I can to help. More than anything, I want my boys and my sister back."

Troy leaned forward, momentarily ignoring his food. "So what are some basic tenets of what these people believe? Is there something in their system of belief that could explain some of the actions they've taken?"

Jeff scratched his chin. "Not that I can think of." He hesitated. "I know you're not a Christian, Troy, so I know that some of this is completely foreign to you, but I'll try to explain the best I can." He took a sip of water. "I guess that the most basic thing for people who call themselves a witch or who practice Wicca is that they follow what is called the Wiccan Rede. It's a twist of the Golden Rule that most people associate with Christianity. It states that a witch may only use magic or spells for the good of others or themselves, never to hurt anyone. Unfortunately, what a lot of them don't realize, and I didn't realize when I was part of it, is that when a witch tries to help someone by casting a spell, a lot of times, it can hurt someone else, no matter how much 'good' the witch intends to do with the spell."

"Interesting." Troy nodded thoughtfully. "So based on this notepad that Jill found, do you know of any one particular person who practices Wicca who may want to find you or Jill?"

"I made a lot of enemies when I became a Christian." Jeff tilted his chair back on two legs and clasped his hands behind his head. "My coven was completely disillusioned with me, and I received several death threats in the following months. God protected me and I haven't heard anything for several years now." He waved his hand toward the notepad next to Troy's plate. "This is the first sign of my past cropping up since before I met Cindy. Somebody *may* have a grudge." He shrugged.

Jill broke in. "Plus, in the journal, their primary investigation was of me with just a few entries about Jeff. So does it make sense that the pure motive behind these notes is vengeance against Jeff?"

"I think you're probably right, Jill." Troy nodded.

Silence blanketed the group. Jeff scraped his chair back and stretched. "Maybe what we need is a good break from stuff like this for awhile. My mind has been going in circles since Bonnie called from the hospital, and I think it's time for a break."

"Right." Troy stretched as well. "We have to leave here by 3 o'clock to make it up to D.C. in good time to get to the gate. We'd better be cleaning up."

"I'll take care of the dishes." Jill scraped her chair back. Suzanne started to protest, but Jill interrupted. "This is your last chance to spend time with your husband for a few days, Suzanne. Don't you dare come into that kitchen."

Suzanne smiled and sank back into her chair. "Oh, Jill. If you insist."

Jill stacked the plates and carried them into the kitchen as Jeff followed with the cups and silverware.

Plunging her hands into the hot soapy water, Jill swirled the suds into a frenzy as her sponge wiped each plate to a sparkling sheen. Jeff had grabbed a dishtowel and was drying a glass. He watched her changing facial expressions carefully.

Jill took a deep breath. "So Jeff, is your past with Wicca what you wanted to tell me about before I got too attached to you?" Her words rushed out in a torrent as if she had needed to spill them before she lost her nerve.

Jeff smiled wryly. "Well, yeah. I guess it came out sooner than I had intended. I would have preferred to tell you in private, but—well, the situation just happened as it happened and I couldn't change it." He chuckled. "Though it feels good to know that I don't have to worry about you finding out before I'm ready."

Jill didn't smile as he expected her to. He set the glass down. "Jill?"

Jill's hands stopped moving in the dishwater. Jeff leaned one hip against the counter and waited.

"I guess we all have our secrets, Jeff. What I'm trying to say…." She sniffed and rubbed one wet hand against her nose. "What you said about God's grace, Jeff., I've known that all my life and I've taught the concept to the kids I've worked with and offered the idea to any of my coworkers that would listen; but, I never applied it to myself until you said it just now."

Jeff touched her shoulder and gently turned her to face him. Dishwater dripped unheeded onto the kitchen floor.

"I dated a guy for three months. Not very long, I know. His name was David. He was respectable, clean, nice, funny. My mother gave me her reluctant stamp of approval on David when I took him to meet her. I wish so much that I had listened to her concerns." Jill's wide blue eyes were full of unshed tears. She fixed her gaze on something behind Jeff's head.

"And then one night, David took me out for a nice evening. It was the whole shebang—the ritzy restaurant, string quartet in the corner, moonlit walk on the pier afterward. I thought he was going to propose; but he raped me. Just like that. I never saw him again."

Jeff pulled Jill against his chest and stroked her hair. He stayed silent as she laid her head on his shoulder.

"I got pregnant, Jeff. I was so confused by what was happening to me that I went to an abortion clinic and—and killed my baby." She shuddered against him. "I told my mom about the rape some months after it happened, but I never could get the courage to tell her that I was thinking of having an abortion. She died of cancer in my second trimester and I caved in to the pressure. A month after her funeral, I went to the abortion clinic, and then moved here to start over."

Hot tears seeped through Jeff's shirt onto his shoulder. He continued to rub her back as her body wrenched with sobs. He could barely understand her next words. "I've been so eaten up by guilt, even knowing that God forgives. I haven't forgiven myself, though. I had purpose in my life, direction. I graduated summa cum laude from college before the whole incident. And then I failed. I failed, Jeff." A fresh wave of sobs broke over her. Jeff tightened his hold, his hand gently brushing through her hair.

"It's okay," he whispered. "Cry it out."

She hiccupped and then took a deep gasping breath. "I've struggled since then to trust people. Even my closest friends, I'd look at with suspicion sometimes. In this situation, I've struggled to trust you and Troy completely, but as events keep happening, I find I have to. Don't take that the wrong way."

She pulled away from him and snatched a tissue from the counter. Wiping her nose she continued. "And I especially didn't want to trust God—not after he let all that happen to me. I've 'forgiven' God now." She smiled tremulously, holding up her fingers to make quotation marks in the air. "But I guess it leaves a lot of emotional scars. My inability to trust is one of them. It's taken some large steps of faith for me to get to where I'm at right now."

Jeff wiped a tear from Jill's chin where it hung ready to drop. "It takes work. Some of the experiences I went through, I found it hard to trust again as well."

Jill nodded and blew her nose again.

"Jill?" She raised her eyes to his face. "It takes a lot of time, too. Don't think you need to rush. Let me prove to you that I'm worth trusting, okay? That doesn't mean I won't make mistakes. But I will do my absolute best to let you see that I am a man who wants first in everything to do God's will."

Jill nodded. "Thanks, Jeff. I—I need to think about this and pray, too, for awhile."

She headed for the door. Jeff looked wryly at the stack of dishes still to be done and moved to the dishwater.

"Oh!" Jill's head popped back around the doorway. "I need to finish the dishes."

Jeff spritzed some water in her direction. "Get going, Jill. We have a long flight ahead, and you need to be refreshed for what's coming up."

"Thanks, Jeff...again." She opened her mouth to say something else and then thought better of it. "See ya."

Jeff turned back to the dishwater, scrubbing a plate hard with the green sponge in his hand, but his thoughts were centered on a vulnerable young woman on the back deck with blond hair as soft as rose petals.

CHAPTER 17

Jill opened her eyes with a jerk. The sun had slid over the roof and her chair cast a shadow on the deck. Her eyes felt gritty and she rubbed them with the heel of her hand, flinching suddenly as they chafed. She looked down at her bare arms. "Oh, no." She pressed her finger lightly on one. A white spot appeared, then returned to a deep red after she removed it. "I shouldn't have slept in the sun."

She stood, gingerly stretched, and moved to the side of the deck where she could see the driveway and the road beyond. Leaning on it, she yawned hugely and watched a few cars move lazily down the street. Jill's eyes followed them, her mind absently going over her luggage to make sure she had everything. Out of the corner of her eye, she noticed a white Ford parked by the curb, almost out of sight from Jill's vantage point. She jerked forward, squinting to get a better view, but the car was too far away to be able to make out clearly. *That can't be it.* She shook her head. *The police sent it to the impound.*

She pulled back from the rail and opened the sliding screen door to re-enter the relative darkness of the house.

Troy looked up from his place on the living room couch. "You look burned."

Suzanne elbowed him in the ribs. "Troy, you're being rude."

"Huh?" He looked confused.

Jill yawned again, sinking down into a cushy armchair. "I'm awake, but I'm not quite with it yet." She blinked rapidly.

"Looks like it." Troy chuckled.

"Well, are we leaving then?" She rubbed her eyes and winced.

"Yep." Troy pushed himself off the couch. "Jeff already took his bag out. Is there anything you need to add to yours?"

"No. I added a few clothes to my stash from Bonnie and bought all the rest of the stuff at the store."

"I'll say you did." Troy laughed and Suzanne smacked him on the shoulder. "Ow! Sorry." He struggled to look apologetic, though a smile still played on his lips. "Well, the car's loaded up and ready to go. Shall we?"

Jill and Jeff simultaneously took deep breaths. "I guess." Jill tried to put spirit into her anxious words. "Let's go get Jeff's boys."

Troy ducked into the kitchen. He motioned discreetly for Jeff to follow him.

"Take a look." Troy pointed out the window above the sink. Jeff craned his head to see, then straightened abruptly.

"You're sure it's the same car?"

Troy shook his head. "Not certain, but it's pretty likely." He rapped his knuckles on the counter. "Well, we knew they were going to be on our tails all the way to England, so we may as well take them along with us." He tossed the keys to Jeff. "You can drive if you like."

"Sure." Jeff turned to the front door, but stopped short as he spotted Jill's silhouette in the doorway.

"I saw a car that looked like theirs on the street, but I thought it was impossible." Jill's breath huffed between parted lips.

Troy looked uneasily at Jeff. "Jill, I got a call before lunch that these guys had stolen the car back from the impound. We didn't want to tell you, because this week is going to be rough, especially on you. We didn't want you to worry more than you already are."

Jeff stepped forward and wrapped an arm around Jill. He rested his chin on top of her head. "Jill, I'm here. And Troy's here. We're not going to leave you. And most importantly, the Lord is here too."

He felt her head nod beneath his chin and he stepped back. She smiled fleetingly and hurried across the hall to the bathroom.

"She's scared to death, isn't she?"

"Yeah." Jeff nodded. "I am too." He turned, opened the front door, and walked out into afternoon heat.

Traffic was heavy all the way to Dulles Airport. Red brake lights blazed down the highway in the late afternoon sunlight, and Jeff turned on his blinker to get into the departure lane.

"Are they still with us, Jeff?" Troy stuck his head between the two front seats.

"Yeah." Jeff glanced in his rear view mirror. "You would think that we would have lost them in all this traffic, but nope. They're five cars back."

"I wonder what they would do if they knew we knew they were following us?" Jill tapped her fingers on the armrest.

Jeff gave a quirky smile. "How does your brain come up with stuff like that?"

"Just a gift, I guess." Jill grinned at him though her eyes were shadowed.

Jeff angled the car in and out of lanes and finally pulled into the parking area. "Everybody out." He tossed the keys back to Suzanne and swung open his door. Popping the trunk, he jogged around to the back to unload their luggage.

Jill tugged her purse over her shoulder and slipped a hand inside to feel for her passport. She had made it a habit to carry all her important information with her at all times. She shuddered as she remembered how close she had come to losing not only all her identification, but her own life the day before. She watched the planes taking off and landing in the golden afternoon sunlight. *God, I have no idea what I'm getting into here. Anyone who uses snakes to deliver a message is someone that—well, I don't want to meet. Please help me to trust you as we walk into this. Keep all of us safe in your hands. I'm afraid, but I'm still going to do this.* She decisively snapped her purse shut before stepping from the car.

Troy stared up at the huge glass building in front of them. "Well, here goes nothing."

Jill hardly heard him. Her thoughts zoomed in on one word. Trust. The concept still eluded her, but obviously God wanted her to understand it. The word thudded in Jill's ears with each step she took. She pushed all other thoughts from her mind. She blindly steamed toward the building, momentarily forgetting her companions.

"Wait up, Jill." She heard Troy's voice some distance behind her. "The general idea was to get to London on the same flight."

Jill turned and waited impatiently at the bottom of the escalator. Troy took the lead and she followed in his path as he tapped on shoulders and excused himself to reach the top of the crowded escalator. A glance behind her showed that Jeff and Suzanne contently waited for the escalator to move them along.

"Alright." Troy reached the top and pulled Jill off to the side. "We need to go pick up the tickets. Then we'll head on over to security."

"Sounds good." Jill watched Jeff and Suzanne make their way over to them. "It's about time." She knew she sounded snippy she didn't care. Jeff and Suzanne looked at each other and rolled their eyes. Jill ignored the look, turned on her heel and began jogging through the airport, mindful of the others' hurried footsteps behind her.

An hour later, the three of them sat aboard British Airways Flight 292, waiting their turn to take off. Troy sat silent and glum across the aisle from Jill and Jeff. The flight attendants were going through their normal routines and Jill stared at a point somewhere behind their heads. Jeff leaned to look out the window. "Sure you don't want a window seat?" he whispered.

"No." Jill winced at the sharpness of her own voice. She immediately apologized. "I'm sorry, Jeff. I'm terrified of flying. I make myself do it, but I hate heights more than anything." She gripped the handles of her seat. "And I hate large heavy objects flying 30,000 feet above the ground, because it seems like they shouldn't stay up in the air, but somehow they do most of the time. I just don't want to be in one when it decides it doesn't want to be in the air and has to crash."

Jeff looked down at her white knuckles. "It'll be okay. I'll just talk to you the whole flight over to make sure you don't think about how high up we are." As his fingers brushed hers, she grabbed them. He obligingly wrapped his large hand around hers.

The motors roared and the plane started to speed down the runway. Jill shut her eyes and leaned her head back. Her grip around Jeff's hand increased in intensity, but he squeezed her hand reassuringly.

"Knock knock." Jeff's voice sounded close to her ear.

Jill relaxed her jaw a bit, though her eyes remained closed. "Who's there?"

"The impatient cow."

"Impat…"

"Moo!"

Jill lips curved up into a smile and a chuckle escaped her throat. "I've heard that one before. But your rapier wit is stunning."

"Think I should go into business? Friday nights down at the comedy club?"

Jill snorted. "No."

Silence. The plane leveled out and the seatbelt light went off.

"Jeff?"

"Yes?"

"Thanks for taking my mind off flying." She opened her eyes. He squeezed her hand. "Glad to see you like my brand of humor."

Jeff gazed in appreciation at the picture Jill made sitting next to him. Her deep blue eyes were highlighted by the sapphire ring on her necklace and her blue knit top. Her blonde hair had spilled over onto his shoulder and he had an irresistible urge to stroke it.

Jill unbuckled and leaned forward before Jeff put his thought into action. "I need to visit the ladies' room."

"Go for me too, will you?" Troy turned the page in his magazine.

Jill made no comment, though she playfully thumped him on the head on her way by.

No more than two minutes had passed before Jill slid back into her seat next to Jeff. She immediately leaned close so her breath feathered his cheek.

Jeff grinned. "Why, Jill, I didn't know you'd be so glad to see me after only two minutes." He slid his arm around her. "What happens if you're away for three minutes? Can I guess? Please?"

"No, you idiot." Her whisper hissed through her teeth and her face flushed a deep crimson. She pulled away ever so slightly. "I'm trying to tell you something, so please listen."

All joking flew from Jeff's mind. He turned to face her directly. "What?"

"The two guys that have been following us caught the same flight as us. They're in the back row next to the bathroom." She chewed her lip. "I figured they'd follow us to London, but I thought we got tickets late enough that they couldn't be on the same flight."

"Did they do anything to you back there?"

"No." Jill shook her head. "The one guy shaved his head, so I almost didn't recognize him at first. The other guy must have a fake mustache. I don't think he could have grown one that thick since yesterday. But they're still recognizable."

Troy stared curiously at them over his magazine. Jeff pointed discreetly to the back of the plane. "We've got company," he mouthed.

Troy peeked briefly around the side of his seat and nodded thoughtfully.

"Would you like something to drink?" The flight attendant stopped in the aisle with the drink cart. She had a pleasant British accent.

Jill leaned back against her seat. "Orange juice, please." The flight attendant nodded and handed her a small glass filled with the liquid. "Here you are. For you, sir?" Jeff shook his head.

Jill flipped the tray down from the seat in front of her and set her orange juice on it. She accepted the small plastic pack of pretzels the flight attendant handed her with a smile, but her hands shook as she opened the bag.

Jeff noticed immediately. "So you know a thing or two about horses? Tell me about them. I've always liked them, but never got good at riding them." He shifted in his seat to be able to see her better.

"Okay." Jill drew a shaky breath. "What do you want to know?"

"Anything at all."

"Okay, well, horses are pretty temperamental so you have to always be wary whenever you're around them. Never stand directly behind them. I did once and have a scar to prove it."

By the time the plane dropped its landing gear over Heathrow, Jeff knew just about everything there was to know about horses and most everything else under the sun. Jill had talked a blue streak, but he didn't mind. He liked the sound of her voice even after it became dry and croaky. She had eventually dozed off.

Troy raised his head and pushed the heels of his hands into his eyes. "We're here already? The flight didn't feel that long."

"You slept most of it." Jeff glanced at his watch and set it forward five hours to London time. "It's 8:30 in the morning. July 30th. Tomorrow's the 31st." As if a bucket of cold water had washed over him, Jeff felt himself mentally shivering in his boots. Tomorrow he might see his sons again. Tomorrow it would all play out.

The plane jerked and shuddered as it touched down on the runway. Brake flaps flipped up and brought the plane to a roaring halt at the end of the strip. They began a slow taxi to the gate.

People began unbuckling, but Jeff's fingers suddenly felt numb. He fumbled with his seatbelt release button and tried to ignore the panic that seeped into his heart.

Jill and Troy had already retrieved their bags from the overhead compartments before Jeff even stood up. They looked at him curiously. Suddenly all he wanted to do was curl up into a ball and cry. It was all coming back—the smoggy London air, the mess, the twisted mess he had made of his life.

"Ready?" Jill's blue eyes watched him carefully. They were clouded with concern. Jeff took a deep breath and nodded. He grabbed his bag from the overhead compartment and moved into the line of exiting people.

It was slow moving getting out of the plane, but eventually they walked up the accordion ramp into the airport. Jeff watched Jill glance over her shoulder several times, but each time, she caught his eye and shook her head. Jeff shoved his heavy thoughts from his mind. He put one hand on the small of her back as he walked close behind her. Troy, with his large size, barreled through the crowds of people toward customs and Jill and Jeff followed in his wake. Jeff felt as though they were walking into a black hole with no way out.

CHAPTER 18

A British police officer met them by the baggage claim and ushered them toward a room nearby.

"Lieutenant Sam Scott, Special Forces for Scotland Yard." The man shut the door on the bustle outside and held out his hand. "I do hope your trip was enjoyable."

"Yes, thank you." Troy gripped his hand firmly and nodded.

Lieutenant Scott shook hands with the other two, then waved to a group of chairs. "Please, be seated." Another deputy was already seated in one of them and he quickly rose when the others headed in his direction.

"Officer Cecil Barnaby." He nodded gravely and also shook each of their hands.

Lieutenant Scott sat down and faced the Americans. "Now, let's have a summary of your story. I've heard the majority of it from Officer Lane here, but I wanted to know your accounts." His deep-set blue eyes swept over Jeff and Jill.

Troy glanced at Jill and Jeff, took a deep breath and began a summary of the situation. Lieutenant Scott's brow furrowed as he nodded.

"So what you're saying is that you want these two to meet whoever has been threatening them at the Tower." His gaze pierced through Troy as he leaned forward.

"That's right." Troy nodded in agreement.

"And you want them to do it alone."

"Yes. At this point, we don't know what the plans are for them, and we don't want to do anything to risk harming the children."

"Well then, we'll jolly well have to do it their way then, won't we?" Lieutenant Scott's fingers absently combed his neatly trimmed goatee, his face intent as he studied Jeff and Jill. "You are aware that this is potentially a life-threatening situation, don't you? Even if we are able to rescue your tots, we can't guarantee that you'll come out of this alive. Though, of course, we'll do our best."

Both Jeff and Jill nodded gravely.

"What about you, miss?" The lieutenant looked directly at Jill. "You don't have children's lives at stake in this. Why are you risking everything?"

Jill chewed on her lip before answering. "But I do have childrens' lives at stake here. Whoever sent the notes to me is the same person who sent the note to Jeff. That person also has Jeff's children and sister in his or her power. The notes said I had to come, and they didn't leave any room for negotiation. I don't want to do anything to jeopardize the lives of Jeff's family." She paused and lifted her chin. "And I think God wants me here."

Troy felt his mouth jerk into a grin. "Can't argue with that."

Lieutenant Scott leaned back in his chair and locked his fingers behind his head.

Troy cleared his throat. "I believe you said you had accommodation for us while we're in London?"

"Yes. Since this situation has been rather last minute and we are smack in the middle of tourist season, I couldn't find any rooms close to the station. You'll be staying at the Lion Gate Hotel. It's across from Hampton Court Palace and next to Bushy Park. You have the last two rooms available."

"Thanks, Lieutenant Scott." Jeff rubbed his eyes. "I'm sure it'll be very comfortable."

The lieutenant smiled briefly. "Well, since it's obvious you all are suffering from jet-lag, let me drive you over. Have you got all your luggage?"

Troy nodded. "How far away is the Lion Gate?"

"It's a fair piece, but it shouldn't be too much trouble. Since it's so directly on site of the palace grounds, perhaps if we get this thing solved successfully, you all will be able to do some sightseeing as well." The lieutenant stood. "Now then, are we ready?"

Troy struggled to his feet. "Lead on."

Lieutenant Scott briskly opened the glass door and led the way back into the bustle of the airport.

Jeff pulled his duffel bag out of the trunk of the lieutenant's car last and followed the other three a few steps up the sidewalk.

"This way." Lieutenant Scott led them across the sidewalk in the late summer heat to the relative coolness under the awning of the Lion Gate Hotel's front door. He pointed to a large iron gate across the busy street. Lions topped the pillars on both sides of the gate and in the park beyond the black bars the group could see battlements. "That gate is the famous Lion Gate that this hotel is named after and beyond it is Hampton Court Palace and grounds. It's got quite a bit of history actually. Are any of you interested in British history?"

Jeff shrugged politely, hoping the four of them could just go inside and check in, but Jill nodded eagerly. "Yes, I think history is fascinating. I'm always interested to learn what I can."

"That palace that you see over there was the dwelling place of King Henry the VIII from the Tudor period of English history. Five out of six of his wives lived in it with him. He had the place restored numerous times and as he was an avid sportsman, he completed an extensive sporting wing to the palace as well."

Jill shook her hair back from her face. "You said it belonged to King Henry the VIII?"

Lieutenant Scott opened the door to the hotel politely and motioned them in ahead of him. "Yes, ma'am. Do you know much about him?"

The group stopped in the lobby. Jill shook her head. "Not a whole lot. I knew he was married six times before his last wife outlived him." She paused. "He had a sort of advisor, correct? A Cardinal Wolsey?"

"Ah yes, Thomas Wolsey. There are several places in this part of the city that we've passed named after Cardinal Wolsey, including a pub. The king did indeed inherit this palace from Cardinal Wolsey soon after the high point of Wolsey's power. I believe I've heard it mentioned that it was a political move on Wolsey's part. He knew he was declining in favor with the king and he knew the king coveted his palace, so he gave it to him as a gift."

"Did it put him back in favor with the king again?"

"Sadly, no. Wolsey became more and more unpopular with the king and eventually had his title and most of his lands stripped from him. I believe he was ordered to be executed at the Tower."

"But he never made it."

"No ma'am, he grew ill to the point of death before his escorts even arrived with him to the Tower and he died elsewhere." He looked at her speculatively. "So you *are* familiar with this part of British history."

Troy broke in. "Actually, that's part of the investigation I still wanted to explain to you yet. I understand I'm meeting with you and a couple of your officers this evening. I'll gladly fill you in at that point."

Jeff shrugged off his duffel bag and looked appreciatively around him. Pointing to the row of windows in the dining room to the left, he asked, "What park is that?"

"It's called Bushy Park. There are several deer that inhabit the park and are very tame. If you get a chance to wander through, you'll probably run into some of them, though I believe the park is closed after dark." He pointed. "You can just see the Diana Fountain there up the street. If you have time, the park is a wonderful place to relax, and you'll likely need to relax after this ordeal is over."

Jeff's shoulders sagged at this last comment. "Yes, you're probably right."

Lieutenant Scott greeted the concierge at the reception desk. Jill, Jeff and Troy waited patiently in the dining room for their police guide to bring the room keys.

"It's better accommodation than I hoped for, that's for sure." Troy fingered a thick linen tablecloth. "I didn't expect such a nice hotel."

"I'm just glad we each have beds." Jill yawned and stretched her long legs in front of her, crossing them at the ankles. "I'm bone weary. I don't want to sleep much now though, 'cause I'll never sleep tonight and it'll take me longer to get adjusted to London time."

"You've got a point." Jeff bopped her on the head with a brochure he was holding. "I say we keep it to an hour and then head out."

"Two hours." Troy stretched his arms over his head.

Jill sniffed. "An hour and a half and that settles it."

The two men chuckled.

Lieutenant Scott stepped into the dining room. "They've given you two rooms at the front overlooking the street. Hopefully the traffic noise won't be overwhelming. They're your rooms for as long as you need them, but hopefully, we'll finish up this case in the next few days."

The beeping of Jill's alarm clock crowded into her fuzzy consciousness along with the noon sunshine. She opened her eyes slowly, for a moment unable to remember where she was.

A knock sounded at the door and Jill groaned as she crawled off the bed to open it.

"Ready to go, Sunshine?" Jeff's voice greeted her as she turned the lock.

"Give me a minute." She opened the door wide for him before stumbling to her duffel bag to dig out her eye-drops. "I slept in my contacts. Stupid mistake." She held the bottle above each eye and splashed a drop of liquid on both sides. Blinking rapidly, she turned to look at Jeff. "Now I'm ready." Tear streaks ran down her cheeks from the drops.

Jeff grinned at her from where he leaned against the doorjamb. "Never could stand to see a pretty woman cry."

"You haven't seen a *pretty* woman cry, yet." Jill immediately clapped her hand over her mouth. "I'm sorry, I shouldn't have said that."

Jeff looked puzzled.

Jill explained. "My pastor at church once told me that even though I've had a past and it's easy for me to view myself as disgusting and dirty, I'm still precious in the sight of God. I need to view myself as God's child rather than a filthy rag." She chewed her bottom lip. "So it's easy for me to come out with comments that tear myself down, but I've been working on trying to see myself as God sees me."

Jill watched him to see his reaction and he nodded thoughtfully. "You're a good example to me, Jill." He cleared his throat suddenly. "I'm proud of you." He eased forward and pulled her into a hug.

Jill smiled as she hugged him back. "I could get used to this, you know."

Jeff pulled away slightly and looked down into her face. "I could, too," he said, smiling, "but I want to be careful. I want to earn your trust—over time. I want to be pure before God as well. I've done things in the past that were not holy, but I want our relationship to be completely God-honoring." He gazed steadily at her. "Do you see where I'm coming from?"

Jill nodded, smiling as peace settled over her. "Yes. Jeff, I think that little speech you just gave did more to help me trust you than anything else you could have done."

Jeff chuckled. "Good." On impulse, he kissed her upturned nose. "Troy's waiting for us. We'll eat lunch on the way. I don't know how long a tour is going to take, and we might want to look around by ourselves as well, so we should probably scoot. The Tower closes at 5 o'clock this afternoon.

Troy hopped out of the cab before the others, then leaned through the window to pay the driver. Jill and Jeff crawled out of the backseat to stand on the sidewalk. Jeff crumpled up the pastry wrappers that were all that remained of the lunch the three had grabbed at the hotel. Jill studied the towering structure before them.

"I'll get tickets." Troy waved cheerfully, striding toward the blessedly short line at the ticket office.

"I never really thought much about the Tower of London till this whole thing started happening." Jill turned in a circle, drinking in the sights. "And I never thought I'd actually see it. London's never been on my list of places to see, though I don't know why."

"You can feel the history just sopping from the walls of this place." Jeff's eyes moved slowly over the stone battlements and tower tops. "So many generations of people have lived since the Tower was built."

"Troy said that the tour guides here are called Beefeaters. They're here to take care of the Tower, but part of their job is to be tour guides.

Maybe we'll get to tour with them."

"Maybe." Jeff's hooded eyes followed various people, suspicion written across his face.

"And here we are." Troy joined them, holding three tickets in his hand. He handed one each to Jeff and Jill. Together they walked toward the structure, their heads tilted to see the top.

"It's huge." Jeff's voice held awe.

"Yep." Jill suddenly felt short of breath. How in the world were they going to find Jeff's family in this place?

A woman in a black rain-proof jacket and hat stood at the entrance, greeting each newcomer and tearing tickets. She took their tickets. "Cheers," she said.

Jill took her stub and pushed it into her pocket, nodding pleasantly to the woman. The three passed through the entrance to the Tower and headed up the stone walkway toward the large courtyard.

Jeff pointed. "Look at the ravens!"

Jill's brow crinkled. "Why are some of them in cages?"

"I've heard that there's an old superstition behind it." Troy leaned on a nearby stone wall. Jeff and Jill stared at him. He blushed. "Hey, it's just a random fact I remember hearing in a high school history class. I'm really not as smart as I look." He winked.

"So what's the superstition?" Jill looked back at the ravens.

"All I remember is that the ravens are tied in somehow to England's monarchy. As long as the ravens stay, supposedly the monarchy will continue, though I think the primary reason there are still ravens here now is because their wings are clipped. Maybe one of the Beefeaters explains it in their tour."

Jill twisted a finger through her hair. "Do you think we should try to get a tour while we're here? I mean, that's probably the best way to get an idea of the layout of the Tower for tomorrow."

Troy nodded. "Good idea, Jill. Let's go get information."

"Do you think they have any idea that we've followed them to London?" Topper peered out the window into the courtyard where three familiar figures mingled in a small crowd of tourists. A Beefeater gestured in front of them, standing on a wall close to the raven cages.

"I'm sure they do." Elliot settled deeper in his chair. "They've proved they're smart. They figured out all the riddles didn't they?"

A voice spoke from the corner. "Their cryptologist friend figured them all out."

"Oh, that's right. You were following them that night, Lee." Elliot glanced in his direction. "After Topper lost them at the hospital, I thought sure we were stuck."

"You're lucky she didn't find out about your mistake. You'd be snake bait otherwise."

Topper shuddered.

Lee threw him a disgusted look. "Speaking of which, how did the snakes do on the trip to and from the States?"

"There were no problems, security or otherwise." Elliot kicked his legs in front of him and crossed them at the ankles. "It's surprising what money can do, if you have enough of it."

Topper jumped in, hoping for a change of subject. "What are the instructions for tomorrow?"

Lee approached the window and gazed down into the courtyard. Jill, Jeff and Troy, surrounded by a group of fellow tourists, now followed a tour guide toward a door. "You'll meet them just before noon."

Topper shuffled his feet. "But…."

"Not simple enough for you, Topper?" Lee's words ground into Topper's bones and grated. He nodded quickly.

Lee leaned against the window frame, tapping his fingers on the sill. "It'll be an interesting meeting." Topper and Elliot remained quiet. Lee's face transformed into a leer. "Very interesting," he said, and then a trace of a smile appeared on his thin lips.

CHAPTER 19

Troy cynically eyed the few relics of torture instruments that they passed, the tour guide's words fading into the background. He twisted his lips as he pictured the poor unfortunates who had been subject to these tools.

"Makes you glad we live in the modern era, huh?" Troy nudged Jill as she bent to read an inscription. "Sure would hate to meet up with something like that now." He pointed to a small metal contraption that looked like an upside down V with a loop at the top and two smaller loops at the ends. He squinted at the inscription next to it. "Looks like they shoved the poor guy's head through that top loop there and the feet through the bottom ones, so they were never able to stand up straight. Talk about cramping your style."

Jill groaned. "Ugh, those poor people. I don't see how anyone could be so cruel." Troy shook his head and followed the other two through several more rooms, each displaying extensive information on Tower weaponry and armor used in previous centuries.

At last they stepped back outside into the fresh air. Jill meandered over to a bench and sank down onto it. Jeff and Troy sat on either side of her, though no one said anything. Troy scanned the courtyard and tried to ignore the dread practically seething from the other two.

Troy also tried to ignore the prickly sensation on the back of his neck as his hair stood on end. He had felt much the same way in the hospital lobby a few days ago. He narrowed his eyes and looked around, sure they were being watched.

He finally sighed. "Well, I'll get a cab and we'll go eat an early supper at the hotel." Jill nodded and pushed herself to her feet, Jeff following suit.

No one spoke in the cab. Troy watched Jeff and Jill's sober faces and tightened his resolve to wrap up this case as soon as possible.

Jill decided to go up to her room immediately upon arriving. Jeff promised to come get her in half an hour or so for supper.

Troy watched her walk up the stairs before tapping Jeff on the shoulder. "Did you see them?" He kept his voice low as he motioned for Jeff to follow him to the corner of the lobby.

"No, see who?" Jeff's face suddenly became very intent.

"Our shadows, of course." Troy sank down onto a couch. "The people following us. Only this time, there were three of them."

"How do you know?" Jeff sat on the second couch facing Troy and leaned forward with his elbows on his knees.

"They were always about three displays behind us. Two of them I recognized from Jill's description of them on the plane. The third one was wearing a hooded sweatshirt with the hood was pulled up, so I couldn't see his face. There was something familiar about the way he stood though. I wish I could remember!" Troy blew out his breath in exasperation and grabbed a magazine off the table between them. He opened it and stared out the window.

"You're completely sure it was them?"

"Positive. Like I say, I saw two faces clearly."

Jeff nodded thoughtfully. "Well, we knew they were following us to London. I guess I shouldn't be surprised that we've spotted them once already."

Troy shook his head. "I just can't think what was familiar about that third guy. I hope I think of it before it's too late." He glanced down at his magazine. "I'm meeting with Sam Scott and a couple of his assistants on this case after supper. We're going to work on a couple more strategies in case…," he pause and glanced up sharply at Jeff's face.

"In case what? No, never mind, I know. In case something happens to Jill and me."

"Yeah." Troy studied Jeff's face and felt relieved that he didn't look too worried. "Man, how do you do it?"

"Do what?"

"Through the whole course of this investigation, you've never once flipped, like I know I would if I were on your end of it; or on Jill's."

Jeff stared at Troy, then grinned briefly. "I would flip if it were all up to me, if *I* were the one that everyone was depending on; but I'm not." He leaned back and propped his feet on the coffee table. "Jesus is the only one that can get us through this, and I know beyond a shadow of a doubt that he won't let us down." He shrugged.

"Jeff, honestly, what if you get killed?"

"What's the worst that could happen, Troy? I die, but I go straight to heaven to be with God. In my opinion, that's about the best thing that could happen."

"But what about your boys, Jeff? They still need you here. And if I'm not mistaken, I think Jill might wish you'd stick around, too."

A slight blush covered Jeff's face, but he removed his feet from the coffee table and leaned forward. "You're absolutely right, Troy, and it's because of my boys and Jill and those around me I love that I'm going to do my best to be careful and stay alive. All I'm saying is that I have complete confidence that God has this situation under control and I'm going to leave it in His hands."

Troy snapped his magazine shut and tossed it back on the sofa table. He wasn't sure why he felt irritated. "Well, I'm glad you've got all confidence in your God, but just the same, I'm going to make sure I have my gun and cuffs in working order and that I work with only the best law enforcement." He pushed himself to his feet and stretched. "Time for supper?"

"I guess so." Jeff stood. "I'll go get Jill." He headed for the stairway and Troy turned toward the dining room.

"Anybody up for a walk in Bushy Park tonight?" Jeff pushed back his plate. The three had sat at their table for a long time talking and Jill had noticed the dark looks in their direction from the staff.

Still somewhat stiff from the long plane ride, Jill nodded eagerly. "Anything to stop me from thinking about tomorrow." She rubbed her aching legs. "If I even had a small clue what was going to happen…, but all I know is that someone is going to meet us somewhere outside the Tower. After that, who knows?"

Troy nodded. "Well, I'm having a brainstorming session in about fifteen minutes with Lieutenant Scott and a couple of others, so I won't be able to come, but enjoy the fresh London air." He chuckled as Jill snorted. The London air was not what she considered fresh at all. It had the big city scent of diesel, fuel, smog and cigarette smoke.

Jill pushed back her chair, smiled at Troy and headed for the exit. She turned at the door to wait for Jeff. Jeff stood and slapped Troy on the back. "See you later."

Troy grinned after them. "See you, lovebirds."

Jill hurriedly pushed the door open, thankful for the cool evening air on her flushed cheeks. She heard Jeff's footsteps jog to catch up with her. They turned through the gate into Bushy Park and slowed their pace. Jill lifted her eyes to the orange-gold sky. "Beautiful."

Jeff pointed to the lake in the center of the park. "Let's head over there." A statue stood in the middle of the moss-covered water. "This must be the Diana Fountain that Lieutenant Scott mentioned."

"There's no water coming from it." Jill squinted at it. "I wonder why they call it a fountain? It's pretty though." Beyond the statue, a calm landscape greeted them. A dog barked and a boy ran after it. To their right, a couple of university students threw a Frisbee back and forth. Jeff could see four or five bicyclers through the trees, meandering along a shaded stretch of grass.

Jill sank down on the short grass next to the lake and watched her reflection between the pads of moss. She sighed. "Isn't it strange? In the middle of the hustle and bustle of the city, there's such a place as this, that's quiet and calm—and safe."

Jeff squatted down next to her, gathering a few blades of grass and releasing them one by one into the pool. He didn't say anything and Jill felt comforted by his silence.

"My life has been so hectic since—was it only two days ago that all this started?" She picked up a twig and pulled it through the water, watching the ripples fan out behind it. "I guess I feel like my life is like this park in a big city. It's a confused mess with lots of pollution and dirt.

Somewhere in all of that mess though…," she paused, looking out over the trees again. The sky grew darker and small twinkling stars began to appear.

"Somewhere, Jesus decided to live and make a resting spot where I can come and get some perspective." She blew out her breath. "Right now, Jeff, right here…, I don't care about tomorrow or the fact that we may not even live through this. All I know is right now, I'm happy."

Jeff threw down the last of the grass and hugged his knees, rocking on his heels. "I know what you mean." He gazed at the statue in the middle of the small lake. "Troy asked me about that before supper. He wanted to know how I could be so peaceful about this whole situation when it feels like my world has turned upside-down. I don't know, Jill, I guess we all need to find our resting spot. I had forgotten where mine was until this all happened. Then when they took my boys and I felt so helpless, God showed me His resting spot through this."

Silence blanketed them for a minute, then Jill shifted around to face the entrance to the park, her back to the fountain. Her eyes took in the blaze of splendor in the distant western sky. "I guess I never would have met you if all this hadn't happened. Even if nothing else happens between us, Jeff, I'll always count our friendship as valuable. It's helped me to trust when I didn't think I would ever be able to again."

Jeff turned to sit beside her, his back to the fountain as well. He nodded at the huge building across the road from the hotel where they were staying. "Can you believe someone actually lived in that palace and called it home?"

Jill chuckled. "Yeah, I wonder how many times they got lost just getting to the bathroom."

"You think they had bathrooms back then?" Jeff sounded surprised. "Don't you think they would have had outdoor ones?"

"Oh, I don't know." Jill shrugged. "Maybe they were technologically advanced enough to figure out indoor plumbing by then. Maybe if all goes well, we might get a chance to tour it." She heard the excitement in her own voice and laughed at herself.

"Just Hampton Court Palace or any of the other palaces around here?"

"This one looks pretty fascinating to me. It's right on the bank of the Thames, it's huge, and Henry the VIII lived in it. Sounds like a lot of good history to go with it."

"You're just a history nut in disguise."

"You've got me pegged." Jill chuckled. "Not really. I just enjoy finding out what I can about places."

Jeff tilted his chin back and gazed at the night sky. "Look," he said pointing, "almost a full moon. Tomorrow should be the fullest."

Jill hooked her arms around her knees. "It's really clear this evening. Usually you can't see anything in the city." She pointed to a familiar formation of stars in the sky. "Look, the Big Dipper."

She glanced at Jeff to see that the stars no longer held his attention. She gazed at the moonlight reflected in his eyes and felt a shiver run up her spine as he drew his head close to hers. His hand came up and cupped her chin. Her eyes widened and she saw his lips touch hers, felt the moist sensation. A shock soared through her and her back stiffened. A thought skittered across her mind. *He's not David.*

Ever so slowly, she relaxed, sliding her eyes shut for the kiss. She felt his strong hands on the back of her neck, pulling her closer. Her thoughts skittered in all directions and she slid her fingers into his hair. She could feel the prickly stubble of his chin where he hadn't shaved that morning. The kiss deepened.

Suddenly, as if by a signal that both of them heard, each instinctively broke the kiss. Jeff tenderly stroked Jill's hair, his face still close to hers. "I want to be worthy of your trust." He slid his hand slowly down her arm and laced his fingers through hers and rubbed his thumb along the back of her hand. "You've honored me by telling me your past and I want to honor you by not taking advantage of you."

Jill nodded in the semi-darkness. She licked her lips. "Thanks, Jeff."

He smiled and leaned forward again, catching her lips once more with his and then pulled away. "And that's so you know that I didn't kiss you because the stars are out and it's an almost-full moon. I really want to see where this goes."

Jill felt any reservations she had melting away. "Me, too."

Jumping up, Jeff dusted off the seat of his pants. "Ready to go back?"

"Yep." Jill gave him her hand to pull her up. She looked over his shoulder at a man walking swiftly toward them.

"This park closes at dark." The uniformed security guard pointed toward the gate. "You both need to leave immediately."

"Yes, sir, we were just heading out." Jeff curled his fingers through Jill's and they walked back toward the inn.

Troy pulled two of the chairs in his room away from the window and motioned Lieutenant Scott and the two men accompanying him to sit. The lieutenant sat, but the other two continued standing. Troy shrugged and took a seat on the bed.

Sam Scott introduced the two men. "This is Sergeant Peabody and Lieutenant Hicks." Troy nodded pleasantly to them. Neither smiled back. Both men had shrew looks, as if they had been through too much and encountered more than they wanted to share. Sam took the gun from his holster and laid it on the table, sighing as he settled back in his chair.

Troy motioned toward the gun. "I've been under the impression that Scotland Yard doesn't carry guns."

"Most don't," Sam said, nodding at the weapon. "Our unit has only recently begun allowing a few of us to carry them, mostly those on Special Forces and a few in higher command. It's been a big debate in the department."

"Well, then." Troy sighed and rubbed his hands together. "This is a pickle of a situation, and we don't have a lot to go on." He reached into his suitcase and pulled out the three notes that Jill and Jeff had received. He handed one note to each of the three men. "This is the primary evidence that we have. As you can see, they're riddles and codes, but our specialist deciphered them for us." He waited. The men quickly perused their notes, then traded them off for another one. "You'll notice the reference to Wolsey in one of them. That's why Jill was surprised to find out that Hampton Court Palace used to be Cardinal Wolsey's before he gave it to Henry the VIII, Sam."

The lieutenant nodded, looking thoughtful.

Troy took a breath and continued. "It does seem that the main gist of the notes has been directed at Jill, though Jeff is worse off at this point than Jill with his sister and two children kidnapped. Our main worry right now is to have them returned to us safely. Once we succeed in that, the status quo is shifted and we don't need to play by their rules anymore." He shrugged. "Until then...."

Sergeant Peabody interrupted. "About this lawyer fellow. Can you describe again what you found at the crime scene?"

Troy nodded. "Certainly. My partner, Officer Lee, and I went to review the situation. We had been assuming that the perpetrator had entered the office through the window."

Troy pulled out his notepad and grabbed a pen. "This is how the office was laid out." He drew a square for a desk, an opening for the door into the hallway, and another opening to the right of the desk for the door into Jill's office. Behind the desk, he drew another square with two bars at right angles to represent a window. He pointed his pencil to the window. "But as I examined the situation, I realized that the murderer didn't enter through the window. There were no fingerprints and there was a fine layer of dust across the sill, with no evidence of it having been disturbed."

He paused and chewed on the end of his pencil. All three men had leaned closer and were studying the crude drawing on his notepad. Troy continued, "The autopsy came back with the report that Mr. Bradley was shot at fairly close range. Not only that, but he was shot from the front. The back of his head was destroyed by the bullet's exit."

Sam glanced up from the drawing. "Did any suspects come to light as you investigated?"

"Yes." Troy straightened on the bed. "Directly outside of the office, hanging next to the door, Mr. Bradley kept a small turquoise notepad and a pen for people to leave him messages if he was in conference or on the phone. According to Jill, people would quickly scribble on these sticky notes and plaster them to the glass panel on his door. This he could see from the inside and would know that someone had left him a note."

He pointed to the turquoise piece of paper in Lieutenant Hicks' hand. "The note you see there is a note from that notepad. It was printed with painstaking neatness, as you see, so according to my deduction, it must have been written before the murder was actually committed. Once the shooting happened, the next several steps occurred very quickly with Jill returning to the office and finding Mr. Bradley dead. Since it had been written beforehand and only employees and partners of the firm are allowed anywhere close to Mr. Bradley's office, I decided then that this had to have been an inside job."

Sam leaned back in his chair. "Didn't you mention that Jill overheard two strangers in one of the back hallways? How do you think they entered the building if no one outside the firm is allowed in that area?"

"I'm guessing that the inside suspect let them in through a back entrance."

"Do you have any idea who that might have been?" Troy nodded. "Yes. I have reason to believe that the younger Mr. Bradley, Mr. William Bradley's son, is the murderer."

CHAPTER 20

The officers stared at Troy. Sam nodded slowly, his look speculative.

Troy put down the diagram of the office and leaned forward, digging his elbows into his knees. "While Jill and Jeff were running around town with last minute details, I called a few people." He ticked off some names on his fingers. "I called William Bradley's sister, Doris Farrell. When I questioned her, she mentioned that her nephew, Edward Bradley, had gotten into a huge fight with William a year or so back. Although William allowed Edward to stay on as partner in the firm, he cut him out of his will. She said she didn't know what the row was about."

Troy pulled up a second finger. "Then I called William's pet charity, Shenandoah Mental Health Clinic. Interestingly enough, Phil Snyder, the director, informed me that William had just sent him a letter. It mentioned that 'a member of his family was, he feared, suffering from a state of mental illness induced by cult activity of some sort.' He wanted to discuss the situation with Phil at a more convenient time. Unfortunately, William died before that could happen."

Sam narrowed his eyes. "The evidence does seem to point to Edward as perpetrator."

Troy raised his third finger. "The third person I called was Edward Bradley. His housekeeper answered and wouldn't give me much information other than the fact that Edward was suddenly called out of town the day after his father's murder." Troy planted his fists behind him and leaned back. "I'd be highly surprised if we don't find him in London before this is all said and done, wrapped up somehow in what's going on with Jill and Jeff."

Silence descended. The window had turned dark. Troy pushed himself off the bed and closed the curtains.

Sergeant Peabody's voice drew him around. "So what's our course of action tomorrow?"

Troy opened his mouth to respond, but Sam jumped in. "We watch." Sam turned to face Troy. "Lane, they recognize you. I don't think you should be anywhere close to Jill and Jeff tomorrow."

"Hold on here, Lieutenant. With all due respect, I've been on this case from the beginning. I'm obligated to follow it through."

"Granted." Sam's expression didn't change. He nodded calmly. "I'm not saying you shouldn't follow it through. What I am saying, however, is that your face is too recognizable. They won't meet Jill or Jeff while they see you hulking about. Let us monitor the situation." He nodded at Hicks and Peabody. "We've arranged to set up a command post close by and you will certainly be needed there."

Troy waged an internal battle, pushed back a stubborn answer and nodded in acquiescence. "You're right, of course. I'll wait at the command post tomorrow unless and until the situation changes and we should need to set up a chase."

"Right." Sam stood up. "In the meantime, I suggest, gentlemen, that we all get a good night's sleep. We'll need clear heads tomorrow."

"Yep, 'cause my brain's still fogged over from jetlag." Troy chuckled.

Sam shook Troy's hand. "Good night, then, sir." The other two men nodded at Troy and the British officers exited the room.

Jill squinted her eyes at the bright light from her hotel window. She rolled over in bed as a knock sounded at her door.

"Who is it?" Silence.

Jill leaned on her elbow and focused slowly on the door to her room. An envelope appeared in the crack between the door and the floor. Jill sat up straight. Throwing back the covers, she touched her bare feet to the floor and padded over to the door. She slid the chain in its slot and slowly turned the handle. Her heart thumped in her ears. She thrust her head into the empty hallway and narrowed her eyes. Closing the door again, she picked up the envelope, slipped her finger under the flap, and tore it open. Her fingers shook as she gripped the enclosed paper and read the words in front of her. She clamped her jaw and strode to the phone on her nightstand. Dialing Jeff's extension, she waited for him to answer.

"Hello." Jeff's gravelly voice drifted over the line.

Jill studied the paper in her lap and twisted a strand of hair around her finger. "Good morning."

"Hey, beautiful. You're up already?"

"Yeah." Jill sighed. "Hey, Jeff, can you meet me downstairs in 15 minutes? Bring Troy."

"Huh? Okay, yeah." Jeff paused. "Uh, is everything okay?"

"I think so, but come anyway, just in case."

"We'll be right there."

Jill reread the words on the paper, though each letter was already burned on her memory.

Good morning, Sunshine. Please be early today. We'd like to take care of business as soon as possible, hence, no delays. And don't forget your seal. We'd like to have this meeting go off without a hitch; and no seal would indeed be a hitch.

The note was signed with the same pentagram that had been used as a signature on all the journal entries Jill had found. She blew out her breath in frustration. "Well, it sure would be helpful if you would tell me what my seal *is*." She glared at the door. "How am I supposed to bring something that I don't even know about?" She threw the paper on the bed and headed for the shower.

Troy glanced over the paper at the breakfast table. "It's the same print as in all the notes, so they're probably all written by the same person. I guess we'll find out today who that person is." He took a hearty bite out of his scone.

Jill looked down at her untouched plate of food and set her fork down. "I'm too nervous to eat." She leaned her chin on the heel of her hand. "Any ideas yet on what my seal would be?"

"It's probably too late now anyway." Jeff scraped some marmalade over a piece of toast. "If you had a seal, most likely it's still at home; unless you just brought a bunch of random trinkets hoping one of them would be it." He took a huge bite.

"I didn't." Jill ran her finger around the edge of her glass and chewed nervously on her bottom lip. "I didn't even get home to pack before we came. I had to buy all my stuff, remember?"

"Well, I wouldn't worry too much about it." Troy pushed aside his plate and leaned back in his chair. "Hopefully they'll be open to negotiation, and they've got to make some allowance for the fact that you have no idea what they're talking about with the seal."

Jill straightened up and clutched the edge of the table, hope flaring through her. "Maybe Zachary was wrong. Maybe the note didn't really mean a seal, but something different."

Jeff and Troy were silent. Jeff stirred his tea slowly, his eyes resting sympathetically on her.

The spark of hope smothered and died. Jill slumped back over the table. "Then again, there's really no other possibility of what it could be."

Troy glanced at his watch. "It's time."

Jill allowed Jeff to hold open the cab door for her as she climbed in. He quickly followed.

Jill settled herself on the seat and clamped her jaw to keep her teeth from chattering. "Jeff, all at once, I—I'm terrified. I have no idea what I'm stepping into or who these people are."

Jeff wove his fingers through hers and gazed into her eyes. Without looking away, he prayed, "God, we're in a situation here that's really testing our trust in you. Protect us by your strength. Give us wisdom to know what course of action we should take when the time comes. Let me see my boys and my sister again today. And even if we don't—or can't—see them again," Jeff choked and struggled to continue, "don't let our faith in You waver. We pray this in the name of Your Son. Amen."

"Amen." Jill whispered the word and willed her shoulders to relax. Her stomach still felt like she was on a roller coaster ride, but at least now she could feel the safety harness.

Jeff pulled back the right flap of the vest he wore. He lifted a small black box from the inside pocket, just enough to show Jill the lights blinking on it. He glanced up at the cab driver, then back to Jill and winked.

"What is it?" she mouthed.

She strained to hear his answering whisper. "Tracking unit. It's how Sam and Troy are going to track us if they take us somewhere."

Jill's fingers relaxed their death grip on her shirt. "Good." She cleared her throat and continued in an audible voice. "I guess I didn't really think about this before, Jeff, but you've got some idea of what kind of people we're going up against."

"Yes." Jeff's mouth tightened into a straight line.

"Is there anything you should tell me so I can be prepared?"

"Jill, they're normal people that usually lead fairly successful lives as businessmen and women, or in England, lords, ladies and wealthy persons who claim a title of some sort. Like I've mentioned, most of them adhere closely to the Wiccan Rede, but there are nuts in every bunch." He turned to gaze out the window. "I'm willing to bet that it's a nut that's arranged this meeting."

"Did you know any—uh—nuts in your past when you were a witch?"

Jeff didn't answer for a minute, then he cleared his throat. "Well, we all believed then that anyone could believe whatever way they wanted—that each person could choose his or her own religion and that what was right for one person might not necessarily be right for another." Jeff shook his head. "No, that's not completely true either. There was no right or wrong; everything was right. Reminds me of that verse at the end of Judges in the Bible where it talks about how each person did what was right in his own eyes. Behavior like that brings a lot of upheaval. After I became a Christian, most people didn't care that I had, so I went back to try to show them the truth. They took offense right away because I was claiming that there was *one* right way. That's when I made some enemies. No one person stands out in my mind right now as becoming a 'nut' who would violate the Rede, but there were several who were definitely leaning in that direction when I left."

Jeff fell quiet and Jill didn't ask any more questions.

The turrets of the Tower of London loomed before them and the cab driver pulled to the curb. "Here you are, sir."

Jeff looked at Jill and both took deep breaths. "Ready?"

Jill nodded decisively. "Let's go."

Jeff paid the driver, then guided Jill over the sidewalk toward the Tower.

Troy handed cash to the cab driver and glanced quickly in both directions before crossing the street. He shoved his hands in his pockets, hunched his shoulders and ducked his head, hoping no one would recognize him.

The window of the van he was walking past cracked open. "Psst, in here."

Troy reached quickly to open the passenger door and a pair of hands pulled him inside, shutting the door behind him.

Sam nodded to him. "It's good to see you made it on time."

Troy took the seat next to Sam in front of the laptop, nodding to Barnaby who was wedged in on Sam's other side. "Any action yet?"

"No." The lieutenant spoke into his headpiece. "The subjects have just arrived. Everyone positioned?"

"Affirmative." Troy could hear several voices reply.

He glanced out the windshield at the Tower. "How many people in the field?"

"Seven, all told." Sam pointed to the small computer monitor in front of him. "Jill and Jeff are here." He pointed to a blinking dot moving slowly around the Tower toward the Tower Bridge. "Peabody and Hicks are covering the northwestern point of the Tower and have the first visual on Jill and Jeff. We've got Turner and Wheeler on the southeast corner." He pointed to two more dots. "Norse is north of the bridge keeping an eye on anyone coming and going across it." Another blinking dot hovered on the right side of the screen. "Powers and Southerland are covering the whole grounds."

"Looks good." Troy hovered closer to the screen, watching intently. "We're positioned fairly close to the bridge ourselves."

"Yes." Sam nodded at the gigantic structure in front of them. "I thought we'd have decent access to both the Tower and the bridge from here, and we're still obscure in this location."

A loud beeping sounded and Troy clapped his hand to his belt. He pulled his pager off to read the number. "That's headquarters in the States." He fumbled for his cell phone to make the call.

"Yeah, Carol? Kyle just paged me. Can you patch me through? Oh, that was you?" Sam eyed him from his side of the van while Barnaby continued to watch the screen intently. "You got a call?" Troy snatched a pen and notepad off the dashboard. "Okay, I'm ready. What was the message?"

He felt his brows crease in confusion. "John said what? Are you sure that's right?" His pen slipped from his hand as he reached to scratch the back of his neck. "Okay, thanks Carol. You too. Uh-huh. Bye."

Sam stared at him. "What was that all about?"

Troy's eyes were glued to the Tower and his fingers gripped the door handle. "Jeff's brother is out of his coma and he just started talking. We've got to get both Jeff and Jill away from the Tower and out of here. They're in way over their heads."

"But what about his lads? You know he'll never go for it."

Troy opened his mouth to reply, but was interrupted by a voice crackling over the speaker. "Command post, we've got company."

Emily uncurled her cramped legs and pushed herself to her feet. Her rear was fast asleep from the hours she had been sitting on the stone floor. She could feel the numbness creeping down her legs.

"All right boys." Brian and Brandon looked up at her. Her heart nearly broke at the trust she saw mirrored there. "I'll race you around the room. Three laps and winner gets a prize as soon as we're out of here."

"What prize?" Brandon's voice sparked with interest.

"Something really special. How about a day at the lake with your brother and dad and me? We'll take the boat, too." Emily smiled brightly at the little face, trying her best to keep the anxiety from her voice.

"Yeah!" Brian jumped up. Brandon quickly scrambled behind him, not willing to be left behind.

Emily pointed to a crack between the stones in the floor. "Okay, we start right here and then run like crazy around the room three times. No cutting corners. Winner takes the prize. Ready?"

Brandon jumped over the line in his eagerness. "Hold it, Speedy." Emily pulled him back. "Okay, here we go. Ready, set, RUN!" Her voice echoed around the hollow room and she let the boys take the lead while she jogged easily behind them. Brandon's mouth opened wide in delight and Brian laughed as he sprinted around the perimeter. He easily passed his younger brother, but then good-naturedly ran in place while Brandon passed him again before he followed once more. Two laps had passed and Brian had the lead on Brandon. Just before he crossed the finish line he stopped, waited for his little brother, and grabbed his hand. "Wait, Brandon. Let's finish together."

Brandon grinned and squealed and the two of them together jumped over the finish line. Emily's eyes pricked at the compassion Brian showed for his brother. "A tie! I never would have believed it! I guess we'll just have to spend a whole weekend at the lake now. One day isn't enough for two winners."

She chuckled over the boys' excitement. It felt so good to get their blood pumping again and enjoy a few worry-free moments.

The heavy oak door swung open, colliding with the wall behind it. "*What* is going on here?"

Emily squatted quickly and pulled the two boys into her arms. "Nothing. The boys needed exercise. So did I. We had a race." The steel in her voice was unmistakable.

The woman stared at them, an eternity passing in a few seconds. With a jerk, she turned and motioned to someone in the hall. "Bring them to the aquariums. You know what to do."

"Yes, my lady." A man entered the room, a gun evident and grasped tightly in his hands. The woman in the pantsuit exited and the man jutted his chin in the direction of the hallway. "Come."

CHAPTER 21

Sam touched his earpiece. "Don't let them out of your sight. Norse, you follow. Powers and Southerland, head to the bridge."

"Right-o." A pause. "Hey, what the—?" The static on the other end suddenly increased, then went dead.

"Norse?" Sam strained to see the far end of the bridge. "Norse, can you hear me? Where's the bloomin' dot?" The blinking light that had shown Norse on the screen had disappeared. There was no answer. "Blimey." He looked desperately at Troy. "I think they've got Norse." He gripped the edge of the laptop. "Powers, Southerland, can you see what happened?"

"Sorry, Lieutenant. We can't see Norse. He's gone from his position."

Sam's alarmed eyes flew back to the screen. "Jeff's light has gone off. Someone must have gotten hold of their tracking unit. Whoever it is must be near the bridge. Southerland, I need a visual—now!" Sam ran frustrated fingers through his hair.

Barnaby slammed a fist against the door, muttering dour words under his breath. "Hang it all, they've got to be somewhere."

Sam took a calming breath. He lowered his voice back to normal pitch. "Scour the area. We're moving in."

He turned to Troy, but Troy was already taking the steps to the bridge three at a time. He disappeared immediately from sight behind early morning traffic. "Blimey." Sam's jaw clenched. "Where's the bloke think he's going? I can't keep anyone in sight."

Jill leaned over the railing on the sidewalk of the bridge, gazing at the Tower, Jeff close beside her.

A voice spoke on her left side. "D'you think they recognize us, Topper?" Jill caught her breath and sidestepped onto Jeff's toe. To his credit, he didn't even flinch.

The large man from the scene of her car crash stood before her, as big and intimidating as earlier. His smaller counterpart moved quickly to the other side of Jeff, glancing around him at the heavy flow of tourists. His head was indeed shaved, though the larger man had gotten rid of his fake moustache.

Jill's breath sped up and her back grew rigid. Before anymore words were spoken, the big man reached across Jill, flipped Jeff's vest open and snatched the tracking unit. He dropped it on the pavement and ground it beneath his heel.

Jill felt Jeff flinch as the plastic casing splintered. His voice sounded strained. "That was mine."

"Of course it was, mate. And I just took it. Don't think about making a fuss if you want your tykes back, yeah?"

Jill met Jeff's gaze and saw her own fear reflected in his eyes. He swallowed hard and managed a tight smile. "It's okay, Jill."

The big man ignored him and turned on Jill. "Did you bring it?"

"Bring what?" Jill jerked her attention back to the man. She was still recovering from the fact that they couldn't be tracked.

"The seal, o'course. The seal for m'lady." His accent was much heavier than what Jill had remembered when they were in America.

Jill pulled back her shoulders, assuming an air of confidence. She stuck her hands in her pockets to conceal their trembling. "I received the instructions to bring the seal, only whoever 'm'lady' is forgot to detail exactly what my seal was, so I have no idea what you're talking about."

The big man stepped menacingly nearer. "You didn't bring it?" His hand moved slowly to his pocket.

The smaller man gasped and choked. "Wait!" A few passers-by glanced their way. Topper looked around the bridge. He continued in a quieter voice. "Wait, Elliot. Her Grace needs to decide. Maybe she did bring it or maybe she can get it easily."

Elliot stopped, his eyes narrowed, then nodded. "Follow Topper." He motioned to his partner. "I'll be just behind you, and if you value your lives or the lives of your tots, you'll not try to do anything stupid." He planted a hand on the center of Jeff's back. "Get a move on." Jill's back was stiff as she turned to follow Topper. Her lips felt numb. Jeff touched her back with his fingers. "I guess this is a good time to trust, huh?" he whispered.

"Shut yer yaps." Elliot laid a heavy hand on Jill's shoulder. "No talking 'till we get to where we're going."

Topper led the way to the end of the bridge and hurried down the stairs to the walkway by the Tower. Jill glanced around at the people milling beside them or behind them and tried to catch someone's eye. People seemed shy of looking directly at her though. Elliot poked her back from behind. "Keep your head down," he growled.

Jill immediately dropped her eyes and studied her shoes as they stepped rhythmically in front of her. They reached the bottom of the stairs, blending in with the crowds around the Tower.

Topper led the way up the pavement between the Thames and the Tower. Jill glanced up now and then, hoping desperately to catch a glimpse of Troy. Each time she did, she received a knuckle in her back and a warning grunt from Elliot.

They reached a side gate to the Tower. An older man in a black waterproof jacket sat in the guardhouse shaking his head at any passerby that tried to walk in that way. He repeatedly jerked his thumb toward the corner of the Tower where the main gate was. Topper made his way toward the guard and stopped directly in front of him. He handed him a note and the guard glanced down swiftly to read it. A moment later, he nodded and motioned Topper and the three people with him through a side archway of the Tower.

Jill strained to read what the note said on the way by, but the print was too small. She did see a flowing signature at the bottom, but before she could make it out, they were inside the archway.

Instead of walking straight into the main courtyard, Topper turned right and stopped in front of a wooden door in the wall of the archway. He pulled a key from his pocket and inserted it into the keyhole. He pulled back on the handle and the door creaked slowly open. Jill took a deep breath and followed Topper into the damp darkness. She could feel Jeff close behind her.

"This way." Topper's voice floated in front of them. Jill couldn't see a thing. She tentatively placed one foot in front of the other, holding tightly to Jeff's hand. Elliot's deep bass suddenly boomed impatiently in the darkness. "Get movin'. There are no steps for a ways yet."

Jill quickened her pace. Dim light glowed at the end of a very long passageway. She squeezed Jeff's hand and they hurried forward.

Troy watched Jill and Jeff, sandwiched between two men, disappear into the Tower's side archway. He jumped impulsively into the heavy traffic crossing the bridge, narrowly avoided the bumper of a red Peugeot and sprinted toward the stairs on the other side. He reached the bottom of the steps and scrambled toward the archway in time to see the short, bald man in front open a second door inside the portal and lead the rest of them in.

Troy strolled casually by the guard, sat down on a nearby bench overlooking the Thames and glanced around him. The guard returned to his stool in the guardhouse. Troy tapped his fingers together, his mind whirling with ideas, most of which he immediately discarded.

He suddenly straightened. Behind the guard, Troy could see another man in uniform walking swiftly toward the gate to relieve his co-worker. Troy stood up, leaned casually against the stone wall and stared unobtrusively outward over the Thames. Just as the replacement guard reached the guardhouse and said a few words to his fellow employee, a teenage boy ran toward the two guards, huffing and puffing for all he was worth.

The boy gasped for breath. "I saw—a man." He blew out and tried to take another lungful. "He was—floating in the Thames along this bank—couldn't tell if he was dead—his face was above water, but it was all white and blanched. I don't have a mobile. Can you help?"

Both guards bent attentively toward the boy. "You did right, lad. We'll call about it right away. You'll stick around for any questions?"

The boy's breathing had lessened and he nodded vigorously. "It was amazing. The man was chained to a post on the rail and everything."

The guards glanced at each other. One scratched his head. "And you couldn't tell if he was dead?"

"I don't think so.... I couldn't try to get down for a closer look—it's a good three meter drop. But he might have been breathing." The boy's eyes were huge.

One of the guards looked at the other. "You'd better go with the lad to check out the situation. I'll call 999."

"Had any other people seen the man yet?"

"Not yet that I could tell." The boy shook his head. "He was wedged right up against the edge of the overhang. I just saw a shoe and leaned for a closer look, and that's when I saw him. As soon as I got a good look at him, I started running over here. There might be more people now who have seen him."

"Let's go take a look." One of the guards jogged down the walk, the boy running to keep up. The other guard walked toward the guardhouse to place the call. Troy, now hidden in the shadows of the archway, slipped silently through the wooden door, thanking his lucky stars for the distraction and the fact that the tools on his belt could easily pick an old-fashioned lock.

Jeff's eyes had grown accustomed to the dim light as he and Jill stepped into the room. Before them was a wide staircase leading down into a huge circular stone room. In the middle of the room, set in a semi-circle, were three large, glass cases. Blue light filtered from inside the cases. Jeff's gaze swept the room but he couldn't see anyone in the shadows.

"Keep movin'." Elliot's finger prodded him in the back. "Down the stairs."

Jeff swallowed and pulled Jill along with him as he stepped forward. The sound of clapping filled the air.

"Well done, well done, if I do say so," said a voice with an American accent. Jeff jerked his head to search the shadows to his right. "I've got to say, I'm impressed with how well you all figured out your clues."

A man stepped forward into the center of the blue-lit room, a toothy grin on his face. Jeff's neck muscles stiffened. "I know you." He searched his memory. "Where have I seen you before?"

The man smiled pleasantly. "You must mean the place where I work. I'm Neil Lee and I work with Troy Lane at the police department in our pleasant little valley in Virginia."

"Yes, that's right," Jeff said, narrowing his eyes, "and I remember, too, that Troy didn't like you, not one little bit."

Lee laughed. "There's little love lost between us then. Ah well, I won't be working with him much longer anyway, once we see what you've brought. It will be of considerable value." He rubbed his hands together, his eyes sparkling greedily in the dim light.

Jill spoke up. "Why did you give us riddles and clues to come find you? Why not just tell us where to meet you? It would have been a whole lot easier."

"The clues were a test." A misty voice drifted from behind Lee. "I wanted to see if the carrier of the seal was worthy of it."

Jeff froze at the sound of the voice, puzzle pieces suddenly falling into place in his head. He strained his eyes to see past Lee and could make out a tall slender silhouette at the far end of the room. The person approached. Her hour-glass figure was enhanced by the jet-black hair swept away from her shoulders and tied into an elegant knot in the back. She wore a black pantsuit, looking as if she had just stepped out of a corporate office.

"What are you doing here?" Jeff's stiff jaw barely allowed the words out. From the corner of his eye, he saw Jill's eyebrows wing upward in surprise.

The woman laughed. "Jeff, it's good to see you again. You haven't changed much." She stepped closer to him, gazing at him from under her dark lashes. "I've been enjoying getting to know your children. They look like their mother, yes?" She idly reached out her fingers and brushed one of his curls behind his ear.

Like a whip, Jeff's hand slapped hers away. "I should have known that you would have been behind all this."

The woman's eyes blazed. "Oh, come off it, Jeff. Who else do you think would have wanted you back after all these years?"

"I'm telling you, Celia, you better not have harmed one hair on their heads, or I'll make sure you'll pay for it, duchess or not."

"Will you?" Her penciled eye-brows flicked upward. Her unsmiling eyes told him she intended to do nothing of the sort.

Jill's tremulous voice broke the heavy pause. "Do you know her, Jeff?"

"Oh yes." Celia smiled cruelly. "He knows me well. Have you forgotten just how well you knew me?" She directed her question to Jeff. His fingernails bit into his hand as he prayed for strength not to snap her dainty neck. "And now I have your children and your sister—there." Not breaking eye contact with Jeff, she pointed a manicured finger toward the tops of the glass boxes.

Jeff's gaze shot upward at the sound of three winches creaking. Three shadowy figures suspended from ropes swung above the glass boxes—or as Jeff suddenly comprehended—aquariums. The blue lights brightened and Jeff could see long thin shapes slowly twisting and coiling in the bottom of the aquariums. Snakes. Jeff tasted bile in his throat. He swallowed convulsively. Ropes belted the victims around their stomachs. Their hands and feet were bound tightly and gags were stuffed in their mouths. Blindfolds covered their eyes. One of the boys moaned.

Jeff tore his eyes from them. "Let them go," he whispered to Celia. "They haven't done a thing." He rubbed his forehead. "It's all my fault. My sin, visited on my children—my family."

"Sin? Yes, it was a horrible thing to do, leaving." Celia chuckled. "We'll see what happens to them—if you do everything I tell you."

Anger burned through Jeff. "Never!" He spat at Celia's feet. "I'll never serve you again." He stepped forward threateningly but stopped abruptly at the soft click of a gun cocking.

Lee's soft voice drifted lazily over him. "I wouldn't try that if I were you."

Celia gazed at Jeff, amusement in her eyes. "Lower the ropes."

Jeff and Jill watched in open-mouthed horror as all three helpless people swung lower over the aquariums.

Troy pulled the door swiftly shut behind him, desperately listening past the sound of his own thudding heart. No sounds came from the other side and he breathed a sigh of relief. He left the door unlocked, pushed gently on the door from the inside and the crack of light widened. He let the door fall shut again, thankful that he could make a quick escape if needed.

Quieting his breathing with an effort, he crept along the passageway. He could see a dim light in the far distance, and he hurried along the downward slope toward it.

As he drew near to the entranceway, he slowed to a stop, tiptoeing the last few steps toward the door. What he saw made him draw in a sharp breath. Jill and Jeff and an unknown woman stood stock-still in an eerie pose, while none other than his one-day partner, Lee, stood nearby with his gun cocked and ready. On the ends of three thick ropes, three bound people slowly descended toward three glass aquariums. Snakes coiled and slithered across the bottoms of the aquariums. The two men he now recognized as the men who had followed them in the States watched the scene with pure enjoyment on their faces.

Troy grasped his own gun firmly in his hands. Taking a deep breath, his leg muscles tightened as he prepared to jump headlong into the room.

CHAPTER 22

"STOP!" Jeff roared.

Celia lifted a finger and the ropes halted. All were squirming now and the smallest one—Jill assumed it must be Brandon—whimpered.

Celia raised an eyebrow. "You wish to say something?"

"Don't hurt them…please." Jeff's voice broke. "Just tell me what you want and I'll see what I can do."

Celia smiled. "Very well." She turned abruptly to Jill and bit out her words. "Did you bring the seal?"

Jill sighed. "As I've said before, I have no idea what seal you're talking about. As far as I know, I've never owned a seal of any sort."

"Ah, but you have." Celia's lips curled upward at the corners and her voice took on a condescending tone, as if speaking to a simple child. "It has been in your family for generations—all the way back to the time of Henry VIII, King of England."

Jill's mouth swung open. She stared incredulously at Celia. "But I didn't know I was in Henry VIII's lineage."

Celia burst out laughing. "You aren't. Your blood is not noble at all. You belong to the house of Cardinal Wolsey, in the line of an illegitimate child. Wolsey," she spat, "was common born and a commoner he died. You see, Jill," her voice returned to its musical ebb and flow, "your ancestor and my ancestor were the worst of enemies. It was my ancestor that finally caused your ancestor's death, but not before Wolsey had hidden the seal that proclaimed all rights and privileges to what should have been my ancestral home—Hampton Court Palace."

Jill felt like her head was trapped under twenty feet of water. "Hampton Court Palace?"

Celia seemed surprised at her reaction. "Why, yes. Surely you know that at one time, Wolsey had owned Hampton Court Palace, which he gave to Henry the VIII when he knew he was falling out of favor with the king."

Jill shook her head to clear it. "So, you're in Henry's lineage?"

Celia laughed again. "Oh, no. No, dear, my ancestor was the great Duke of Buckingham."

The name meant nothing to Jill and Celia stiffened. "Enough. I have no patience with ignorance. Do you not remember seeing a ring anywhere, given to you by your mother before her death?"

Jill's hand flew to her necklace, most of which had fallen inside her shirt. "My ring?" she gasped. "But that's not a seal."

Celia's eyes were pinned to Jill's hand. "The ring is on a chain, yes?"

Jill looked down at her hand. Drawing a deep breath, she plunged in. "I'll only let you have it if you let the boys and Jeff's sister go— unharmed."

Celia smiled slowly. "We could possibly arrange that."

Jill gulped in surprise. She swung her gaze to Jeff. His eyes looked troubled. "No."

"What?" Jill stared at him.

"It's too easy. The ring for my kids and my sister. Come on, Celia. I know your cruelty too well." He folded his arms across his chest. "I know you want something more. Let's have it then. Out with it."

Celia's mouth twisted upward on one side. "You're correct, Jeff. You do know me well. And yes, I want something more." Turning her back to the two of them, she drifted to the first aquarium. She leaned close to the glass and gently stroked the exterior of the cage. "My precious darlings," she crooned, "are you hungry? Don't worry, Mummy will feed you soon. Have patience." She smiled down at the tangled mass of snakes. She turned and strolled slowly past Jeff, running her fingertips lightly along his chest. She dropped her hand and commanded, "Follow me."

Just behind Jeff and to his right, Elliot and Topper held open two large wooden doors leading to another long tunnel. This tunnel was well lit with flaming torches. Celia walked rapidly toward it.

"Wait," Jill cried. "What about the children? What about Jeff's sister?"

"They will keep." Celia glanced back over her shoulder. "I want to show you something."

Jill hesitated, looking frantically at the swinging whimpering bundles. Jeff swallowed noisily, his face in utter agony.

"Move." Lee moved into Jill's line of vision. "I don't mind using this weapon, but Her Grace the Duchess doesn't like messes."

Jill and Jeff did as they were told and Elliot and Topper fell in behind Lee. As soon as they had passed through the portal, the doors swung slowly shut on noiseless hinges. Jeff turned his head toward Lee. "Lee, how did you ever get away with what you're doing—you, a police officer of all things?"

"I've got brains. I know how to get in and out of situations easily. And most of all, I don't care about people—only money. That's how I got to where I am."

Jill slowly shook her head. "What a sad life you've lived then."

"Oh, no, my dear, never sad." Lee allowed a glimmer of a smile to show. "Only wealth and luxury can make me as I am."

"Then may I never be rich in the ways of this world." Jill jerked her shoulders angrily.

"I don't think you need to fear that." Lee's smile widened to a grin. "Her Grace will see to that. She will take everything."

"As long as we get Brian, Brandon and Emily back."

Lee chuckled. "We'll see what Her Grace's plan is."

Jill glanced at Jeff but neither said anything. She had noticed the shadow of a large man slip inside the door through which they had entered and follow noiselessly at a distance. She tried to reassure Jeff with a look. He looked puzzled but gave her a small smile.

In front of them, Celia halted and held up a finger. Topper hurried ahead of the group and gripped the large brass handle of a massive set of doors. The left door slowly ground open to the company. All of them entered into another dark room, this one containing a huge pentagram on the floor in front of them and a large circle chart lit in violet light on the main wall.

Jeff stopped short at the sight of it. "Oh, no," he whispered.

Jill didn't hear him. She glanced around, confused. "Where are we?"

"Underneath and slightly northwest of the gift shop." Celia waved off the question as it was of little importance. "Jeff, surely you remember this."

Jeff's eyes were glued to a spot at the lowest point in the circle on the wall. It read, *August 1st, Lammas.*

"Tomorrow." Jill heard Jeff clamp his jaw.

Jill's eyes grew wider. "What is it?"

"Lammas, my dear, is a sabbat, along with all the other sabbats listed on this circle." Celia waved her hand at the bright violet light casting a glow from the wall. "It is a time sacred to Artemis, the Greek goddess of the moon and the hunt. And to add to this time," she continued, "tonight is a full moon, which of course we always celebrate, so there will be a large festival tonight in Bushy Park. I'll reveal the rest of my plan then—when the seal is safe."

Jill looked to Jeff for confirmation but his jaw was set. "Celia, I want my kids and my sister back. And I want them back now. You can have your seal for whatever horrible motives you've got, but you will let me have my family."

Celia smiled cruelly. "But Jeff, I'm not done with them yet. Also, you wouldn't say that if you really knew what my plans happen to be." She pinpointed the two men behind them. "Elliot, Topper." She turned and exited the room through a small door in the stone wall in the corner of the room.

Elliot stepped forward and yanked Jill's wrists behind her. She could feel the rough bristles of a thin rope as he wrapped her wrists together tightly. Topper did the same for Jeff.

"Now we wait." Elliot gave a final tug to Jill's rope. She gulped. Lee laughed at them from the corner where he stood, then made himself comfortable on the floor.

Troy pulled his ear away from the door through which he had been listening and stared up and around him. The smoky haze of the tunnel was getting on his nerves. He had visions of himself bursting into the room, killing Elliot, Topper and Lee, then dragging Jill and Jeff out, but he had no idea how many reinforcements the duchess had and how close they might be. And he didn't want to do anything that would jeopardize the lives of all three of them. *Six of us.* He thought of the three hanging over the aquariums.

At least I can go back and free Jeff's sister and the kids. That takes away the duchess' leverage. Jill and Jeff might be able to bargain their way out of this if I do that. He turned and hurried silently up the hallway.

Reaching up for the hanging brass ring, he pulled the heavy door towards himself. It swung slowly open.

The room hadn't changed since he had been in it several minutes ago. Both of the boys still whimpered and Emily kicked her bound feet as hard as she could. The motion swung her in jerky circles.

Troy glanced cautiously around him, his ears straining for any noises. He approached the aquariums warily. The snakes seemed to be restless in their cages and Troy spied a digital thermometer set on each one. *No wonder. She's got it warmed to their natural habitat climate. I bet they're all ready to hunt.* He glanced from the aquariums full of huge rattlers to the one directly under Emily with eight-foot boas wrapped heavily around some logs. He shuddered. *She's some kind of sick nut.*

He looked above the cages. All of them had an open top. Heat lamps lined the upper edges all the way around. He glanced quickly over his shoulder. There was no other furniture in the room.

"Emily," he whispered. She jerked her head toward him, her feet instantly still, her body continuing to swing freely. The boys stopped whimpering, though they still shook.

"I'm going to cut you down," Troy whispered. "You're hanging over an open snake cage, so it's going to be tricky, but I think I've got a plan."

Emily nodded, her long hair obscuring her blindfold and face. A ledge ran around the aquarium at waist-level. Troy took a deep breath and placed his shoe on it. He hoisted himself up, reaching as high as he could, and managed to wrap his fingers over the top ledge. *About four inches width, I think.* The warmth from the heat lamps scorched his fingertips. He gritted his teeth through the pain and strengthened his grip. He swung his right leg up as far as he could. His right foot touched the top of the next cage over, but slipped. Troy struggled to keep his grip as his body crashed against the cage. *Calm. Keep calm.*

Troy took a deep breath, then with every bit of strength from his abdomen, he swung again. This time his foot caught the rim. Straining with all his might, he quickly followed the motion with his left leg. Both feet now wrapped over the rim. He pulled the rest of his body up and lay fully extended on the four-inch rim. His breath came in gasps. He glanced warily at the floor ten feet below and wiped the sweat from his upper lip. Pushing himself into a crouch, he inched his way to the center of the ledge. Soon he was directly across from Emily. A gap of three feet stretched between him and the swinging woman.

"Emily, I'm cutting you down first." Troy kept his voice to a whisper. "And then you can help me keep my balance when I cut the boys down."

She nodded her understanding.

"Can you see at all through the crack at the bottom of your blindfold?"

Emily shook her head.

"Okay." Troy glanced nervously behind him. "You're about ten to twelve feet off the ground. Directly under you is a large cage full of snakes. You're about three feet above it, with close to three feet on either side of you to the edge of the cage." Troy looked uncertainly at the snakes below him. "My plan is to try to get you swinging enough to make it to the side of the cage. Once we do that, I'm going to cut your ropes." *This is crazy.* "If we fall, it's probably going to hurt. But we'll try to fall outside the aquarium if we have to. Personally, I'd rather jump."

Emily nodded again.

"Okay, here goes." *Come on, Troy.* He rubbed his sweaty hands on his shirt. His fingertips throbbed where he had scorched them on the heat lamps. He flinched and cleared his throat. "If you believe in prayer, now might be a good time."

Troy took a deep breath and blew it out. Ever so slowly, he uncurled his legs, putting all his weight on the balls of his feet for extra balance. He gripped his knife in his left hand, and crouched forward.

"Ready, Emily?"

She nodded again, her hair flopping over her face.

Troy took another breath and allowed himself to fall forward. The rope was in front of him and he caught it. Momentum pushed Emily away from him and he frantically gripped the edge of the aquarium with the toes of his shoes. *Should have kicked off my shoes.*

His feet steadied. Troy could feel his abs, calves and hamstrings cramping under the strain. With a grunt, he wrapped his right arm around the rope and tucked it into his shoulder. Immediately, the weight on his muscles lessened a bit.

"Okay," he gasped. "New plan. I'm going to cut the rope around your ankles now. *Then* we'll try to get back to the edge."

Again Emily nodded. Now, inches away from her, Troy could see her trembling. She pulled her legs towards herself as far as she could till Troy could reach her ankles. The sight of the snakes directly beneath him played on his nerves. He shook his head and sawed at the rope. The last strand broke free and Emily's feet spasmodically kicked outward. Troy's feet lost their grip on the ledge and both of them hung free.

For one wild panic stricken second, Troy almost lost his grip on the rope. Emily hung against him, completely still, and Troy took a deep breath to calm himself. The rope cut into his hand. Troy swung his legs forward as far as he could, then back. Forward, then back. The rope began to swing like a pendulum. Troy's shoe contacted the ledge again. He frantically gripped it, one foot on the outside of the aquarium and one resting on top of the heat lamps on the inside. The rope abruptly stopped swinging.

"Okay." Troy blew out a heavy breath. "Sorry about that. Now, I'm going to try to cut your blindfold, so you can see where you're jumping, okay?"

Emily nodded again and Troy painstakingly switched his knife to his right hand, his left arm now wrapped securely around the rope. Carefully edging his knife under her blindfold, he sawed upward. "You've got a lot of trust in me." *Good girl. Don't mess up, Troy.*

Troy kept sawing. With a snap, the last thread of the blindfold broke free and the cloth fluttered down into the aquarium where one of the snakes slowly glided over it. Emily twisted her head around to look at Troy and her huge eyes pled with him.

"I'll get your gag off as soon as we get to the ground. Right now, we can't waste any time at all."

She nodded again.

"Okay, here's where it gets tricky." Troy looked at the rope above them. "I'm going to cut the rope. We're going to *try* to stay balanced so we can jump down. But if you feel at all off-balance, fall *backward*, not forward. If there is a God, we won't be snake food today."

Emily nodded her understanding.

Troy nodded back and smiled what he hoped was a reassuring smile. "Here goes." His arm ached and he brought his knife up to saw the rope above Emily's head. Sweat rolled into his eyes and burned. He blinked the moisture away. His knife broke quickly through the strands.

"Last strand." Troy felt Emily tense against him. The rope snapped. Troy's feet slipped from their anchor position and he automatically whipped his body backward, grabbing Emily in his arms as he fell. He saw the ceiling circle as he arched through the air and he landed with a grunt on his left shoulder on the hard stone floor.

He groaned. "Ouch! That's going to leave a mark." He struggled to his elbows, rubbing his sore shoulder. He saw the rope hanging free from the ceiling. "Emily?"

He made it to his feet, a shooting pain piercing his shoulder and collarbone. Emily stood up just a foot away, the gag still in her mouth and her hands still bound. Troy's knife had fallen from his hand when he landed and he painfully leaned over to pick it up. Sawing through the cloth around her mouth, he finally broke it loose and quickly pulled the gag from her mouth.

Emily licked her lips several times to moisten them. "Thank you." She cleared her throat. "Quick, do my hands. We've got to get the boys down."

"Yep." Troy whirled her around and sawed quickly through her bonds.

She briefly rubbed her wrists, then ran over to their cages. "Brian, Brandon, we're going to get you down. Just do everything we tell you, okay?"

Both boys nodded.

"Here." Emily braced her rear against the lower ledge of Brian's aquarium. Facing Troy, she gripped her hands together to make a stepping stool for him. "Should make it slightly easier than last time. When you put your foot here, I'll lift you higher."

"Emily, I'll crush your hands if I step on them."

"Just do it," she snapped. "Sorry, I don't want to be rude, but I'm not going to take time to be polite when we've got to get out of here—now."

"Gotcha." Troy stepped onto her hands and caught the top ledge as Emily hoisted his foot from below. His shoulder shot painful fireworks, but Troy gritted his teeth, ignoring it.

Emily, tall and athletic, hustled around to the other side of the aquariums, hopped up on the ledge and grasped the top of the aquarium with her fingers. She swung herself easily to the top. Both she and Troy crouched on opposite sides of the cage, panting. Troy allowed himself a brief second of admiration for her finesse.

"Brian," Emily whispered. "We're going to get you down like I got down. This man is going to cut your ropes off your legs first and then your blindfold so you can see to jump. And then we're going to jump off the edge together as soon as the rope is cut, okay? Brandon, you listen, too. We'll have to do it the same way for you both."

Troy eased himself to a standing position. He concentrated on the rope in front of him. "Emily, as soon as I get y'all out of here, I've got something to tell you with regards to both of your brothers. It's really important, so if anything happens to any of us, I've got to get the message to you. Got it?"

Emily nodded at him, wide-eyed. "I'll remember. You hurry."

"Ready, Brian?" Troy crouched forward. "You're going to swing for a minute when I hit your rope, but we'll get you out of this."

Brian nodded.

Troy fell toward the rope and grabbed it with his right hand. The momentum shifted both of them and he lost his footing. He and Brian swung close to Emily and she reached out with one arm and grabbed the rope below Troy's hand, pulling it back to her ledge.

Troy swung his feet around to balance next to Emily. Sweat trickled in his eyes again and his left shoulder shot pain through his arm. Emily cradled Brian with both arms while Troy sawed through Brian's bonds. The loose pieces of rope, the blindfold and the gag fell into the cage below. The snakes, disturbed, shook their rattles in a quick rhythm. The last thread gave way and Brian's rope popped upward with its loss of weight. Emily's grip tightened on Brian and Troy steadied both the woman and the boy so they didn't fall.

"You're okay." Emily rubbed Brian's back. His arms clung to her neck and his eyes were wide with fear. "Here, Brian, hang on to this man for a minute and I'll jump down and catch you when you jump, okay?" Reluctantly, Brian allowed himself to be pulled into Troy's arms. Emily nimbly jumped the distance to the ground, landing in a squat on the floor. She held out her arms. "Jump," she commanded.

Brian trembled, but he mutely did as he was told. He landed safely in her arms, though the impact knocked her off her feet and they rolled on the ground. Emily quickly pushed herself back into a standing position and pulled Brian to his feet. "Now for Brandon."

Troy nodded from the top of the cage, and crouching, made his way slowly to the far end. Emily ran back around the end of the aquariums to the front so she could be on the opposite side of Troy. She swung herself to the top ledge again. Brian followed and watched anxiously from his place on the floor.

"Here we go, Brandon. We're almost out of here." Troy kept his voice even and low, the comforting tones calming the shaking form.

"Shh," Emily snapped. "What's that?"

Both fell silent immediately. "Voices," Troy whispered. Two men's voices were heard at a distance, moving slowly up the tunnel from the room that held Jeff and Jill.

Emily's wide eyes stared into Troy's. "Hurry," she mouthed. Troy immediately stood up and jumped to the rope, not even attempting to keep his grasp on the ledge this time. It swung him to the far side and Emily grabbed Brandon as Troy found his footing on the ledge next to her. "Hurry, hurry, hurry." The voices were getting closer.

Troy sawed through Brandon's ankle ropes. "Don't worry about his blindfold," Emily whispered. "Just get him down."

Troy nodded, his hand gripping the rope above Brandon, and frantically sawed the thick rope. The men had almost reached the room now and Troy's hand slipped. His knife dropped with a sickening thud right in the middle of the snakes.

Emily desperately stood, pulling back with all her might on the rope, and grasped the last few threads between her teeth. With a snap, the rope gave way, and she, Troy and Brandon all tumbled onto the stone floor. Brandon landed on top of Emily. Troy had managed to get his feet under him. "Come on, Brian."

Brian stared at the door that was just about to open. He turned immediately at the words from Troy. Troy gave a hand up to Emily, threw Brandon over his uninjured shoulder and ran across the room toward the exit.

They had no sooner disappeared through the doorway than they heard a shout behind them. "Oi! They're gone!"

"Run." Troy spread an urgent hand on Emily's back and nudged her in front of him.

Emily took off with Brian clinging to her hand and Troy stayed close on her heels. Troy could hear footsteps thudding behind them. Up ahead, he could see the crack of light at the bottom of the entrance doorway.

"Get through that door," he panted.

The sound of a shot ricocheted off the stone walls, the sound deafening in their ears. A new pain burned Troy's side. Gritting his teeth, he ran even faster, the exit just in front of them.

Emily hit the door, throwing it open into blazing sunlight. Brian stumbled out after her. She grabbed his hand and hauled him to a nearby Tower employee.

"Help! I need help." Her breath came in hysterical pants. She felt tears running down her cheeks. She glanced wildly behind her, then gasped. Troy had made it out of the tunnel with Brandon in his arms, but had hit the ground, blood pooling on the stones underneath him.

The door swung slowly shut. It didn't open again. She gathered Brian and Brandon to her and allowed herself to sob into their hair.

CHAPTER 23

"You okay?" Jeff's whisper shook Jill from her thoughts. They sat back to back, their hands tied together, and they leaned on each other for support. Topper was the lone guard in the room. The other two men had left the room a couple of hours before. Topper watched them closely but said nothing.

"Yeah." Jill heaved a sigh. "I'm just thinking."

"What about?"

"About water polo." She snorted. "Obviously, Jeff, about escaping with nobody getting hurt."

"Any ideas yet?"

"Nope. But I'm working on it."

"Hey you, Topper." Jeff raised his voice to the guard. "What time is it?"

Topper glanced at his watch. "A quarter past five."

"That late?" Jill leaned her head back against Jeff's. "We've been here for hours!"

Jeff shifted. "How much longer are they going to keep us in this room?"

"Her Grace will decide."

Jeff's shoulders slumped. "I wish I knew why she was doing this. And I wish I knew what her plans were for my kids. If she had it out for just me, this wouldn't be so hard."

Jill was silent. Then she took a breath and asked, "Were you and your sister very close?"

"We used to be." Jeff sighed. "Back when we were kids. We used to gang up on John, since he was the oldest." He swallowed hard. "But then I started getting mixed up with the wrong people. Ran away from home just before I turned 18 and decided to see the world. Scraped together what little money I had earned and blew it all on a plane ticket to Europe. I had decided I would get a job over here and do things the way I wanted to do them. My parents had an awful time dealing with it. Then I got invited by a friend to my very first sabbat and that's where I ran into Celia." He sighed again. "I was such an idiot." Discouragement filled his voice.

Jill twisted her wrist in the rope, then decided that was a mistake. The bristles cut sharply into her skin.

"Not an idiot, Jeff. Just not aware of what you needed."

"And what was that?"

"Christ's love, of course." Jill twisted her wrist again. The rope, though tied very tightly was sliding down her slim wrist. She stretched her fingers outward, bunching her knuckles closely together, making her hand as small as possible. The rope stuck hard when it reached the base of her thumb, but slowly and painfully, Jill inched her hand outward. Her knuckles collapsed around each other and Jill winced. The raw scratches that the rope left in her skin throbbed painfully, but after the knot passed the base of Jill's hand, it became easier from there. She withdrew the last of her fingers, but left her hand firmly behind her back. Topper still watched them closely. Jill's brain searched frantically for more topics of conversation to help cover any sounds of movement.

"So tell me about the church you attend." Jeff's voice cut into her thoughts.

Jill moved her fingers to work on the knot attaching her left hand to both of Jeff's. "It's small. Only about sixty people attend on any given Sunday. But I like it—it's got great community. And the pastor is wonderful. Really gets into his sermons." Her fingernails clicked as they slipped off the knot. Jeff seemed to sense that she was doing something and straightened to make it easier for her to reach the knot.

Topper stood suddenly from the bare floor where he had been sitting.

Jill looked up with wide, panicked eyes, sure she had been caught. He wasn't looking at her, though. The Duchess marched back through the small doorway through which she had exited.

Without pausing, she made straight for them. "I suppose you want to see your kids again," she said without preamble.

"Of—of course." Jeff stuttered in his relief.

She stared hard at him, then at Jill. "Come." She turned on her heel and strode out the small doorway again.

Topper hurried over and hefted Jeff up by the arm. Jill quickly followed, her hand still bound. Topper, not glancing at their wrists, grabbed both of their arms and pushed them forward. They sidestepped their way awkwardly toward the door. Topper threw it open, and both of them entered into yet another dark hallway.

Jeff and Jill followed Celia around two or three more curves. They rounded one last corner and Celia flung open a door. Late afternoon sunlight and city heat dazed them both. Jill vaguely recognized the Tower in the distance, and the Underground station right across the road from them.

Celia turned sharply. "Topper, take them to the park. Wait until the rest arrive, then prepare them."

"Yes, Your Grace." Topper bowed. He pushed Jill and Jeff forward, his small size belying his strength. A white paneled van sat at the exit to the tunnel and he opened the back two doors for them. "In you go."

Jeff struggled on, dragging Jill with him again, and Topper slammed the doors. Jill closed her eyes as she heard the motor start and felt the vehicle begin to move.

Sam was having a hard time of it. After Troy had disappeared into the crowd, Sam got back in contact with the agents surrounding the Tower to see if they could spot Jill and Jeff, or his agent Norse.

"Hang it all, they can't have taken Norse. too." Sam spoke into his radio. "Keep your eyes peeled. I'm heading to the Tower." He nodded to Barnaby. "Stay here for a bit."

Barnaby's eyes narrowed. "Yes, sir."

Sam slammed the door on his van and touched his earpiece. "I'm coming in," he mumbled.

"We copy that." Southerland's voice cracked with static. "Will we meet you at the bridge?"

"The bridge," Sam confirmed.

He jogged up the stairs onto the busy bridge, his eyes darting here and there. "Has anyone laid eyes on Lane?"

Negative answers were thrown back to him through the static. "Blast. Where did he get to?"

"We have a visual on you, Lieutenant," Southerland's voice crackled. "We're heading your way."

A second later, two men casually strolled close to Sam.

"How in the world did they give us the slip?" Powers muttered.

"No idea." Sam popped his knuckles in frustration. "But now we've got seven field agents–six, minus Norse–all standing around like blasted idiots and no one has the first clue where to look."

Powers looked back toward where the command post van was parked. "What's that?" He pointed.

Southerland and Sam stared at a quickly swelling mass of people along the stone wall by the Thames, no more than 50 feet behind where the van was parked.

"What are they looking at?" Sam shielded his eyes with his hand. "It's too bright out here."

"I'll find out." Southerland broke into a jog.

"Wait." Sam caught up with him. "I'll go with you." He spoke into his mouthpiece. "All agents on standby."

The three of them spread out and hurried over to the crowd. Upon reaching the scene, Sam pushed his way through the people till he reached the front. He was on the bank of the Thames, the Tower behind him and to his right. A Tower security guard stood next to a husky boy in his teens. The guard had a transmitter to his mouth, explaining the situation.

Sam saw what the boy was staring at and gulped hard. Norse floated in the water of the Thames chained to a metal post on the bank of the river. His face was above water, but red liquid—Sam breathed in sharply as he realized it was blood—trickled from his head and stained the water around him. Norse appeared to be unconscious, or dead, Sam thought with a slight tremor.

Sam reached in his back pocket for his badge. He stepped up to the guard. "Police." He waved his badge in front of the guard. "What's going on here?"

"Over and out." The guard finished his speech and nodded to Sam. "I'm glad you're here, sir." He motioned to the boy. "This lad happened to see this man chained in the river and he ran for help. I was the first person he found. I've just finished informing the Tower of the situation and they're in conversation with your headquarters. I can have them cancel the call since you're already here.

Sam shook his head absently. "Don't worry about it. I'll contact them." He gazed down at Norse. "Norse, mate, you've had a rough day."

"Yes, sir." The guard pointed. "He looks to have been lobbed upside the head too. Can't tell what the medics will have to say about this."

"Contact the Tower and have them call for an ambulance. We need to get him out as soon as possible."

"Yes, sir." The guard immediately spoke into his transmitter again.

"And get these people out of here," Sam added irritably. His assignment was not going as planned and his perfectionist nature balked at the developments.

The guard again nodded in agreement, once more finishing his communication with the Tower before moving to block the scene from the public. The boy who discovered Norse stayed put. "I need to witness." His voice was firm.

Sam walked a slight distance away and spoke, "All agents continue surveillance of the Tower. I've got a situation here I need to take care of. Notify me immediately if you spot any parties involved, especially Sergeant Lane."

"Yes sir," came the responses.

Sam glanced at Powers and Southerland from the corner of his eye. They had moved back from the scene and headed once again toward the Tower. He went back to the guard.

"I'd like to know how some person managed to do this to Norse without any tourists spotting them."

"It's hard to say, sir. This area is more secluded since most of the tourists stay on the other side of the bridge. Was he in surveillance, sir? Because it wouldn't have been anything for someone to knock him on the head, chain him to this post, and drop him in the river. It could have happened in a matter of just a few seconds."

Sam felt a crick in his neck as he looked down at his agent. "They had it set up." He shook his head. "They were just waiting for Jill and Jeff to walk on the bridge."

The telltale wail of a siren sounded. A large white and neon yellow van swung to the curb's edge, followed swiftly by a fire truck.

As a fireman hooked himself to safety gear and rappelled his way down the bank, Sam pulled his unit close to his mouth. "As soon as I get Norse on the ambulance, I'm heading to the Tower. Any signs of anyone?"

No response.

"Do you read me?"

Still nothing.

"Blast!" Sam hit the wall with his fist. "I've got to get over there." He jerked his earpiece from his ear.

"Sir?" One of the firemen stood behind him.

"Yes," he snapped as he turned. His face was twisted with frustration and the fireman took a step back.

"I just wanted to give you the status. This man is alive, but he's lost a lot of blood and has been unconscious for so long that if we don't get him to the hospital right away, he probably won't make it. The paramedics have him on a gurney now."

Sam glanced up. Norse had been cut free from his chain. Paramedics carefully lifted his agent into the back of the ambulance. Sam trotted over to one of the paramedics. He pulled his card from his pocket and handed it to him with instructions to contact him from the hospital when he could receive any information.

The paramedic nodded, then climbed into the back. The siren wailed and the van pulled away from the curb. The fire truck followed soon after and the siren's wail gradually disappeared into the distance. The Tower guard looked at Sam.

"Sir, did you need the lad for questioning?"

Sam nodded. "Yes. I'm heading to the Tower, though. I've got surveillance happening that I'm supposed to be overseeing, and my transmitter's gone out."

The guard looked curious, but didn't ask questions. Instead, he motioned for the boy to precede them and they walked quickly in the direction of the Tower. Sam glanced at his watch and was shocked to realize that the whole scenario had taken an hour and he still had had no word on Troy, Jill or Jeff.

The transmitter on the guard's belt crackled and Sam overheard an urgent voice. "All units report to White Tower immediately. There's been a shooting. One victim."

The guard straightened and began to jog toward the Tower, Sam and the boy following quickly behind. The guard touched his transmitter again. "Identification of victim?"

There was a moment of silence, and then the transmitter crackled. "He's an American police officer. His name is Lieutenant Troy Lane."

CHAPTER 24

It was dark in the back of the van. The only light came from a small window at the front just behind the driver's seat. Jill and Jeff jounced along with the potholes in the road.

"We're going to Bushy Park now, I guess." Jill faced Jeff. One hand was still tied, but the fingers on her other hand picked at the tight knot.

Jeff nodded. In the faint light, Jill could see trails of moisture on his cheeks. Her own eyes welled up with empathy. She rubbed her nose with the back of her free hand and bent over the knot.

"Stupid knot." She yanked on it in frustration. "I got my other hand out. Seems like it should be easier to get this one out, but my hand's so swollen now from all the pressure that it's five times its normal size." She jerked at the knot desperately and felt one of her nails chip. She sat back and blew out her breath in a huff.

Jeff's voice sounded hollow. "Do you think she's...killed...my kids yet?" He stared straight ahead.

Jill paused, studying his face. "I don't know, Jeff." She softened her voice. "I honestly have no idea. You seem to know her pretty well. Do you think she has?"

"No." Jeff sighed heavily. "But I could be wrong."

The van lurched suddenly, throwing Jill and Jeff off balance. Jeff rolled back to a sitting position, dragging Jill's arm with him. Jill's eyes were wide as she listened. "We've stopped." The driver's side door slammed. "Quick!" She scooted around behind Jeff again, her back pressing against his, and pulled her free arm tightly behind her. The back doors swung open, the glaring evening sunlight stunning their eyes.

"Come along then." Topper grinned cheerily at them.

Jeff scooted toward the opening, pulling Jill with him. They found themselves in a secluded driveway, a lush green park spread directly in front of the van. A black iron fence kept the van from entering the park, but Topper pulled out a key and inserted it into a padlock resting on the latch of a huge gate.

"How do you have a key for the gate to a public park?" Jill studied the iron bars.

"Her Grace has special privileges." A snide grin on his face covered Topper's face. "She's got powerful influence around here."

"It's too bad she can't use her influence then to help people," Jill bit out.

"I think the Duchess would beg to differ with you. She only does what she knows will be good in the end. The greater good…and all that."

"I don't see how she thinks that torturing small children and innocent people will turn out to be good."

"Then you will find that the Duchess is much wiser than you."

"Wiser, my foot," Jeff mumbled. "If I've ever seen an act that is more demeaning and intended to bring hurt to anyone, then a pig just flew past my head."

Topper spun on him. "No one asked your opinion, so you can shut your yap right now." He gripped the iron bar of the gate and swung it slowly open. "Enter."

Jeff stepped forward through the gate. Jill stumbled after him. Her jaw locked with intense dislike of the man before them.

Topper shut and locked the gate again, then led them slowly through some copses of trees. He stopped at the start of a path leading through some dense trees. At the end, Jill could see a barn. She glanced behind them. The road was barely visible here.

"You're to stay here for the next couple of hours until dark. I'm going to untie you, because you'll be given something different to wear, but I think you know better than to try to run for it. That is, *if* you want your children back alive, you'll know better." He reached for the rope twisting their hands together and Jill heard his sharp intake of breath.

"You little cheat." Topper jerked her around to face him. "Thought you'd escape, eh? It's lucky Elliot knows his knots. When we tie you again, you won't be able to get out so easily."

Jill's mouth narrowed to a firm line and she didn't give him the satisfaction of a retort. She heard his knife saw through the rope and felt the blessed release of her swollen hand. She and Jeff rubbed their wrists for a second, both of them searching the landscape.

"Come with me." Topper led them down the path toward the barn. Arriving at the large doors, he grasped the handle of one and pushed it along its roller to the side.

Bright light lit the inside. Jill and Jeff stepped tentatively forward. The interior was not barn-like at all, but rather richly decorated and furnished. Couches framed the middle of the room and long low tables were set up in front of each couch. There was a sidebar to their left and rich tapestries hung behind the couches to their right, sealing off some rooms.

At the sound of their footsteps, a man entered the room from behind one of the tapestries.

Jill gasped. "What are you doing here?"

Emily was shaking an hour later as the questions continued to bombard her. A nice policeman was asking them, but the emotions and anguish that had been her constant company for days had brought her to the breaking point. Brian and Brandon did not leave her side. They huddled against her, Brandon's thumb stuck in his mouth, a habit he had dropped years before.

At one point, the policeman asked if she had happened to overhear the name of her captor in the last several days. Emily's mind flashed back to the last interview she had been privy to while she swung from the rope above the aquariums.

"Celia." She thought a moment. "Up until the rescue, the woman was only referred to as 'Her Grace' or 'Duchess,' and no names were dropped until I heard my brother talking to her."

An odd look crossed the policeman's face. "You said she was called 'Duchess?'"

"Yes, sir."

He tapped his pen on his notepad, his look serious. After a moment, he sighed. "Right, well, there are some things we're going to have to check into further. For right now, though, I suggest you get some rest—you and the children. It would be best to take them from this scene for now."

Emily nodded. "You're right, of course, but I do have a question. Who was the man who rescued us? And how is he connected with all of this?"

The policeman looked surprised. "Oh, I thought you would have known. His name is Lieutenant Troy Lane. Your eldest brother's partner."

"Troy?" Emily gasped. "I've never met him in person, though I've heard my brother mention him hundreds of times." She bit her lip, thinking. "But John's in the hospital in a coma. Was that only a week ago?"

"Yes, and now Lane is in hospital as well. It's a dangerous business." The officer smiled at her.

Emily stood up. "I've got to get to the hospital right away. Troy told me in the middle of rescuing us that he had a really important message having to do with both of my brothers. I've *got* to talk to him!" Her voice had risen to fever pitch at this point and both boys looked even more frightened.

The officer's eyes flashed to the boys. "Miss Siegle, what about these lads?" He smiled reassuringly at them. "You need to be with them, but let me send some officers to the hospital to see what Officer Lane needed to say."

"No." Emily shook her head. "I'll let a couple of officers come along and the boys can stay in the car with one of them, but I've got to hear what Troy has to say in person."

The officer opened his mouth to protest when another officer appeared next to the bench where Emily and the boys were sitting.

"Certainly, you must go to the hospital and I'll accompany you." The new officer held out his hand. "Lieutenant Sam Scott."

"Emily Siegle," she stuttered in surprise, "and thank you." She breathed a heartfelt sigh.

Sam studied her face briefly for a minute, then turned on his heel. The questioning officer nodded sheepishly. "We'll have a car ready for you in a minute. Follow me, please." He rose and led the trembling threesome toward the main gate. Outside, a whole row of squad cars lined the street.

"Lieutenant Scott will be with you shortly," he said crisply. "In the meantime, you may have a seat in this car right here." He motioned to the closest one.

"Thank you." Emily smiled at him.

She ushered the boys into the back seat of the car, then climbed in after them. The young officer stood just outside her door, his eyes watching the area around them carefully. Sam hurried out of the gate toward them.

"Alright, let's go." He opened the right hand door and jumped in. The other officer scurried around to the passenger side and folded his long legs in as well. A siren wailed loudly. It took Emily an instant before she realized that it belonged to the car she was in. The city streets and stopped motorists flashed past as the squad car sped through town.

Sam parked the car in front of a massive, glass-covered building. An overhang protected a small cul-de-sac. Cars pulled through it as patients were admitted or discharged from the hospital. He left his lights flashing and swung his door open, then grasped the handle to the back door and opened it for her.

Emily nodded. "Brian, Brandon, you'll stay here with...." She stopped, realizing she had never gotten the younger officer's name.

"Barnaby," he filled in for her.

"You'll stay with Mr. Barnaby for a minute while I run in." She looked the boys in their eyes and took their hands firmly in her own. "And I promise that I'll be back out in just a couple of minutes. We're going to go find your daddy after that."

Both boys still had traces of tears on their cheeks, but they nodded silently.

As she turned to climb out of the car, she noticed Barnaby pull an electronic version of Hearts from the glove compartment. "Here lads, see what I've got here? Have you ever played Hearts?" Barnaby turned to better face the boys. With a smile playing across Emily's lips, she stepped out to meet Sam and walked swiftly beside him into the hospital.

"Surprised to see me, Jill?" The man grinned. "Though I'm not as surprised to see you. I would have been very surprised, however, if you hadn't shown up."

Jill's jaw locked. "What do you mean, Mr. Bradley?"

"Only that I played an important part in bringing you here." He breathed deeply through his nose and exhaled. "It is such a wonderful feeling knowing that all your efforts have paid off."

"Why did you fire me, Mr. Bradley? It didn't have anything to do with the firm's decision, did it?" Jill felt the lead ball in the pit of her stomach again.

"No, it didn't." Edward Bradley chuckled. "The firm has probably been wondering what ever happened to you. I'm sure they've hired someone new by now to replace their remiss employee."

Anger spiked through Jill. "How do you think you'll get away with being here, skipping your father's funeral and all that, without being suspected of—of...." Jill glanced wildly around.

"That's just it," Edward said and laughed again. "You're not exactly sure what I'm guilty of, are you?" He walked forward toward the couches and motioned for them to sit. "Allow me to enlighten you."

Jill glanced at Jeff, then at Topper. He nodded threateningly. She and Jeff moved forward, settling gingerly on a couch facing Edward.

He popped his jaw, his facial features twitching. "I don't think it's any secret." He rubbed his chin. "The relationship I had with my father wasn't great. He hated me and I hated him. He had quirks, I know, and most of the time, we could tolerate each other's presence, at least in the company of others. I watched him carefully all the time. I hated him so much that I tried in every way to be as little like him as possible. I have always dreamed of being a lawyer, so I couldn't give that up. But he liked to fish, so I hate fish or anything to do with them. He enjoyed his family and wife. So I never married, nor had any desire to have children. He believed in a god who is the father of the world, therefore I decided to believe in a goddess, mother of nature. My father hated me even worse when he found out that our beliefs had separated. On one memorable evening, he told me he was cutting me out of his will."

Edward paused there, as if waiting for questions. Jill and Jeff gave him none.

He sighed. "So we had a huge argument. While I had to see him at work, we ignored each other as much as possible. And as this was all going on, I began to see how much he valued his relationship with his young secretary. Oh, nothing sleazy. I'm sure he saw you as the daughter he never had." He stared at Jill as if daring her to deny it.

"Yes, I admit that we were close." Jill frowned. "What does that have to do with you?"

"One day, I headed to my father's house. I wanted to clean the last of my things out of my old room. I didn't intend to let him know that I was there. I was simply going to go in and get what I wanted." He was starting to sweat now, his face white and his nostrils flaring. "I heard him talking to my aunt on the phone in his study, mentioning how he planned to redo his will to cut me out, obviously confirming what we had already discussed. He wanted to add someone new to it. Can you guess who the new person was? Of course, you can," he continued without waiting for an answer. "Jill Lyon, of course! The same young woman that I had been keeping tabs on for three months."

"What?" Jill leaned forward. "I'm in Mr. Bradley's will?" Then, as if suddenly realizing it, she sputtered, "You were following me, too?"

"Of course. Oh, I forgot to explain. I told you that I believe in a goddess, mother earth and all that. I joined in with a coven in the area, and somehow, word got to me that a very powerful witch from England wished to find you, Jill Lyon. She needed you for a great purpose, and of course, since you were quickly becoming more and more despicable to me as time passed, I contacted Her Grace; hence, the reason why you are here."

A long moment of silence passed as both Jill and Jeff digested this information.

"But why tell me all this?" Jill sat back and glared at him. "I can have you arrested once we get back to the States and you'll go to prison for a very long time. Kidnapping, imprisonment, defamation of character— the list goes on."

"Ah." Edward leaned forward and trained his gaze on Jill's face. "But you're not going back to the States, now are you?" He smiled widely, his teeth glinting in the bright glow from the top of the barn.

CHAPTER 25

Emily peered around the corner of the private room where Troy had been placed. A nurse bustled around the foot of the bed, checking monitors and instruments. She turned at the sound of the two new visitors.

"He's just out of surgery." She spoke in a whisper as she smiled at them. "It's best just to let him sleep now."

Emily nodded politely and she and Sam edged into the room. The nurse gave a final pat to the bed covers and hurried out of the room, nodding pleasantly to them as she passed.

Sam inched forward, apprehensively dodging the monitors and wires that were hooked up to Troy. "Lane." He glanced over his shoulder at the door. "Lane!" He placed a hand on Troy's uninjured shoulder and shook it gently.

Troy groaned, his eyes blinking open. He stared at Sam, his eyes dulled in confusion. "Where am I?" His words slurred together.

"You're in hospital, Lane. Hey mate, can you come awake enough to give a message to your partner's sister, Emily?"

Troy's eyes moved slowly from Sam's face to Emily, standing just behind the lieutenant.

"Sounds familiar." He gulped convulsively. "Need water."

Sam glanced up at Emily, then nodded and fumbled with the water pitcher and paper cups next to the bed.

Emily leaned over Troy. "Troy, do you remember rescuing me and my nephews just a few hours ago?"

Troy's eyes slid shut, his lips moved briefly, then his breathing evened out into the steady rhythm of slumber.

Emily desperately grasped both shoulders. "Troy!" She shook his shoulders gently. "Troy, I need you to remember what you were going to tell me. Please, please wake up and remember."

Troy groaned. His eyes opened again, still dull and confused. "Can't remember," he slurred. "Too hard."

Sam lifted the cup close to Troy's mouth. "Here, Lane." He held it to the injured man's lips. "Drink."

The water trickled down Troy's chin over day-old stubble. A little managed to make it into his mouth.

"I think the medication is too strong." Emily straightened. "He just can't get past the fog."

"I've been put under before." Sam glanced at her. "It's no picnic trying to wake up from it."

Sam's radio crackled. A garbled voice came through the noise. Emily couldn't quite make it out, but Sam glanced up sharply. "Bushy Park, of course!" He snapped his fingers. He listened a minute longer, then turned to Emily. "Did you catch that?"

She shook her head. "Too much static and too low."

"A passing motorist called in a sighting of a man and woman who seemed to have their hands bound. They were being let into Bushy Park by a back private entrance." He glanced back at Troy. "I've got to get over there. It's probably Jeff and Jill that they saw."

Troy's eyes were open again. "Jeff an' Jill," he mumbled. "Had a message. What was it?"

Sam was poised to leave and Emily seemed prepared to hurry after him, but they both stopped short at Troy's words.

The nurse who had been in Troy's room several minutes ago came bustling around the corner. "Here, here, what do you think you're doing?" She flapped her arms at the two adults. "The patient needs his sleep and you're disturbing him."

"Hold on a sec." Troy's voice was clearing, his words less slurred together. The nurse glanced in surprise at Troy.

"Well, you're a beauty and no mistake." She patted his arm. "I've never seen anyone come out of anesthesia quite that fast, especially after major surgery."

Troy looked slowly from Sam to Emily. "I remember listening to someone talking about Jill and Jeff. They were going to be taken to Bushy park—was it this evening?" His hand moved to his stomach where Emily was sure he must be in some pain.

"So I needed to tell you that." He nodded at Emily, his head wobbling a little. "And then there was something else, too."

The nurse patted his arm once more. "You need to rest, dearie. You can tell these people your message later, alright?"

"Get off me." Troy feebly pushed aside the woman's hands as she tried to tuck his covers closer around him. "That's it—it's coming back." His eyes started to close again. With an effort, he jerked them back open.

"I got a call from my head office in the States. John's out of his coma and talking. I didn't get to talk to the dispatcher for long." He shook his head this time to clear it, then clutched it with his hand. "Ooh, that hurt. Anyway, the dispatcher said that John had mentioned a coronation of some sort. Somebody was supposed to be crowned at a certain point and that in order for this coronation to take place, Jill has to be killed. She didn't say how John knew all that…." His voice trailed off.

Emily swiftly knelt by Troy's bed. "Troy." Urgency laced her voice. "Is Jill the woman that was with my brother in the snake chamber?"

Troy's eyes had shut again. "Y-yes, I think so," he mumbled. "Not real sure of anything now, though."

Emily looked up at Sam. "If what he says is true, we've got to get them out of there before any more time passes."

"I'm sorry, ma'am." Sam's polite expression infuriated Emily. "We won't be allowing you to accompany us to the park."

"Oh, yes you will." Emily stood to speak, her voice harder than flint rock. "And I'll tell you why. I've been in this from the beginning, have endured more than most people ever could have, and I intend to see it through. My brothers are both part of this and you won't be able to keep me away."

Sam opened his mouth to speak, but Emily planted her hands on her hips. "Stop wasting time telling me I can't go when you know good and well that I will go no matter what. You can't stop me and we've got to get a move on."

The nurse's eyes swung back and forth between them. "Look at the pair of them, fightin' like cats and dogs." She clicked her tongue, then motioned to the doorway. "Now if you don't mind, I have a patient who very much needs his sleep and you've been enough of a disturbance for one evening."

Sam raked a hand through his hair and glared at Emily. "I could lose my job over this."

"Then deal with it." Emily glared right back at him. "I'll leave you free to do your job, but I intend to be on site when we go to get Jeff and Jill, and if you won't let me, I'll take a cab straight over to the park right now, and 'accidentally' stumble into wherever they've got my brother hidden. And then you'll be stuck with another hostage to free. I mean it." She stood so close to Sam now. Her nose almost touched his.

Sam narrowed his eyes. "Fine. You American women are too stubborn for your own good anyway. If you want to put yourself in more danger, what's that to me? What do I know? I'm just a police officer anyway." He turned on his heel and strode from the room. Emily glanced once more at Troy, who was sound asleep again, and hurried after the lieutenant.

Jill's head was bowed as she sat on the couch and stared fixedly at her knees. Jeff scooted closer to her and gently rubbed her neck. She sat stiffly, not seeming to realize or care that he had done this.

Edward Bradley had gone. Only Topper remained in the room and now he moved forward. "It's time to go." His voice broke the silence.

Jeff looked up. "Where to?"

"Not you." Topper nodded at Jill. "Jill's got to get ready for the ceremony this evening. Her Grace wants you to wait patiently."

"Oh, does she?" Jeff snapped. "Well, she can just...."

Jill laid her hand swiftly on Jeff's knee. "Hush, Jeff." She looked significantly at him, a light flickering in her eyes. "You need to stay here. *Listen* to me, okay? You've got to *listen*." Her black pupils were wide and seemed to communicate something.

Jeff minutely shook his head. *What are you saying?*

Jill squeezed his hand and rose from the couch. Topper pushed her to one side and grabbed an ugly looking length of rope from one of the drawers in the sofa table. He tied Jeff's hands tightly together again, then extended the rope to his ankles and tied those tightly together as well.

"Insurance. Just to make sure your stay with us is a long and comfortable one."

He grabbed Jill's upper arm and marched her around the couches and through the tapestry across from Jeff. Jeff watched them go. *She really wants me to listen. This barn isn't very soundproof. Maybe I can hear something important.* He sat quietly on the couch, hands bound, listening.

Topper led Jill into a small room in the back of the barn. It sported a king-sized bed, an ornate dresser and two wide closets. Jill noticed immediately that there were no windows in the room.

Topper released her arm and strode quickly to one of the closets. He pulled out a white, clingy gown and tossed it on the bed. Then he jerked open a door next to one of the closets. Jill could see a sink and a mirror inside from where she was standing.

"Her Grace commands that you bathe, then put this on." He motioned to the gown on the bed. "We will come get you when it is time."

Jill stared at him. "What's going to happen?" She bit her bottom lip.

Topper's eyes narrowed. "You'll find out when it's time to find out. Leave your necklace on." He backed toward the door of the room. "You don't have much time, so I suggest you get moving quickly."

He opened the door and walked out, shutting it firmly behind him. Jill heard a lock click. Her eyes filled with tears. *Where are you now, God?*

Jeff heard Topper's footsteps walking swiftly toward the room where he was sitting. He strained his ears for any sounds of where Jill might be, but he heard nothing.

A door slammed, the sound coming from the west side of the barn, behind the tapestries. Topper's footsteps stopped, then retreated. Jeff assumed he must be going to meet whoever was at the door.

He leaned forward and shut his eyes, his face screwed up in concentration. His mouth twisted with dislike when he heard the Duchess' voice wafting through the tapestries.

"Is she ready?"

"She is getting ready now, my lady."

"And Jeff? Where is he?"

"In the main room."

"He has not found out about his children?"

"My lady, what about them? I have been with Jill and Jeff the whole time and have heard nothing."

The Duchess' voice dropped slightly, but Jeff could still make out the words and his heart somersaulted. "They escaped."

Jeff's breathing quickened. If his children were no longer prisoners, there was no more point in being careful. He could escape, be with his children again—free.

He was on the point of trying to untie his knots with his teeth when he heard the Duchess's voice again. "I want Jeff there to watch Miss Lyon's ritual sacrifice. Front row seats, do you understand?"

"Yes, m'lady."

"He needs to learn that once he covenants himself to me, he can't run—ever."

"Of course, m'lady."

There was a pause in the conversation. Then the Duchess' voice returned and Jeff caught the note of steel in it. "Topper, that goes for you, too. I'm aware of your mistakes in America, and I can't allow that to happen again. I'm afraid I'm going to have to punish you."

"Oh, m'lady, please." Topper's voice suddenly rose to almost a shriek. "Please, m'lady, I won't fail you ever again. You have my word on that, m'lady."

The Duchess laughed cruelly. "Your word? *Your* word? What's that to me? Horse manure. Now go watch Miss Lyon's door and do not let her escape."

"Yes, m'lady."

Topper's feet went one way and the Duchess' heels tapped briefly in another. A door slammed and all was silent once again. The quietness rang in Jeff's ears.

Please, God. Thank you that my children are safe, but please don't take Jill in their place.

A tiny cough sounded behind him. He angled his head to look. A partition blocked his view of any intruders, but he was certain he had heard something.

A breath of a whisper came to his ears. "Jeff."

Jeff jerked around even further. "What?" he whispered back.

A head peered around the corner. Jeff immediately recognized Sam Scott. His heart leaped. Sam opened his mouth to whisper something, but the door on the western side of the barn slammed again and pointed heels clicked in his direction.

Without a sound, Sam faded behind the partition and Jeff turned quickly to face the front.

CHAPTER 26

Barnaby could tell by the look on Sam's face that the lieutenant was furious about something.

Emily had climbed back in the rear seat of the vehicle and had begun quietly playing with the boys, but Sam flung the door open, slammed the car into gear and spun his tires as he screeched away from the front entrance of the hospital. Barnaby wisely held his tongue.

"We need to get a full report on the Duchess' history." Sam turned right. "Seems like there's some people in this world that have to *control* everything that happens around them and she might be one of them." He shot a seething glance back at Emily. She ignored him.

"Got it." Barnaby jotted down a note for himself.

"I want you, Southerland and Rogers to head up three contingents of officers to Bushy Park as soon as we get back. No uniforms; we need to look like pedestrians. By dusk, each officer must find a place to hide near to the Duchess' hideout."

"But sir, we don't know where the hideout is, do we?"

"I've got a hunch. If it plays out, then I know exactly where it is."

The squad car pulled up at the police station not many minutes later.

"All right, lads." Sam turned around. "I've got a room set up here just for you. It's got toys and games and films, and if you want to take a nap, we have two air mattresses all ready for you. We'll be coming back to get you in just a little while. Does that sound like a plan?"

Brian and Brandon both looked apprehensive. "What if someone comes and takes us again?" Brian asked.

"They won't." Sam reached back to ruffle Brian's hair. "We've got this building so locked up and barred down that it would take a whole army to break in. And our biggest, strongest police officer has agreed to play with you the whole time we're gone."

Brandon was distracted by the army concept. "A whole army? Like the Marines?"

"Well, close." Sam winked. "Of course, this is England, so they're called something different, but we can pretend that they're Marines." He paused, his eyes quickly glancing at Emily. "Of course, your aunt decided not to stay."

"Boys, you know that I need to go try to find your dad, right?" Emily interrupted. "And that you really are very safe here. Do you feel very scared now?"

Brian shook his head and Brandon imitated him. "Not really now, Aunt Emily." Brian glanced back at Sam. "And if we get scared, we'll just pray, and that always makes us feel better."

"You do that." Emily took his hand. "In fact, let's pray right now."

She bowed her head, the boys immediately following suit. She was surprised when she heard the slight rustle of Sam and Barnaby bowing their heads and a lump formed in her throat as each man quietly echoed her "Amen."

"All right, let's get on with it then." Sam opened his door.

The five of them exited the car and entered the station. Barnaby went one way and Sam and Emily pulled the boys toward a small room at the far end, opposite the entrance.

Emily opened the door and caught her breath. Toys and games and books lined the walls and a small television sat in one corner. Two air mattresses lay to one side, already inflated.

"Wow." She looked at Sam. "How did you have time to set all this up?"

"It's been several hours since the incident, so we had time to add a few things, though we've had this room here for a few years. Our chief has young children and every now and then will bring them to work after they leave school."

Brian and Brandon had rushed into the room, gazing in delight at everything. Brandon ran to the corner and pulled out a soccer ball.

"Are you boys going to play football all night then?" Sam grinned at their excitement.

"No, we do soccer better." Brian passed the ball to Brandon. Sam looked confused, then his expression cleared.

"Of course, I had forgotten that Americans call it soccer." He touched Emily gently on the shoulder. "Shall we go?" he asked quietly.

Emily looked up and nodded. "Yes, I suppose it's time."

Sam wheeled on his heel, walking to the next office over.

"Griffith, the lads are here. Keep an eye on them for us, will you?"

"Will do." The big man rose from his desk and stretched. "Time for a play break anyway." He slid past Sam and entered the play area. Sam motioned for Emily and she followed, glancing over her shoulder for one last look. The boys were shrieking with laughter as they tossed the soccer ball back and forth over Griffith's head, laughing uproariously as he lunged to catch it and purposely missed.

Emily shook her head in amazement. "It's hard to believe that they can so easily leave behind the experiences of the last few days, Lieutenant Scott."

Sam's eyes surveyed her speculatively. "Oh, it hasn't passed yet. They're young and yes, they can recover quickly, but I'm sure they'll have nightmares for awhile." He paused, his eyes warming. "And please call me Sam."

Emily felt heat flood her cheeks. *Emily, don't be silly.* "Okay, Sam it is."

They were at the exit to the parking lot and Barnaby hurried over. "They're waiting for us in the car park outside." He motioned.

Sam glanced out at the dozen or so officers standing on the pavement outside. He grabbed an earpiece out of Barnaby's hand and handed it to Emily. "Here," he said brusquely. "If you're coming along, you're going to need this."

He let go before Emily had quite taken hold of it and she almost dropped it. Sam turned on his heel and strode outside. Emily sighed in frustration. "Thanks," she told the back of his head.

It was a deep dusk by the time Emily and Sam crept into the park. The attendants were closing the gates and last minute pedestrians were being escorted out.

A security guard accosted them almost at once. "I'm sorry, sir, ma'am, but the park is closed after dark."

Sam held up his badge and introduced himself. "Lieutenant Sam Scott. I believe headquarters has already informed you that we would be here."

The guard scrutinized the badge and finally gave him a nod of approval. "How many do you have here?"

"Eleven officers." Sam glanced around. "Twelve with the lady." He jerked his thumb toward Emily.

The guard nodded. "Go on in. I'll inform the rest of security that you've arrived."

"Thanks."

Emily shivered as they made their way along the fence to the west. "I feel like I'm doing something wrong." Emily glanced behind her. "I've never really had to sneak around before."

"Get used to it." Sam kicked a fallen branch aside. "The night is still young. There'll be lots of sneaking from here on out."

Emily took a deep breath and moved closer to Sam.

The barn towered above them, black in the moonlit grounds. Sam touched his microphone. "All units in place?"

"Affirmative," came the response.

Emily's straightened her leg from its cramped position at the base of a massive tree.

"I'm going in." Sam glanced around. "Wait for my signal."

He crept to the edge of the tree's shadow, peering in all directions, then flung himself across the moonlit space to the barn's edge.

Feeling his way across the wall, he felt the familiar shape of a door. Finding the doorknob with little difficulty, he turned it quietly.

"East door is unlocked," he whispered. He could hear his heart beating in his ears. No sounds came from the interior. He edged inside, catching a glimpse of light several yards to his right.

Putting his hands in front of him, he felt his way inch by inch toward the light. From his position, he could see one side of what looked like a living room. He listened carefully, but couldn't hear any noise. He took a risk and peeked.

Not more than two yards in front of him, the back of Jeff's head confronted his vision.

He ducked back around. He could hear faint voices from the far end of the barn, but his heart beat too loudly to hear what they were saying.

He peeked again. "Jeff!" he whispered.

Jeff's head swung around. He looked frightened and opened his mouth to speak, but then Sam heard heels clicking in his direction. He ducked back behind the wall, risking a whisper into his microphone. "Halt the plan." He began feeling his way back toward the door. "I don't see Jill."

Jill spent most of her time praying fervently as she soaked in the hot bath she had drawn for herself. Suddenly, she realized that her prayers had turned less from pleas for herself and more to petitions on behalf of Jeff, his children and his sister, for their reunification and safety. As she realized this, a deep peace settled over her. It suddenly didn't matter anymore what happened to her. Now she needed to concentrate on becoming enough of a distraction for Jeff to be able to escape.

Before she could think too much about this, a knock sounded on the bedroom door. With a small cry, Jill jumped straight up in the tub, splashing water all over the floor. She hastily grabbed a towel hanging on the rack and wrapped it around her.

Topper's voice came through the barrier. "I'm giving you a five minute warning. Then I'm coming in whether you're ready or not." Jill heard a nasty chuckle.

She let out the breath that she realized she had been holding and waited for his footsteps to fade from the outer room. She snatched up the dress he had given her to wear, pulled it over her shoulders, and paced to the full-length mirror behind the door of the bedroom.

The dress was loose, for which she was thankful, but the material clung to every curve in her body. She tugged the fabric away from her chest, releasing it to fall back and cling once more. She gulped and closed her eyes. *What time I am afraid, I will put my trust in you. Help me, Jesus.* She returned to the bathroom and lifted her necklace from the sink, the ring sliding evenly along the chain. She unhooked the clasp and slid it around her neck, linking the hook to the chain again to secure it. She returned to the mirror in the bedroom. "If I'd only known you would be this much trouble." She shook her head as she looked at the sparkle of blue against her chest. "I should have buried you with my mother." She lightly traced her finger over the engraved words around the edge of the stone. *One Truth. God, you are the One Truth. I'm sure I'm about to have someone try to convince me otherwise, but I'll stick with you, I think.* The peace she felt seemed to settle more fully over her. *Not think.* She shook her head at her reflection. *Know. I know you are the One Truth.*

The door opened swiftly, this time with no knock, and bumped into Jill as she stood in front of the mirror.

Topper eyed her critically, his gaze sweeping from her head to her feet, pausing long enough to take in the ring hanging low on her chest. Jill crossed her arms over it, shaking with disgust for the man in front of her.

"It's time." He laid a heavy hand on her shoulder. "I'll take you to the main room."

"I hate to see you in bonds, Jeff." Celia smiled at him from across the room. Her fingers lightly brushed the back of a couch, trailing slowly along the fabric as she came closer. "If only you would come back to me, you would be so much happier."

"How so?" Anger laced Jeff's voice. "You've shown me what you're capable of, Celia. I could never be happy with a person who portrays such cruelty to innocent humans."

"Oh? Such a pity. You used to, you know—be happy with me." She gazed at him as she crossed the room and sat down next to him, her thigh pressing against his. She brushed his jaw line with her fingertips, then tickled his thick hair. "Because after tonight, Jeff, you and I will once again be together. You know that's the reason I had you brought here. It had nothing to do with the unfortunate Ms. Lyon, though I think it's a shame that she seems so attracted to you. It's hard to love someone when you're dead."

"Love?" Jeff snorted. He twisted to face her. "What do you know about love, Celia? You who claim to have loved hundreds of men? You know, you're absolutely right—it really is hard to love someone when you're dead, and you've been dead for years, Celia. That's right." He nodded when he saw her eyes spark and her finely penciled brows lower. Her hand jerked back to her lap. "You don't know what life is because you're so bogged down with trying to take it away from anyone and everyone who can ever get close to you. You keep trying to take other people's lives so you can live on them, like some drunken goddess who intoxicates herself with power. You're power crazed, Celia. You wouldn't know love if it kicked you in the …."

"You've said enough," Celia interrupted. She stood, shaking. Her eyes snapped fire. "I don't know love, you say. Well, I'm smart enough to see you making sheep's eyes at Jill Lyon, and don't think I haven't guessed that you've fallen in love with her. And what if she's gone tonight, Jeff—pouf! Killed because you love her. How would that make you feel for the rest of your miserable life? And I have the power to do that—or not do that. What's your choice?"

Jeff was silent, his fists clenched so tightly that cramps shot up his forearms. "That's what I thought." She leaned toward him. "Come with me." She pulled a sharp knife from the neckline of her low-cut dress and sawed through his ropes. Replacing the knife, she walked quickly to the north door of the barn, opposite the one through which he and Jill had entered. She turned and saw he hadn't moved. "Come, Jeff," she snapped. "People are waiting, and we mustn't be late."

CHAPTER 27

Sam's ears rang with the intensity of the words slung between the two people on the opposite side of the partition. The door latched behind them as they exited the barn and silence blanketed the building.

Sam worked his way slowly back to the west door, easing himself outside again. He flattened himself against the black siding of the barn and whispered, "Southerland, take your unit and follow the Duchess."

"Copy." It spoke well for the officers and their training that Sam neither heard nor saw any movement following his command.

Sam glanced toward the corner of the barn. "Barnaby, keep your unit here and watch the barn. If you catch sight of Jill, follow her. But don't interfere just yet with the Duchess' plan. We can't move in 'till we can get both Jill and Jeff together."

"Yes, sir."

"Emily and I will follow Southerland."

He glanced to the tree where he had left Emily. He could see her dark shadow still squatting beneath it. He gazed in all directions, then dashed across the moonlit ground to join her.

She looked up at him. "Are you ready?" she mouthed.

He nodded. Together, the two of them slipped from tree to tree, as silent as the night around them.

Jill preceded Topper to the well-lit living room of the barn, glancing in all directions for details to her surroundings. She wanted to be as well informed as possible so she could create a distraction for Jeff to escape. When they reached the living room, Jeff was nowhere in sight. Jill halted. "Where is he?"

"The Duchess has other plans for him." Topper prodded her back. "Come on, out the door."

"I'm not moving until you bring him back here." Jill crossed her arms stubbornly.

Without warning, Topper's hand whipped back and smacked her hard across the cheek. Her flesh stung and involuntary tears filled her eyes.

"That's for not obeying immediately." Topper pushed his face close to hers. "When the Duchess commands something, it's not for us to stand around talking about it and especially not for you, her prisoner, to refuse her anything. Now, get moving." His hand went to his belt and he slid a wicked-looking knife from its sheath. "If I have to ask you again, my knife gets to do a little talking."

Jill's eyes widened and she swallowed hard. She turned her back to him, willing herself to walk, not run, out of the door. The darkness of the night swallowed her up. She found it hard for her eyes to adjust.

"Do you see the path in front of you?" Topper's voice reached her ears. "Follow it until I say to stop. Then don't move another step until I tell you it's alright."

In the moonlight, Jill could make out the faint beginnings of a trail that led into a wooded area. Putting one foot in front of the other, she moved forward.

With each step that she took, courage flowed back into her veins. With each new amount of courage, she found herself praising God for giving her the willpower to continue. She even laughed softly.

"What are you laughing at?" Topper's voice lashed like a whip. "I didn't give you permission to laugh. I'll pull out my knife yet if you don't watch it."

Jill stifled a chuckle. *Either I'm really not afraid anymore, or I'm just really tired and things just aren't connecting.* She glanced backward at Topper. *I just have to be enough of a distraction to get Jeff out of there. That's all that matters.*

They had walked quite a ways by this time and Topper's voice came softly to her ears. "Stop."

Jill halted. In front of her, she could see firelight flickering through the trees. The sound of many people talking quietly filled the air. The chatter had an excited ring to it, an expectancy that something was about to happen.

Jeff sat in the middle of a small clearing, staring fixedly at a crackling bonfire. All around him mingled people he didn't know, dressed in black, dark green or deep purple robes. They were talking with each other, laughing excitedly at certain points, then immediately hushing as if they had made too much noise. A large decorative table stood at the far end of the clearing, a huge pentagram painted across the whole center of it. Jeff shuddered as he thought what would most likely happen on that table. He searched the clearing for any possible methods of escape.

Two of the figures across the clearing caught his eye. He immediately recognized Troy's co-worker, Lee, and Jill's ex-boss, Edward Bradley. Both of these men wore dark robes and grinned maliciously in his direction. Apparently, he was the topic of their discussion. Jeff turned his face away from them, hopelessness filling him.

Celia had disappeared as soon as she had led him into the clearing. She now emerged from the woods, dressed in thick black robes, her eyes flickering exultantly in the firelight.

She raised her hands. "Attention."

Quiet immediately settled over the group. The figures moved slowly to form a circle around the bonfire. Jeff looked around, not bothering to rise from his position. The flickering light gave a strange effect to the faces, creating a hollow look in the shadows under their eyes.

"The time has come." Celia spoke quietly but each word drifted around the group, distinct as the ring of a bell. "Bring her!"

Jeff heard the shuffle of footsteps and he swiveled his head to look behind him. Jill, dressed in a white sheath of material stepped into the firelight, followed closely by Topper. Her eyes searched quickly and found him and a tiny smile formed on her lips. Jeff raised his eyebrows. How could she smile when she knew what was going to happen? A sudden thought hit him like a rock in the pit of his stomach. *Maybe she doesn't know.* Just then, her right eye-lid dropped in an almost imperceptible wink and Jeff sucked in his breath. What was she trying to tell him?

Two of the dark-robed men stepped out of the circle and grasped Jill by her upper arms. They led her quickly toward the large table. The circle of witches widened, then reformed again to include the table in their midst. One of the men hefted Jill onto the table, forcing her backward to lay her head on the solid stone. There was no sign of struggle and she lay there peaceably. One of the men fastened her wrists to the table. The men melted back into the circle.

A low melodious laugh issued from Celia's mouth. She breathed in deeply and smiled on her gathering. "After many years of waiting, I have my goal at last." She walked slowly from the edge of the circle across the clearing to Jeff. "I have my revenge." Her voice snapped like a whip across Jeff's shoulders. She laid one hand on his head, stroking it affectionately. "And," she continued, "I have my heritage." Here, she turned toward the table at the end and walked slowly toward it. Her eyes narrowed as she gazed at the white-robed figure lying on it.

"Many years have passed since the rightful rule of kings and queens. Our country is no longer a true monarchy, but is merely run by the fools it produces. As you all know, I have the sole right to the throne of England, and only royal blood shall sit on the throne. Tonight, I will claim my heritage and England shall know of it tomorrow." She gazed down at Jill, whose wide eyes were fixed on Celia's face with a mixture of pity and scorn.

Celia drew up to her full height and hissed, "Do you dare to scorn me, you ignorant piece of vermin? I will show you my rights."

She whirled and faced the circle. "Five centuries have come and gone since my ancestor, the Duke of Buckingham ruled England from behind the throne. Henry the VIII was little more than a puppet. The Duke gained the king's favor through cunning, but he had a mortal adversary by the name of Thomas Wolsey, the king's own cardinal." She began to pace, her hands clasped tightly behind her.

"Thomas Wolsey weaseled his way into Henry's good graces. He rose to a power almost equal to that of my ancestor, the Duke. He attained great wealth, but fortunately for my ancestor, Henry was of a rather jealous nature. When Wolsey's wealth became too great, the King began to speak with the Duke about removing Wolsey from power. The time was ripe for the removal of Wolsey as things were because Wolsey was unpopular in public opinion. He had also failed in all his attempts to secure a divorce for the King from his first wife, Catherine of Aragon. Wolsey, conniving creature that he was, persuaded the King that he was to be trusted. To prove this, he gave the King a present, his home estate of Hampton Court Palace."

Jeff glanced at the rest of the assembly. *Well, Celia's obviously a few bricks short of a load, but are the others really buying this?*

Celia focused her gaze on Jeff. "This was only a temporary fix, because soon after, Wolsey was arrested for high treason with a charge of attempting to negotiate a French invasion into England. He was sentenced to the Tower of London to be tortured and killed. Even though the charge of treason was a brilliant strategy on the part of the Duke to be rid of him once and for all, Thomas Wolsey fell ill soon after he was arrested. On his way to the Tower, he died."

Celia briefly fell silent, gazing around the circle at each face. "How does this qualify me to sit on the throne of England, you ask? When Wolsey died, he left an heir, an illegitimate son. Even though he was a man of the church, Wolsey bequeathed on his bastard son everything that he owned, which at the time was still a considerable amount. When Wolsey died, he had only one thing left, something of the utmost value." Celia turned slowly and leaned over Jill. "Shall I tell you what it was?" Her gray eyes stared piercingly into Jill's blue ones. "It was a ring, a ring of such value that few in England could compare." With a cry, Celia suddenly grasped the chain of Jill's necklace and jerked. The chain popped and hung swinging from Celia's extended hand.

"This seal!" Celia's hand shook. "This seal is the seal that once belonged to my ancestor, the Duke, who, like me, was accomplished in the practice of magic. He, like me, desired to sit on the throne of England and he found a way to make it possible. He found an old parchment written nine hundred years before his birth by the original invaders of this great island. These fierce warriors formed seven kingdoms: the kingdoms of Northumbria, Mercia, Wessex, Sussex, Essex, East Anglia, and Kent. They outlined a treaty among themselves. Anyone who owned or overtook the land on which they stood and could produce the seal with which they sealed their agreement, would have the complete loyalty and command of themselves and their descendants. They performed a trial by fire to hold such an oath in place for centuries to come and sealed it with this seal that you see here." She held up the ring, sparkling in the firelight. "They wrapped the seal in protective materials and buried it deep in the earth, never to be unearthed, until my ancestor found it many years later, entombed underneath one of the deepest passageways of Hampton Court Palace.

"However, the ring was stolen from him one night when he returned from a hunting trip. He never found out who had taken it." Celia fell silent, her gaze sweeping over the faces flickering in the firelight. "After a thorough search of ancient documents and artifacts, I discovered two years ago the will of Thomas Wolsey. It bequeathed to his son, among other things, a blue sapphire ring, which oddly enough was very similar to the one stolen from my ancestor. I spent the next two years tracing Wolsey's ancestors to the present generation until, lo and behold," Celia laughed, "his genealogy narrowed down to one solitary young woman, living in the United States of America, who had no idea that she held one of the most powerful antiquities in the history of the world."

Celia paced back toward the table, moving around to stand behind it. She faced the circle, a smile playing on her lips. "Unfortunately," she trailed a finger lightly along the table, "the trial by fire created by the authors of the pact included a ceremony which required a blood sacrifice from anyone who wished to take the ring by force. I cannot claim the ring until blood has been spilled. We are gathered here to do the deed." She slowly drew a silver-tipped knife from the neckline of her low-cut robes, watching it glint in the firelight. A subdued chant slowly swept around the circle.

Jeff's hair on the back of his neck prickled as he slowly rose to his feet. "Celia!" He glanced wildly around at the robed figures on all sides of him. They all seemed entranced as each person stared at the scene. He and Jill were trapped in a ring of maniacs.

Celia ran her fingertip over the edge of the blade, the razor keenness of it slicing a tiny slit in her skin. The rest of the circle slowly closed in tighter, the chanting growing louder and more intense. All eyes were riveted on the woman in white on the table.

Celia laughed, a taunt in her musical voice. "Jack fell down and broke his crown and Jill came tumbling after. Such a pity." With a jerk, she raised her knife over her head.

CHAPTER 28

"Hold it," Jill sat up suddenly. During Celia's speech, she'd tried to collapse her knuckles again as she had done before. Her hands shot pain signals at her brain, but Jill had steadily ignored them. They throbbed and chafed now, but Jill focused on the knife in Celia's hands. The chanting stopped abruptly. Members of the coven looked at one another in surprise.

Celia's eyes spat fireworks. "Who bound this woman?" She glared accusingly around the circle.

One of the men who had placed Jill on the table drew back in fear. "Please, my lady, I—I don't know how it happened...."

"Silence!"

"I'd like to know a few more things before you kill me." Jill turned her eyes on Celia's face. "I have a right to know."

"You have a right to nothing." Celia advanced slowly back around the table. "Your only rights here are to listen to my commands and then submit to them, or suffer a horrific death—worse than what I have planned for you."

Jill held her breath, then released it quickly. "Help me, Jesus," she breathed.

Celia jerked. "*What* did you say?" The circle of robed people seemed to lean in closer.

"I said, HELP ME, JESUS!" Jill shouted. She scrambled to her feet in a flash, jumped off the far end of the table, nimbly darted between two sets of hands that reached for her and ran into the woods. Tree branches slapped her face. She grasped tree trunks as she swung herself from side to side to dodge them. Before she had gone twenty yards, a burning pain pierced her hand. She jerked her eyes to her hand on a tree trunk. A knife quivered between her fingers, cutting into the flesh between the index and middle fingers.

The two-second pause was enough. Two robed men grasped her upper arms and half dragged, half carried her back to the circle of firelight. There was no mercy this time. The men roughly shoved her back against the table and tied ugly ropes tightly around her wrists and ankles, cutting off circulation. As she lay prostrate, unable to move, the pain in her hand throbbed mercilessly.

She turned her head to the center of the clearing. Jeff was gone. Jill felt a pang in her heart. *I'll miss him.* She willed her muscles to relax. "Thank you, Jesus." She lay still.

Celia marched to the center of the circle, sweeping her dark robes wide. "You three, search the woods. I want Jeff back and I want him now. Get going." Three robed figures dissolved into the darkness.

At that moment, Jill heard a whisper. It was so faint, she was sure she must have imagined it. "Jill!" She jerked her head toward the woods.

Jeff tried desperately to quiet his panting as he squatted at the foot of a tree. He could barely see the flicker of firelight from the clearing, but he knew he had to get back to save Jill, somehow. He was sure the Duchess would have missed his presence by now. Sure enough, he spied three dark shapes slip into the woods, twigs and branches crackling beneath their feet. He looked wildly around, searching for a place to hide.

Sam wrapped himself close against a tree, his pistol in hand and cocked. He had lost Emily at some point and his heart pounded as he tried to plan how he was going to take control. He could see his fellow officers spread wide around the circle from tree to tree. There were only eleven of them and forty or more people filled the clearing. He motioned Barnaby over. "Take Austen and see if you can't find Jeff. I saw three men go into the woods after him."

Barnaby nodded, motioning to the officer next to him, and they stole softly into the darkness.

A headache pinched Sam's temples. Nine officers. Forty men and women, most likely armed in some fashion. If he wasn't careful, they could have a full-scale war on their hands. They did have the element of surprise in their favor, though.

Celia had worked herself into a towering rage by now. "I want blood and I want it now!" she screamed, throwing caution to the wind. "I will claim my throne and my inheritance. Little pimples like you can't stop me from taking what is mine!" She stomped her tiny foot, her crazed eyes glaring around the circle. Certain members of the coven began to look a little frightened. A couple of them looked ready to run.

Emily leaned out from the bushes toward the table not a yard away. "Jill," she whispered again. "Catch this." She gently tossed a small pocketknife to the table. It landed with a tiny clatter near the tips of Jill's fingers. Jill stretched her fingers to grasp the handle, but succeeded only in knocking the knife back to the edge of the table. It teetered precariously and dropped to the ground. She heard a frustrated sigh from the bushes and she turned her head to search out the source. Celia was still shouting and none of the coven members standing near Jill's table seemed to have heard the noise.

Celia whirled. "I'm ending this immediately." The knife in her hand gleamed in the firelight like burnished bronze and a faint red glow glimmered from its tip.

Jeff crashed through the underbrush, no longer caring about the noise he made. The three men careened around trees after him. He could hear Jill's pending doom in the clearing and he headed straight toward it.

Emily leaped from the bushes as Celia slammed the knife downward toward Jill's throat. Jill's mouth swung open in horror, but Emily's strong arm caught the witch's wrist just before she could plunge the knife home.

Celia's astonished face stared at Emily. "You!" she screamed. Emily held her wrist firmly. The circle of witches stood in stunned silence. No one seemed to know what to do.

Celia recovered first. Her left hand fumbled with something in the pocket of her robes. She pulled out a small handgun. She smiled and pointed it straight at Emily.

"Say good-bye, dearie."

Jeff burst into the clearing opposite the table, tackled the first two witches in his way, and scrambled over them toward Celia, his arm outstretched to stop the inevitable.

The crack of a gunshot ricocheted off the trees. Emily's eyes widened and she staggered back from the table, her face contorting as she stumbled. Jill's terrified gaze followed Emily as she tottered to one side. But it wasn't Emily who slumped to the ground. Celia crumpled onto Jill, the small gun and knife falling from limp hands. Dark moisture soaked through the back of her robe, spreading in an ever-widening circle.

Sam Scott stood at the other end of the meadow, his gun still hot from the discharge. He kept his weapon at eye level. "Everyone on the ground," he shouted. "Move!"

The eyes of the witches flickered from him to ten other men as each officer stepped from the woods. The three men who had chased Jeff were already handcuffed. Barnaby and his partner prodded them into the clearing. Slowly, one by one, the witches lay prostrate on the ground and the officers commenced their search for weapons.

Jill's eyes filled with tears. "Thank God." She began to sob in earnest.

Jeff ran to the table, tears streaming unchecked down his cheeks. He grabbed the small knife on the table and sawed through Jill's ropes, sitting her upright.

"Emily." He choked. "Jill, you're alright." Emily flew around the table, throwing herself into her brother's arms. He hugged her tightly, his other arm reaching out and pulling Jill into the hug. "Thank God, thank God." Jill buried her head in his chest and cried harder. It was over.

EPILOGUE

Jill's heart melted when Brian and Brandon spied their dad for the first time since the kidnapping. Sam had driven Jill and Jeff back to the police station to pick up the boys. After that, they planned to stay at the Lion Gate Hotel for a long and satisfying rest. As soon as Sam pulled open the doors to the station, two bodies hurtled from a room at the back. "Dad! Dad!" The yells echoed across the hallway.

"Boys!" Jeff dropped to his knees in the entryway, holding both arms open wide. The boys crashed into him, their arms strangling his neck. Jeff struggled to hold them as close to himself as possible. Tears streaked all three of their faces.

"We missed you, Dad." Brian jumped up and down. "I tried to keep Brandon safe, though." He straightened as he dropped his voice to a whisper. "I had to have a little help."

"Son, I couldn't have asked for a better protector for your brother. I'm just so glad you both are okay."

"We don't have to go back there again, do we, Daddy?" asked Brandon.

"Where, son?"

"The scary room with all the snakes?" His lower lip trembled.

"No! No, Brandon." Jeff rubbed his small son's back. "You don't ever have to go back there again. And that woman will never bother you again, so you put her out of your minds, okay?"

The boys nodded. Jeff pushed himself to his feet, taking both of his sons by a hand. "Boys, I want you to meet a couple of people that have come to mean a lot to me in the last few days."

Brian nodded, but Brandon fixed his eyes on Jill. "Are you going to be our new Mommy?"

Jeff choked on a cough as the rest of the group chuckled. He opened his mouth to reply, but Jill stepped forward and bent to Brandon's eye-level. "Hello, Brandon. I'm Jill and I'm very glad to meet you." She held out her hand, which Brandon shook gravely.

"But are you going to be my new Mommy?"

Jill paused, glancing up at Jeff. "We'll see, Brandon. I don't think your Dad nor I know the answer to that yet."

Brian leaned in front of Jeff and whispered, "That means that she and Dad are *dating*, Brandon. Evan says that's what grown-ups do when they don't know whether or not they'll get married."

Jeff snorted. "All right, Mr. Know-It-All. Why don't we go back to the hotel before we make any earth-shattering decisions about who is dating who."

"Who is dating *whom*." Jill corrected him with a smug smile on her face.

Jeff chuckled. "Smarty-pants."

Sam opened the door. "Cabbie this way." He motioned to his car parked by the curb. The group followed him from the room.

Jeff stepped into Troy's hospital room. "Hey, stranger." He grinned at the invalid.

Troy looked up from the chair he was sitting in and set aside the book he was reading. "Boy, am I glad to see you. I'm sick of being cooped up here. Every time I thought I'd check out, I had some sort of spasm with the injury and the nurses wouldn't stop fussing over me until I went back to bed." His voice sounded as if he had hugely enjoyed it.

Jeff grinned. "Life's hard, isn't it?" He glanced at the small bag on the floor. "This all your stuff?"

"Yep." Jeff leaned over to pick it up. A nurse breezed in the door, pushing a wheelchair.

"Well, Mr. Lane, we've enjoyed having you here." She grinned at him.

"Although I'm sure you didn't enjoy it nearly as much."

Troy gave her a grudging smile. "Maybe next time I visit, I'll be a little more talkative and more fun to be around." He stood. "Of course, that would entail not getting shot in the ribs and being unconscious most of the time."

"Well, you'll just have to try harder next time not to get shot in the ribs. Perhaps you should have them aim for grazing your leg next time. I'm sure it's not nearly as painful." The nurse laughed as she helped him into the chair.

Jeff had a cab waiting at the exit doors of the large building. Troy straightened carefully from the wheelchair and sank down onto the cushioned back seat of the taxi. Jeff hurried around to the other side and jumped in. The driver put the car in gear and pulled away from the curb.

They made small talk for a minute, both of them keenly aware of the trauma of the last couple of days. At last, Jeff cleared his throat. "Troy, I got hold of Bonnie after we were rescued, and she filled me in on most of what John had said, but Sam told me you had gotten a run-down from your unit in the States on the day we were taken. I wondered what your version of what happened to John was."

"I didn't get a lot of information in the van," Troy explained, "because I had to make it quick, but then I called back to headquarters yesterday to find out the rest of the details." Troy shifted in his seat to put less pressure on his bandages.

"John was shot at WalMart on his way home from his shift at work. He had to pick up a tie for a dinner this past weekend, which he never went to, obviously.

He was in the men's clothing section. Around one of the rows, he overheard two men talking about this thing they had to do. One thing led to another. At any rate, he figured out the guys were talking about murder. He didn't have his weapon on him, so he was going to call for backup, but before he could get out unseen, the two men discovered him, showed him their weapons, then told him to walk in front of them from the store.

The one guy put the gun back in his pocket and they followed him out to his car. John sat in the driver's seat. The other two climbed in, one in the back and one in the passenger's seat, and threatened him. He tried to lead the conversation to get more information and he learned that there was some sort of coronation happening for a very important lady, but they never would name who she was. They said that she, meaning Celia, had to kill one of the people she was capturing in order to make this ceremony happen.

"John told me that he had his gun in the consul of the car, and his hand was just two or three inches from it. So while they were all wrapped up in telling him this, he was inching his hand toward it. The guy in the front all at once just seemed to think that the guy in the back was talking too much and he told him to shut it. At that second, John got hold of the gun and was swinging it around to face them when he heard a shot and then remembers waking up in the hospital several days later."

Jeff sat in stunned silence for a minute. "I had no idea. It's crazy how far-reaching your actions can be, even years later. I had no idea when I knew Celia before that she could go so far out of control. Then, she was just a little on the wild side. This time she was insane. There's absolutely no other explanation for her actions or for the things she commanded other people to do."

"Yeah, I'm sure she was a nutcase. And I'm just glad Sam got both of y'all out of there before something worse happened."

Jeff nodded. "In a small way, though, I feel sorry for her. The way I was going ten years ago, I was asking to wind up just like she did. It's too bad that she didn't make the choice to get out of it while she had the chance."

"Don't be too sorry." Troy shifted his weight on the seat cushions. "She was about to make a kabob out of Jill, and I don't ever feel too bad for anyone like that who gets their slate wiped. It's called justice."

Jeff nodded, but didn't say anymore. He stared reflectively out of the window.

Jill sank into the deep cushion of the chair with a sigh. The hotel dining room was quiet this morning and Troy smiled at her from his place in the chair across the table from her.

"Sleep well?" he asked.

"Better than I have in… well, days, I guess, but it feels like years." Jill laughed.

"Good, good." Troy rubbed the back of his fingers, studying them intently. "Jill," he began.

Jill immediately heard the weight behind his words. "What do you need, Troy? Can I get you anything?"

"No." He shook his head. "I just wanted to ask you or Jeff something. I know y'all are both Christians and, well, I've never had much use for God. Thought I could pretty much handle everything on my own just fine. But this weekend I realized…," he paused, smiling wryly. "I stood by feeling completely helpless as I realized that you all had more than just a dispute on your hands—that your lives were actually in danger and that I was a mere man who had no more control over anyone's universe than an ant on the ground." He leaned forward, wincing from the pain in his ribs, then went on intently.

"I promised God that if he spared your lives and those of Emily, Brian and Brandon, that he could have my life too. I know." He chuckled at her look. "I'm not supposed to bargain with the Creator of the universe. I guess he saw fit to spare my life anyway." He looked up at Jill. She felt the tears puddle in her eyes and spill over the edges.

"Aw, I didn't mean to make you cry, Jill." Troy smiled at her, and then grew serious again. "But will you help me?"

Jill nodded vigorously. "Of course. It would make me so happy." She took one of his large hands in hers and both of them bowed their heads. When they looked up again, Jeff stood behind Troy's chair and had a hand on his shoulder.

"Welcome to the family, brother." He gave him a playful punch in his bicep.

"Thanks, Jeff." Troy swiped back, then winced. "Though I never thought I'd have to be in the same family as you." He sighed deeply, exhaling his breath as far as it would go. "I feel so peaceful now," he exclaimed. "Can't wait to go home and tell Suzanne about it!"

"You could call her now," Jill suggested.

Troy looked down at the carpet. "Well," he said cleared his throat. "I guess I'd rather tell her in person. It might help her understand a little better."

"Of course." Jill nodded. "Speaking of which, when are we leaving anyway?"

Jeff collapsed in the chair next to Jill. "Sam got the tickets for us already. Our flight's scheduled to leave on Thursday."

Jill inhaled the fresh morning air as she sank onto a bench in the park next to the Hampton Court maze. She eyed the battlements ahead of her and nodded to an early morning tourist as he meandered past.

"Thomas Wolsey," she whispered, her gaze returning to the castle. "It was good to meet you." She paused and thought. "I hope that you found your peace with God before you died." She pulled her sapphire ring from her pocket, turning it to catch the light. She rubbed her thumb gently over the inscription *Veritas Unum*. "I hope you found the One Truth." She jerked from her reverie when she felt a hand on her shoulder. She squinted up at Jeff.

"Ready to go? We've got to catch our flight."

"Yeah." She stood up. "You know, Jeff, it's sort of bittersweet, this lesson that I've learned about trusting. It seems that in a way, we humans have to fail first before we can trust in God. Thomas Wolsey did that, or as Celia put it, he broke his crown. I wonder if in the end, his crown was mended?"

"I don't know." Jeff winked at her. "You're the history buff, not me, remember?"

Jill smiled and turned back for one last look at the Cardinal's palace.

"Is your crown mended, Jill?" Jeff asked after a moment.

"I think so." Jill sighed. "I've learned to trust from the Master of teaching. Not that I'll never forget to trust again, but I've come a long way."

"Me, too." Jeff wrapped both arms around her and kissed the top of her head. "Me, too." He tipped her chin up and kissed her lips softly. "Come on, let's go." They walked back up the path toward the Lion Gate.

"You really think Troy's feeling up to a long flight home?" Concern washed over Jill's face. "He was pretty badly hurt."

"Yeah, but you know Troy. He was in good spirits when I went to pick him up at the hospital. Said none of the nurses wanted to let him go. Probably wishful thinking on his part." He chuckled. "But he was all excited when I got to the hospital—just got word from his boss in the States that he got the promotion he was looking for and that Lee is no longer going to be in his hair at work. He and Ed Bradley are returning to the States in chains."

"I don't have much pity for them." Jill frowned. "They brought it on themselves."

Jeff smiled as he looked down at her. "Brian and Brandon are waiting with Troy, Emily and Sam at the airport." He suddenly threw his arms open wide, taking a deep breath. "Jill, it feels so *good* to know my boys are safe and sound. Like a massive rock just rolled off my chest. You know?"

"I know." Jill squeezed his hand. "So, what's up with Sam and Emily anyway?" She shot a sly glance in his direction.

Jeff grinned wryly. "Oh, I hear that he's already got a ticket to the States to visit a certain young lady that I'm related to." He laughed, then sobered. "But with Celia's death, he's in a lot of trouble with Scotland Yard, and they dropped him from their department."

Jill's mouth dropped open. "But if he hadn't shot her, I'd be dead and she'd be free to keep on doing the evil she was doing."

"It's the way they work, apparently. Celia was a prominent duchess, and even if a death like hers is justified, it's hard to make the public see it that way. It's too bad really. He was a fine police officer. He's struggling with the decision, but Scotland Yard is leaving some options open, so he might be rehired at some point. I guess we'll see."

"One day at a time," Jill murmured. "All things work together for the good of those who love the Lord."

"You said it." Jeff laughed. "And I couldn't agree more."

•

ABOUT THE AUTHOR

Tamara Shoemaker lives in the Shenandoah Valley of Virginia with her husband Tim and their three beautiful children. She spends her days maintaining sanity in her house, not always successfully, and passes the nights occasionally cranking out a book.

25111337R00131

Made in the USA
Lexington, KY
13 August 2013